Murders aplenty

Colin Ian Jeffery

For
'The Jollies'
Hoping to give a smile and a chuckle

Forest Publications
Copyright© 2023 Colin Ian Jeffery

First edition

No part of this book may be reproduced or transmitted in any Form or any means, electronic, mechanical, photocopying, or Otherwise, without the express written consent of Colin Ian Jeffery

Chapter One

Ronald Bartholomew Perkins liked to consider himself a successful businessman, his business murder at which he was imaginative, a master of disguise, cunning and devious. Middle-aged bachelor of average height, with slight pot-belly, sandy-haired going bald, who in a poor light could pass as being moderately handsome, and thought by some ladies of a certain age beguiling with charming personality. Perkins is a member of the local parish council in the little English village of Bumstead-on-the-Wold in the Surrey hills with its little Saxon church, St Freda the Ever-Ready, and bell tower without bells.

So far he has led a charmed life and been lucky, indeed, when he joined the local golf club having never played golf before he achieved a hole-in-one the first time he teed off. Popular with villagers who accepted his story of winning the lottery and taking early retirement from working as a solicitor. But it was a cover story for his thriving murder for hire business, and he plans to retire on his fiftieth birthday when he will buy a villa in the south of France with a vineyard and make his own wine, and considers himself a wine connoisseur with modest rack of wines in his cellar.

The villagers consider him a quiet mannered gentleman who grows roses and can complete the Times Crossword in under an hour, and likes playing chess and the piano. Musically he is in demand by the vicar, the Reverend Sydney Bloom, to play the church organ in cold weather because he is the one in the village other than the eighty-one-year-old organist, Miss Jessica Kemble, a retired music teacher who suffers with arthritis and can play only on warm days when she can move her fingers without pain.

Perkins mother, Miss Hetty Rose Perkins, tall and willowy with hardly a recognizable female shape, once thought of herself as being a perpetual virgin until going on a day's trip to the seaside town of Brighton by coach on a factory outing when she was thirty-four, and sharing a bag of fish and chips with a drunken Scotsman ending with her conceiving her son on a pebble beach under the West pier. The father, a dour middle-aged Scottish Celtic football supporter, work-shy who lived on unemployment and his parents hand-outs. He was in Brighton visiting his married sister, Annabell Watkins, wife of the beach Punch and Judy man, who off-season or in bad weather sold cockles and whelks from off a stall on the promenade.

Wearing a kilt with a football supporter's scarf, the drunken Scotsman met the shy naive Hetty Perkins as he came reeling unsteadily out of a fish and chip shop with a bag of battered cod and chips. On seeing Hetty he leant against a lamppost to stop himself from falling over and leered at her, and fancying what he saw chatted her up speaking with a guttural Glasgow accent that only fellow Glaswegians would understand. Hetty, not understanding in her gullibility he was bargaining to share his fish and chips with her for having sex with him. "Have as many chips as you want, lassie," he slurred giving her a saucy wink of an eye and showing her the bag of fish and chips to tempt her.

She thought, being unworldly, that he was being kind and generous and not negotiating for sex with a piece of battered cod and a few chips. "Oh, how very kind of you," she cooed with a shy smile, and blushing she took a chip and ate it.

"Come this way, lassie," he mumbled, thinking she had agreed to his bargain, and taking her by the hand led her into the shadows under the pier where they stood eating fish and chips. When the moon momentarily disappeared behind a cloud he quickly made his move and fumbling with her clothing raised high his kilt and gave her both a baby and his remaining cod and chips. He never did give his name and was the first and last Celtic football supporter to know Hetty in the biblical sense. Indeed, he was the only man ever to know her in the biblical sense, and she would often recall wistfully in later years how it was the best cod and chips she ever had.

Perkins committed his first murder while at school, an all-boys school, a short-trousered twelve-year-old spotty third-former in his second year at St Beckett's College, a minor public school in Bridgewater, Somerset, where he suffered with bed wetting, acne, homesickness, and a Latin master who was keen on discipline.

The school, with fees £12,000 a year (Perkins won a scholarship), was famous for producing two Prime ministers, eight bishops, seventeen high court judges, a rabbi and a persistent flasher on the London underground tube train circle line.

At school Perkins played a fair game of chess and was good at cricket, a fast bowler feared by opposing teams. His reason for committing his first murder was for being put into detention by his

Latin teacher, Mister Cyril Cooper, for falling asleep in class when he should have been studying his Latin Grammar.

The detention meant he could not perform his fast bowling for an important inter-house cricket match, and because of his absence his team from Kemble House lost and he was blamed by the boys who did not speak to him for a month. Perkins, angry and humiliated vowed revenge on his Latin teacher.

He murdered the teacher, a keen bird watcher, as he stood on a cliff top watching through binoculars swooping shrieking seagulls out at sea. The young Perkins crept up behind the teacher and shoved him in the small of the back with both hands and away went Mister Cooper over the cliff edge, airborne before he knew what was happening. Perkins never forgot the look of incredibility on the teacher's face as he glanced back over his shoulder as he fell to his death onto the rocks below, and his shrill harrowing cry, "It's double detention for you, Perkins."

Mister Cooper, bald as an egg and fat as a butterball, nicknamed 'Curly' by the boys, was washed-up a week later covered with seaweed on a lonely wind-swept sandy beach below a high cliff. The coroner at the inquest, Mrs Jennifer Hepworth-Brown, delivered a verdict of suicide, saying, "Mister Cyril Cooper took his own life by leaping off a two hundred feet high cliff while in a depressed state of mind."

The staff at Saint Beckett's College believed Mister Cooper, a bachelor, committed suicide over a broken love affair knowing he had a lady pen-friend in China he planned to bring to England and marry, who had recently written to him saying she was marrying the postman who delivered his letters. The boys, with the exception of Perkins, thought they knew the real reason for the death believing the teacher jumped to his death because he could no longer stomach appalling school dinners.

The murder of Mister Cooper taught the young Perkins two important lessons, first that murder was easy to commit and second it had been an exhilarating experience with his need for revenge achieved without being punished for it.

It was Mister Cooper's death and the ease and satisfaction of the murder that made the young Perkins consider having a clandestine pastime when he became a man, murdering and being paid for doing it. His mother wanted him to be a solicitor and he thought he could do both and make a fortune with the money kept in a secret Swiss bank account. Both planning and execution of the murders would be like playing chess an intellectual stimulation at which he excelled. There must be, he thought, lots of wealthy people wanting to have somebody deceased for them. Hate and revenge he knew from murdering his Latin teacher were basic to human nature and were best served cold and never in haste when mistakes could be made. He waited three months following his detention before murdering Mister Cooper.

Perkins, as boy, saw the future prospect of becoming a hired murderer the same as if he was called to the priesthood, which for him would be similar in trust and confidentiality. "Many are called but few are chosen," a Church of England bishop told him at public school when he was thirteen following a Confirmation service. The newly confirmed boys gathered for tea and cream cakes in the chaplain's study, the tea presided over by the bishop, a big-bellied jovial red-faced man with a high-pitched squeaky voice, and misbehaving hemorrhoids, and devotion to cake.

The callow spotty young Perkins hoping to impress the bishop asked him how could he become a vicar, thinking the question would ingratiate him with the bishop, and also please the school chaplain who liked to invite boys he liked to scone cream teas with a naughty squeeze of the knee. The beaming bishop was delighted and told Perkins he must pass all his exams and make his parents and teachers proud. "When you're eighteen I'll arrange for you to attend a Church Selection Board," said the smiling bishop as he patted Perkin's head as if he was a pet dog, "and if they accept you then five years later you'll be ordained and have a nice little church to preside over."

The school chaplain, the Reverend Guy Peacock, a tall beanpole of a man with black greasy hair and neat goatee beard, was so pleased to hear Perkins wanted to become a vicar that he gave the boy an extra-large slice of Victoria sponge cake with three chocolate biscuits and two squeezes of his right knee. The other boys were given a thin slice of Dundee cake and one custard cream biscuit without a knee being squeezed. Perkins had learnt that it paid to lie and to tell people what they wanted to hear; a lesson well learnt by the budding serial killer.

Chapter Two

Perkins committed his second murder while doing National Service in 1956, joining the army from public school to receive officer training at Sandhurst and then commissioned a Second-lieutenant with a parachute regiment. He made his one and only parachute jump leaping out of a plane at 20,000ft and suffering badly with pre-jump nerves leapt too early while the jump light was showing red and not green for go. He fell from the plane screaming for his mother with the parachute automatically opened by the emergency cord attached to the plane. At fifteen thousand feet wet himself and at ten thousand feet fainted. He landed in a field where a bull pawed at the ground excited and impatient to get into an opposite field to service a small herd of cows. Perkins, not seeing the bull, dropped thirty yards in front of the snorting animal with parachute flopping over him covering him like a tent.

The farmer, Gerald Topper, a thrice gurney winner for South Yorkshire (face pulling), a short stocky blubbery man with an abundance of nose hair, was preparing to open the field gate to allow the rampant and highly enthusiastic bull to enter and partake in amorous activities with the cows and increase the herd.

Perkins came to his senses and began pushing aside the parachute and saw the bull and in desperate panic struggled to free himself from the restraints of the parachute harness. The bull charged and Perkins fled. He almost reached the gate when bull caught him and plunged both horns into his buttocks tossing him in the air like a rag doll. He landed on the other side of the gate hitting his head and was knocked unconscious. The farmer with his cowman, Gerald Jerkins, carried Perkins to the farmhouse where they phoned for an ambulance.

The next day Perkins woke in a military hospital bed laid on his stomach after undergoing an operation, disorientated and with life-long mistrust of bulls. The surgeon who operated told him he should not sit down for at least a week and allow his buttocks to heal.

Colonel Bradford Squires, officer commanding the parachute regiment, a tall slender man with monocle and neat trimmed moustache, sat in his office reading with dismay Second-lieutenant

Perkins medical notes sent from the hospital. The surgeon wrote, "Second lieutenant Perkins should never be allowed to make another parachute jump, doing so would be too hazardous for his mental health. But other than leaping out of planes he is in my opinion fit for normal duties."

The Colonel turned to his adjutant Major Richard Barker, a short bulky man, bow-legged from landing badly on several occasions doing the splits making parachute jumps, and asked, "Have you read the medical notes of Second lieutenant Perkins, Dicky?"

"Yes, Sir, I have and it's pretty damning I must say. He can't jump anymore from planes and so he isn't any use to us. We're a parachute regiment and have to jump out of planes."

"Can't we get him a medical discharge and be rid of him?"

"No, Sir, he's been passed medically fit for normal duties except for jumping out of a plane."

"Having an officer in a parachute regiment who can't jump out of a plane isn't good for morale, Dicky. The men won't like it."

"We could transfer him, Sir, to a regiment where he won't need to use a parachute."

"Good thinking, get it done."

"Oh, and we've had a claim for damages, Sir, from the farmer who owns the bull that gored Second lieutenant Perkins. He's demanding £3,000."

"£3,000? But that's a bit steep, isn't it? It was Perkins who was damaged not the bull."

"Not according to the farmer, Sir. He claims the incident has traumatized the bull. Now, the bull refuses to service cows and is showing amorous interest in other bulls."

"Now, I've heard everything."

"What shall I do with the claim, Sir?"

"Pass it on to the War Office, Dicky, let them deal with it. But it sounds like it's a lot of bull to me."

"Yes, Sir. I'll see to it and arrange for a posting for Second lieutenant Perkins. Any suggests where to send him?"

"What about the Antarctic? There aren't any bulls there."

Both men laughed.

It was a month later Perkins was posted to Cyprus as Supplies Officer at an army base where he remained for the rest of his National Service. One frosty morning as he was leaving the officers mess he slipped on an icy step and took a bad tumble, and spent a month on his back in a military hospital in Famagusta with both legs in plaster. He was put in a side-room under the nursing care of ward sister Brenda O'Neal who held the rank of major, a fierce dumpy Irish feminist from Dublin who despised men and treated them with contempt. She ordered her nurses to keep male urine bottles in a freezer so they would be icy cold when used with the same freezer treatment for bedpans.

The worse experience for a male patient at the hospital was having a bed-bath administered by Major O'Neal, carried out furiously with a scrubbing brush and bar of carbolic soap, with no tender area of the male anatomy left untouched by the hard bristles of the scrubbing brush.

Six days after Perkins was discharged from hospital Major O'Neal died in tragic circumstances at a railway station with the only witness being Perkins. When giving evidence before the army court of inquiry he told how the major slipped and fell under the wheels of a passing express train, the body minced and scattered for half-a-mile along the tracks. But the truth was she did not slip. Perkins pushed her. "It was dreadful," he explained, his voice choking with false emotion. "There was nothing I could do to save her."

The inquiry, chaired by brigadier-general Sir John Arthur Needham OBE, WC, reached the verdict it was death by 'misadventure.' Major Brenda O'Neal's body was returned to Ireland in three parcels of mince, and her parents with full military honours buried the parcels in St Mary's churchyard, Dublin, to the wailing bagpipes of the Wexford Girls Pipe Band.

Perkins successfully committed his second murder.

Perkins left the army the following year and entered civilian life on a post-graduate course at Oxford University paid for by the army, where he read law and the occasional girlie magazine. His mother wanted him to be a solicitor and so he put aside his ambition to become a murderer for hire until after graduation. Murder then would be a profitable sideline with him working as a solicitor as his cover for his murdering activities.

It was the annual Oxford and Cambridge boat race on the river Thames which caught Perkins interest as means for raising the money needed to launch his murdering enterprise. He was thumbing through a boating magazine 'Jolly Rollicks' while waiting his turn for a haircut in a gentlemen's hairdressers, a short back and sides, while reading an article on the world-famous boat race. He knew fellow students would be placing bets with a small percentage out of devilment betting on one of the boats sinking. It was the sinking of a boat that intrigued and inspired Perkins imagination.

The sinking of a boat during a race happened five times with the Cambridge boat sunk in 1859 and the Oxford boat in 1925, and both boats 31st March 1912, the Oxford boat the 4th March 1951. The bookies believed the sinking of a boat now impossible with the extra buoyant lightweight boats used for the race and were offering 100-to-one odds against a sinking.

Perkins decided to bet on his own Oxford University boat sinking, thinking it was a sporting gesture on his part. It would be ungentlemanly to bet on the opposition boat then to sink it. He would sink his own University boat. Perkins prided himself on being a sportsman and a gentleman.

Taking his turn in the barber's chair he closed his eyes and relaxed and pondered on ways for raising money needed to place bets. But how was he going to raise the money? Then it came to him in a flash of inspiration. The money would come from the death of a close family member who would leave his mother Hetty everything in a last will and testament. He would kill his grandfather. He had never met his grandfather who disowned his mother when she returned home pregnant from her day trip to Brighton when her bump began to show. "I've put £5 at six to one on Oxford to win the boat race," declared Raymond Bryant the barber brightly, a roly-poly man with wobbling chins, slightly crossed-eyed which worried his customers especially when he was shaving them with a cut throat razor. He interrupted Perkins thoughts with a snip of his scissors next to his right ear. "You'll be doing the same I expect, Sir, with you being a young Oxford gentleman, placing a bet on the Oxford boat?"

"I'm not a betting man," replied Perkins opening his eyes and looking up at the barber with a forced smile, "but on this occasion I think I'll make an exception. I'm feeling lucky."

"Lucky, Sir?" echoed the barber dismally with a shudder thinking of his mother-in-law who regularly came to stay. "I wish that I was lucky with the wife's mother and she'd never come to visit and would stay home."

Perkins nodded and smiled. "Yes, I'm feeling very lucky indeed."

The barber nodded thinking Perkins meant he would be having sex during the coming weekend and walked over to the cabinet where he kept packets of contraceptives. "Would, Sir, like something for the weekend?" he asked and winked an eye knowing how sexually active students were at weekends. It was at weekends when he sold most of his contraceptives.

"Weekend?" echoed Perkins surprised. "What would I need for the weekend?"

"Something to prevent a lady from joining the pudding club, Sir," replied the barber holding up a packet of contraceptives, his best-selling brand, 'Love's Delight,' specially ribbed for extra pleasure and ultra-thin and oiled for slip-a-long delight. The manufacturer printed on each packet, 'Extra Large.' This was so the male recipient could proudly show the packet to male friends and make them feel inadequate, and for women seeing the packet before an amorous encounter think they were about to experience a magnificently endowed male. But the truth was all packets of contraceptives were of the same standard size, stretchable to fit both large and small.

Perkins shook his head. "No, thank you. I'm planning to visit my grandfather and I'll be too busy for the ladies."

"Too busy, Sir," responded the barber pensively with a sigh and thinking of his wife Betty Lou and her overactive libido. "I wish my wife wasn't too busy on Sunday evenings after supper. That's when she's most active sexually and makes demands of me, calling out, "Come on, Raymond, and do your husbandly duty."

Two days later Perkins set about preparing to murder his grandfather, George Oliver Perkins, a retired tram driver living alone in Dorking, Surrey. The old man to be made through cunning deception to name Perkin's mother Hetty as sole beneficiary in his last will and testament. His life then ended and made to look like it was an accident.

George Oliver Perkins never forgiven his daughter for becoming an unmarried mother which he considered immoral, antisocial and shameful. In fury after noticing her swollen belly he packed her bags and threw her out of the family home vowing never to speak to her again. She lived on social benefits and raised her son on a rundown housing estate in south Croydon, Surrey. Perkins was a bright boy and won a scholarship to public school when he was eleven.

Perkins found his grandfather address on a letter written twenty-one years earlier in a drawer in his mother's bedroom when home for half-term from University. The letter was the old man's harrowing reply to one received from his daughter pleading for money to buy food and nappies and toys for her baby. The enraged old man replied:

Hetty,

You are no daughter of mine but a harlot and I never want to see nor hear from you. You no longer exist for me and I have no bastard grandson.

The letter stained with tears his mother wept reading it. Perkins was appalled and more determined to murder his grandfather. He arrived at his grandfather's house dressed in a smart three-piece grey suit, white shirt, dark navy-blue tie, trilby-hat and polished black shoes, wanting to impress the old man. He knocked twice on the red painted front door and the door opened and there stood George Oliver Perkins, shabbily dressed in a faded green cardigan, grey trousers, and blue carpet slippers. Small of stature, chubby, in need of a shave and smoking a foul-smelling brier pipe.

The old man hardly ever left the house except to go shopping or to collect his weekly pension from the post office. He had drastically let his personal hygiene go since retiring five years earlier, and for him old age meant freedom to wash and shave whenever he felt like it, which was mostly a fortnightly event. "What do you want?" he snapped angrily, glaring at the young man standing on his doorstep thinking he was a door-to-door salesman.

"You've a daughter," declared Perkins brightly, studying the old man's wrinkled face, and hoping to see a smile and nod of the head agreeing he did have a daughter.

"I've no daughter," retorted the old man scowling.

"That's not true. I know you've a daughter and her name is Hetty."

"I've no daughter I tell you. Now clear off before I set the cat on you."

"I'm your daughter's son, your grandson Ronald."

"Ah, so you're the bastard, are you," exclaimed the old man angrily and slammed the door narrowly missing Perkins nose. He had met his grandfather and hated him intensely and on the train journey back home to Croydon and to his mother he fantasized on various ways for murdering his grandfather. "Slammed the door in my face when I told him I was his grandson and called me a bastard," he thought bitterly. "Well, he's going to pay for that and for scorning my mother."

One week later at the beginning of the half-term holiday, second-year Oxford University law student Ronald Perkins disguised as a vicar in black suit, clerical collar, false grey beard, again visited his grandfather. He knocked on his grandfather's front door and waited with clipboard in hand. There was no response and so he knocked again this time louder than before, still with no response. He shouted through the letterbox in the singsong voice which he thought vicars used in church when taking services, "Halloo, Mister Perkins, I know you're in. I've got exciting news for you." He heard the old man muttering angrily as he came shuffling down the hallway to answer the door.

The door opened and there stood George Oliver Perkins dressed in a pale blue tatty pullover with food stains, mostly jam and egg down the front, crumpled grey trousers and green carpet slippers, and smelling of stale tobacco. Glaring at his caller he sniffed loudly to show his disdain for the clerical collar because he despised do-goody interfering priests almost as much as he despised door-to-door salesmen and social workers. He held the door slightly open ready to slam it in the priest's face. "Well," he demanded curtly, "what do you want? I'm not interested in going to church nor giving money to charity."

"Good day, Sir," beamed his grandson, getting into his role as a vicar making a pastoral house visit and speaking with a slight lisp to add to his characterization. "I'm the Reverend Jonathan Reed, your new vicar."

"Go away."

"Don't worry. I'm not collecting money. I'm here to give money."

"Well, that's a first," replied the old man contemptuously with a sneer, "a vicar on my doorstep who isn't after money."

"Didn't the Lord Jesus say it's better to give than it is to receive?"

"Which doesn't help me. I'm as poor as a church mouse."

"I've money to give away to a poor and needy elderly gentleman living in my parish."

The old man forced a weak smile, his interest and greed now

aroused and he opened the door a few more inches. "Well, I'm poor and needy, Vicar. How about me?"

"Indeed, so you are, and that's why I've called to see you," replied Perkins. He glanced down at his clipboard as if studying it then looked up at his grandfather, and asked, "You're George Oliver Perkins a retired tram driver and widower of this parish and live alone?"

The old man sheepishly nodded. "Money you say to give away, Vicar? Must I go to church to get it?"

"Oh no, we're not so desperate we pay our congregations to attend church. The requirement for receiving the money is for the recipient to be male, elderly, poor and needy, and of course be of good character."

"Alright, I'll go along with it, vicar, tell me more."

"May I call you George?"

The old man sniffed and wiped his nose on the back of his sleeve and nodded. "Yes, but I'm still not coming to church."

"The recipient doesn't have to be a church-goer only to live in the parish of St Charles the Unexpected and be an elderly gentleman living alone to qualify for the special bequest. But perhaps you aren't interested? There are others on my list I can visit, George."

"I'm interested. Come in, Vicar, and I'll put the kettle on and we'll have a nice cup of tea and a chat about the money. I think I've some custard-creams left in the biscuit tin."

The tea was weak and watery with the two cups made from a single teabag dunked three times dangled from a piece of string into each cup of hot water. George Oliver Perkins was a frugal mean old man who did not like waste nor spending money. "I'm all ears, Vicar," he said as he relaxed into his patched brown leather armchair next to the gas-fire, "now tell me about this special bequest?"

Perkins sipped his tea with little finger raised in the manner in which he thought a well-mannered vicar would do. "Well, it's like this, George," he began, "Lord Kelly of Wexford, owner of Kelly castle with its vast estate and five villages in the Republic of Ireland, has left a bequest to the parish of . . ."

"How much?" interrupted the old man eagerly.

"How much?"

"The bequest, Vicar, how much is it?"

"Two hundred thousand pounds."

"Blimey," gasped the old man, ashen-faced with shock, and for a minute he could not speak then regaining his composure smiled broadly and held out a tin of biscuits. "Have a custard cream, Vicar," he said in a friendly voice. Vicars, he knew liked charitable folk who shared worldly goods and so it was important this vicar should think him generous if he was to be in the running for the bequest money.

"Thank you, George," said Perkins as he took a biscuit. He bit into the biscuit then wished he had not as the biscuit was soggy showing it had been stored in the tin for a considerable length of time. He chewed forcing himself to swallow then put the remaining half of the biscuit onto his saucer.

"What were you saying about the bequest, Vicar?"

"Oh, yes, the bequest, George. Well, Lord Kelly of Wexford died five months ago in most tragic circumstances while foxhunting. His horse refused to leap a farm gate and Lord Kelly flew from the saddle over the gate and landed headfirst into a working combine harvester. Farm labourers working nearby stacking bales of hay didn't hear his muffled screams as Lord Kelly was dragged down into the harvester. The remains of Lord Kelly emerged from the harvester neatly packed within a bale of straw with the bale stacked with other bales to make a haystack.

"Well, at least he was neatly stacked at the end, Vicar."

"Lord Kelly wasn't found for a week and it was the smell of his decomposition body that finally led farm labourers to the haystack and to his bale of hay.

"How ghastly, Vicar." The old man felt quite queasy at the thought of Lord Kelly's remains within a bale of hay, and worried the thought might put him off his supper of brown bread and butter with a smoked kipper. "You were saying about the bequest, Vicar, and I might qualify for it?"

"Ah, yes, George, the bequest. Well, I think you could well qualify. Lord Kelly when he was a young man seduced a pretty young English under-maid called Irene Penny who came from this parish. She went to Ireland to work at Kelly castle when she was eighteen, and sadly it was the same old story I'm sorry to say with a baby conceived on the wrong side of the blanket with the new under-maid having been so many times under Lord Kelly."

"What happened to the girl?"

"When she found out she was pregnant she returned to England thinking she wouldn't get a good reference after being an under-maid so often under Lord Kelly, mostly in his bed and twice on the dining-room table. Distraught, she returned home to her parents who took her in. But Lord Kelly loved her and wanted to continue having her under him, pursued her to England where he wooed and married her in our own little Saxon church."

"How very romantic, Vicar, it brings a tear to the eye," muttered the old man with a fake sob wanting to show he cared about the girl when he only cared about getting the bequest.

"The happy couple returned to Kelly castle following the birth of their daughter Colleen. But Lord Kelly never forgot the debt he felt he owed our parish for his happiness, the birthplace of his beloved wife and daughter. He made a special bequest in his will for the sum of two hundred thousand pounds to be paid to the most deserving elderly widower in our parish."

"And you think that's me?"

"I do, George, but there's something else that's required before you qualify for the bequest."

"Which is, Vicar?"

"The recipient must have a female offspring."

"The money comes tax free?"

"It certainly does, George."

"Alright, Vicar, then you need to look no further. I'm your man. I've got a daughter."

"You have? What's her name? "

"Hetty Perkins."

"Perkins? Ah, then she's not married?"

"Does that matter?"

"No, George, not as far as the bequest is concerned but I thought it might please the bishop to know she's wed and possibly a mother."

"She could very well be married, Vicar, for all I know. She was very flirty getting herself in the pudding club, you know with a bun in the oven!"

"Pudding club? Bun in the oven?" exclaimed Perkins angrily, appalled with the terminology used by his grandfather describing his mother's pregnancy with him. His grandfather was loathsome and deserved all that was coming to him.

"Sorry, Vicar," apologized the old man alarmed to see the effect his words had on the vicar. "I didn't mean to offend you. But I haven't seen my daughter since she got herself up the duff. Ooops, sorry, there I go again. I mean when she was as you bible punchers like to say was with child!"

"Quite so, George. What you said about your daughter was rude and crude and uncalled for."

"Has it affected my chance of qualifying for the bequest?"

"Well, according to the instructions of Lord Kelly the recipient must love his daughter and be able prove it to the satisfaction of the executors of his will."

"But I do love her, Vicar," lied the old man, "absence makes the heart grow fonder and I often think of her. My heart yearns for her and for my dear grandson. Yes, I've got a grandson too, a nice lad who visited me recently."

"You must provide me with proof, George, something that's legal and binding, a document to show there's a loving bond between you and your daughter."

"Legal proof? What sort of legal proof?"

"Well, a document signed by yourself and witnessed by two people of social standing, a document I can show to Lord Kelly's solicitors. I think your last will and testament with your daughter the sole beneficiary would be ideal."

"Then I get the money?"

"Yes, George, then you get the money but less an agreed donation for me. I hope you understand?"

"Oh, I most certainly do, Vicar, I understand.. How small a donation?"

"Shall we say two thousand pounds?"

"One thousand."

"One thousand five hundred or I'll find another recipient for the bequest, George."

"Done, Vicar. Now you'll see that I get the bequest?"

"Absolutely, George, of course I will."

The old man nodded and smiled. "Give me a few days to see my solicitors Skinner, Hardy, and Wickerstaff, then I'll arrange to have the document here ready for you to see. Shall we say you call back on Monday afternoon at tea time?" The old man felt pleased with himself and was planning to revoke the will as soon as the money was paid into his bank account. Hetty would inherit nothing he would see to that.

"Good, then that's settled, George. I'll return Monday afternoon to see the will." Perkins was surprised on how gullible and greedy his grandfather was the wicked old scoundrel. It was then a most chilling thought crossed his mind, 'An apple never falls far from the tree,' and he was just like his grandfather both in temperament and spirit and now he understood with a shudder where the darkness in his soul came from, and momentarily felt afraid of his own evil impulse to kill.

The old man smiled happily and feeling generous he held out the tin of biscuits. "Have another custard cream, Vicar?"

Chapter Three

Two days later on a cold Friday afternoon Perkins disguised as vicar the Reverend Jonathan Reed with false beard and horn-rim spectacles, carrying a battered old suitcase arrived at the gatehouse of a convent with an imposing sign in red letters on a white notice board on the wall next to a big oak door: SISTERS OF MERCY. TRESPASSERS WILL BE SEVERELY PROSECUTED. The Convent surrounded by a twelve-foot-high brick wall topped with broken glass, and three miles from Perkins grandfather's house. It is from the Convent where he will conclude his murderous business with his grandfather, the murder to happen after he has seen the old man's will and verified it signed and legal with the sole beneficiary his mother. He chose the convent thinking it would not be thought by police a pious inoffensive vicar on religious retreat would have anything to do with the murder of an old man three miles away.

The Sisters of Mercy are an enclosed order with no man with the exception of frail ninety-one-year-old crusty Father Gilbert Harper and the bishop allowed previously beyond the convent gates. Father Harper taking weekly communion services and monthly confessions wearing carpet slippers. He is a martyr to corns and chilblains, and visits riding on a decrepit old bicycle from a nearby nursing home where he is a resident. The bishop, The Very Reverend Basil Snell, visits on saint days and at Easter and Christmas, and when the novice nuns take final vows.

Perkins, using both hands, tugged manfully on the sturdy bell rope dangling outside the gatehouse of the convent with a resulting thunderous peal of bells, startling him into releasing the rope and to hold both hands over his ears to block out the sound. The hatchway in the heavy oak door slid open and a wrinkled face of an elderly nun peered out. "Who's there," she asked in a frail cackling voice. "If you're the dustman then your late again."

"Not a dustman," replied Perkins brightly in his vicar's singsong voice not forgetting the lisp to give more character, "but the Reverend Jonathan Reed."

"Jonathan who?"

"Reed. I'm a vicar."

"Vicar? What? Has someone died? Nobody's told me."

"Nobody's died as far as I know. I'm here for a religious retreat to recharge my spiritual batteries and help me to carry on with my parish duties in the coming year. Mother Superior's expecting me."

"We don't give retreats for men. It's women only here."

"I know, but the Mother Superior has booked me for a retreat. She said the convent hasn't had any bookings from women for three months and so she's now accepting clergymen on retreat."

"Oh, well, that explains why it's been so quiet here of late at the guesthouse."

"Yes, because you've had no guests."

"I wasn't told about any vicar coming on retreat and I'm the sister in charge of the guesthouse. I hold the gatehouse keys and it's my duty to see the dustbins are emptied and guests shown to their rooms and supplied with clean towels with a bar of carbolic soap."

"Dustbins?"

"Yes, dustbins. They're the scourge of my life they really are. The dustmen who take away our rubbish are a vindictive bunch. I forgot to leave out a tip for them last Christmas and ever since they've been dropping litter deliberately when carrying the bins out to the truck."

"How upsetting, eh Sister . . ."

"Tulip --- all the sisters are named after a flower."

"Oh, but how original. Now, can I please enter the convent, Sister Tulip, as it's getting rather chilly standing out here?"

There was the sound of bolts drawn and locks turned and slowly the creaking heavy oak door opened to reveal the wheezing Sister Tulip dressed in a black habit, white wimple, and wellington boots. The wellington boots because she had been working in the garden digging up potatoes when summoned by the peal of the gatehouse doorbell.

Sister Tulip, seventy-three, face wrinkled like a prune, thin as a rake, puffed and wheezing with the effort of pushing open the heavy oak door. Plain-faced with bulbous nose she once worked as a waitress at a Lyons corner tea shop in Sheffield from her late teens to her thirtieth birthday, before entering the religious life to become a career virgin and penguin look-a-like nun. She had hoped to find while serving in the tea shop romance and happiness and meet an unmarried man with bad eyesight and his own hair and teeth, who had some knowledge of the female anatomy. But sadly, she never romance and finally with reluctance accepted her destiny lay in remaining a virgin and becoming a nun. But her need for romance was not quenched with putting on a wimple and it bubbled quietly away waiting to erupt like a volcano.

Sister Tulip forced a smile feeling her passions stirring and hormones beginning to race seeing a man close-up and she held out a bony right hand to Perkins. "I'm Guest Mistress," she declared in what she thought was a sultry voice, shaking his hand, "and in charge of hospitality at the convent. If I'd had known you were coming then I would have aired the sheets and put out a new toilet roll in the guesthouse toilet, extra soft and strong that won't fall apart with a second or third wipe. It's just like Mother Superior to keep me in the dark and make a booking without telling me. I'm always last to know anything of importance happening here."

"Bit forgetful is she, the Mother Superior?" asked Perkins sympathetically, as he struggled to free his hand from her vice-like grip, but Sister Tulip was determined to hold on to his hand for as long as possible. It had been such a long time since she held a man's hand and her heart fluttered with excitement.

"Sister Tulip," called out a woman's shrill piping voice with an Irish accent. "I hope you're not misbehaving again and having one of your naughty episodes? We don't want more trouble like the last time when you chased the milkman round the garden and the diary refused to make deliveries for a month." Perkins pulled his hand free from the old nun's grip and turned to look in the direction of the voice and saw a small rotund nun with black habit flapping in the wind, rosy cheeks, in late fifties, striding towards him smiling broadly. "You must be the Reverend Jonathan Reed," she added brightly taking his hand and shaking it warmly. "I've been expecting you. I'm Sister Rosebud the Mother Superior."

The meal that night served in the convent dining room because it was a Friday and a no meat-eating day for the nuns, was a thick green pea soup with crusty bread rolls, steamed fish, followed by cheese and biscuits. Sitting at oblong tables sat ninety-six black habited nuns of the Order of the Sisters of Mercy with eleven novices dressed in white habits. The nuns silent and sitting on wooden benches, and although there was no rule for silence during mealtimes they stared in silence at Perkins, intrigued and fascinated having a man their midst. Perkins sat at the top table feeling uneasy with such an avid interest shown in him.

He sat next to the Mother Superior who occasionally made a loud clucking noise with her tongue showing her displeasure with her nuns for staring at their male guest. "Will you say grace, Vicar?" she asked sweetly when the pea soup was served.

Perkins did not hear what the Mother Superior asked, he was too worried with the nuns staring at him making him think of a pride of lionesses sizing up the meal of the day. "Pardon?" he asked, seeing the Mother Superior looking at him expectantly.

"Grace," beamed the Mother Superior sweetly.

"Grace? Have I met her?

"No, no, Vicar, will you please say Grace for me?"

He was even more confused. "But of course, Mother Superior," thinking Grace was a novice nun who had not yet taken her final vows to be given a flower's name, wanted by the Mother Superior. Standing up he called out in a loud voice to the assembled nuns, "GRACE."

The Mother Superior, startled and flustered, exclaimed, "Grace, Vicar, the prayer said before a meal thanking God for providing the food."

"But of course, that Grace, how silly of me," he muttered apologetically, and feeling foolish said grace and made it short and to the point. "Thank you, God, for this meal, Amen." He sat down crimson faced with embarrassment. It had not occurred to him that with him impersonating a vicar the nuns would be expecting him to say prayers and even worse take services in the chapel, which would be a disaster for a man whose only knowledge of the Common Book of Prayer was that it was used for Church of England services.

Sister Tulip, assisting in the kitchen, entered the dining hall carrying a tray on which was a plate with half-a-dozen oysters and with a flourish she presented the oysters to Perkins. The oysters stored in the freezer for the bishop's next visit who was partial to shellfish, especially oysters. Sister Tulip winked at Perkins as she put the tray down in front of him. "Oysters, Vicar," she declared with a smile, "really good to harden up a man's resolve and purpose."

"Remove the oysters at once, Sister Tulip," exclaimed the Mother Superior angrily. "The vicar doesn't need to have his resolve and purpose hardened up. He'll be having steamed fish like the rest of us."

Muttering under her breath Sister Tulip took the oysters away and returned to the kitchen where she sat brooding in a corner. She sprinkled the oysters with lemon juice and ate them. The oysters could not be returned to the freezer for the bishop with shells having been opened. With thoughts on the vicar and the oysters she sighed wistfully remembering the touch of his hand as they shook hands when he arrived at the gatehouse, which for her had been the most thrilling experience for decades making her passions rise with exciting possibilities.

When Sister Tulip left the table with the oysters the Mother Superior leant across the table and whispered to Perkins, "I think you should lock your bedroom door tonight, Vicar. It looks as if the Bromide drops I put into Sister Tulip's tea aren't working."

Perkins retired to bed as soon as the nuns filed from the dining room heading for the chapel for evening prayers, excusing himself to the Mother Superior saying he was sorry to miss evening prayers but was not feeling too well, bunged up and constipated, and blaming the thick pea soup. This was not true. He simply did not want to spend an hour in the cold chapel for evening prayers. "I'm sorry you're not feeling well, Vicar," responded the Mother Superior sympathetically. "I'll get you a purgative from the medicine cabinet guaranteed to move any blockage. I know because I've used it myself on several occasions with great success."

He smiled weakly and nodded. "Thank you, Mother Superior, that's most thoughtful of you," he said humbly, and thinking that taking the purgative and getting into bed more acceptable than attending chapel and getting his knees sore kneeling for prayers. The yellow purgative was foul tasting which he drank in one quick swallow from a glass. The Mother Superior had poured the dark brown purgative from a bottle labelled 'Purgative to loosen stubborn stools. Not for children or the fainthearted.'

The Mother Superior insisted on accompanying Perkins to his bedroom door in the guesthouse. "I must leave the convent tomorrow afternoon for an hour or two," he told her. "It's on important church business. I've funeral arrangements to make for an elderly gentleman who's soon to die."

"Oh, Vicar, but death's so tragic isn't it?"

"Yes, especially for the person doing the dying."

"I'll pray for his passing to be quick and painless."

"Oh, it'll be quick, Mother Superior, of that I'm certain."

"Oh, that reminds me, Vicar, about you leaving the Convent tomorrow afternoon. You'll miss the bible study group taken by Sister Primrose. She's does a most lively portrayal of Moses and the Ten Commandments, with all the voices including the Pharaoh and a braying donkey."

"Well, knowing that, Mother Superior, I'll certainly be doing my best to conclude my business and be back in time for Sister Primrose bible study group."

"Goodnight, Vicar. Don't let the bed-bugs bite."

"What? The bed's infested?"

"Oh, goodness gracious no, Vicar, of course not," chuckled the Mother Superior. "It's what my dear mother used to say when I was a little girl back in Ireland as she was tucking me up in bed at night."

"Goodnight, Mother Superior."

Perkins entered his bedroom and switched on the light. There was something on the pillow, something that chilled his blood, a single yellow tulip. He knew who placed the tulip there, Sister Tulip, and forgot that as Guest Mistress she had a key to his bedroom. Panicked, he quickly bolted the bedroom door against her. "She might have the key," he thought grimly with a shudder, "but the bolt can only be opened from inside the room." He removed his shoes and switched off the light and fully clothed lay in darkness listening nervously for footsteps coming down the corridor to his door.

Midnight came and went before he fell into a fitful sleep only to wake with a start hearing the rasping sound of the doorknob twisted back and forth. "Cooey," called the familiar voice of Sister Tulip through the keyhole, "are you awake, dear Vicar?" With a groan he closed his eyes began to snore loudly hoping Sister Tulip would hear and think he was asleep and go away. It was ten minutes later before he heard her footsteps shuffling away from his door. The Mother Superior was right and the Bromide drops in Sister Tulip's tea were not working.

It was five o'clock in the morning and still dark when Perkins woke to the loud ringing of a hand-bell outside his bedroom door. "Wakey, wakey, Vicar," called a gruff baritone voice. It was Sister Lilly, broad-shouldered, six foot tall, and the strangest looking of all the nuns. Sister Lilly shaved daily and peed standing up with toilet seat raised. It was her duty to wake the nuns every morning from their beds with the hand bell. "I'm waiting for my operation," she confided as she led Perkins down the stairs to the dining room, "Once it's done then I'll be the woman I've always wanted to be since my schooldays at Broadwood College."

"Broadwood College? But that's a school for boys only."

"Yes," agreed sister Lilly saddened by the memory, "I was only allowed to wear a dress for school plays when they needed someone to pay a female role. Plastic surgeons can do wonders these days and I'm going to have extra-large breasts to go with my height."

When Perkins entered the dining room he found the nuns were already seated and eating breakfast, cornflakes and milk, and chatting away among themselves. Seeing him they fell silent. He sat next to the Mother Superior at the top table. "Did you sleep well, Vicar?" she asked with a smile as she poured him a cup of tea.

"Yes, thank you, Mother Superior," he lied not wanting to tell her about the visit made by Sister Tulip and get the elderly nun into trouble.

"What of the purgative? Did it work?"

He nodded, embarrassed, to discuss his bowel movements with the Mother Superior. "Yes, it worked like a dam bursting," he muttered.

"Oh dear, I hope you weren't still in bed at the time."

"No, I made it to the toilet in time."

Sister Tulip, helping in the kitchen, appeared at the door and shuffled over to Perkins carrying a plate of hot buttered toast. "Eggs this morning, Vicar," she declared. "I hope you like eggs."

"I do, Sister Tulip, thank you."

"How do you like your eggs? Scrambled, boiled or fried?"

"Scrambled."

"Well, I would prefer my eggs fertilized," she replied, winking an eye and making him shudder at the thought.

"Sister Tulip, stop this nonsense at once," exclaimed the Mother Superior angrily, "Go to your room and stay there until it's time for your confession with Father Harper this afternoon. I'll have your breakfast and lunch sent to you --- and with you being a nun you'll have your eggs unfertilized like the rest of us."

It was late afternoon when Perkins disguised as the Reverend Jonathan Reed in black suit, clerical dog collar, trousers tucked into socks to stop them being caught in the bicycle chain, rode a heavy lady's bicycle with a basket on the front. The bike borrowed from the Convent with its reinforced saddle for the indulgent overweight nun. He cycled three miles down leafy lanes to his grandfather's house and knocked on his front door. The old man, smoking a pipe, answered the door and smiled showing his discoloured tobacco-stained teeth. He led Perkins into the living room and presented him with a three-page document. "There, Vicar," he exclaimed brightly, "my will and testament, legal and acceptable by any court in the land, with my sole beneficiary my daughter Hetty."

"I'd like to read it, George."

"But of course, Vicar." The old man handed over the document with each page carefully perused in silence by Perkins not forgetting the small print. He did not trust his grandfather and was pleased to see the document was legally binding. He could not have done better if he had drawn it up himself.

"Can I have the cheque now, Vicar?"

Perkins nodded. "Yes, George," he said, and taking out a brown envelope from his inside jacket pocket he handed it to the old man. "I hope you haven't forgotten your agreed donation for me?"

"Don't worry about that, Vicar," replied the old man curtly. "I'll keep to my side of the bargain. We'll both benefit from the bequest. You scratch my back and I'll scratch your back."

"Good man, George, and I'll see you get all that's coming to you, and without too much delay," replied Perkins, thinking of murdering his grandfather.

The old man took the envelope, opened it and took out a cheque and held it up before the single light bulb in the room and studied it. "Ah, yes," he exclaimed gleefully, "all that money and it's mine, all mine."

"Not quite yet, George. I still have to take your will and testament away with me for Lord Kelly's solicitors to verify it's legal. Once that's done you can cash the cheque at your bank."

"It's legal, Vicar, so why the delay? Don't you trust me?"

"I do, George, but the solicitors acting as executors for Lord Kelly's estate must be certain your daughter is the sole beneficiary before they release the money."

"But I thought Lord Kelly's solicitors were coming here to see it, Vicar." The old man did not want the document out of his sight thinking if anything happened to him while it was in the vicar's custody his daughter Hetty would inherit all his worldly goods, which was something he did not want to happen.

"I thought you understood, George, the solicitors won't be coming here, not all the way from Dublin. No, I have to show your last will and testament to my own solicitors in London so they can vouch its legality. Once satisfied they'll notify Lord Kelly's executors in Ireland, and then, and only then, can you cash the cheque.

The old man was still reluctant to be parted with such a legally binding document. He was planning to destroy the document once the money was paid into his bank account. "How long will you need the document?" he asked curtly.

"Three days at most, George."

"Alright, Vicar," he agreed reluctantly, "but no later than Tuesday tea time."

"Tuesday at tea time it'll be, George."

"Would you like a cup of tea and a custard cream, Vicar?"

As Perkins cycled back to the convent with his mind full of various ways for murdering his grandfather, which now must be done before the old man took the cheque to his bank and it was found to be a forgery. He had four days to kill his grandfather before Tuesday tea time. When he reached the convent gate he had formulated a plan and it would be the old man's pipe that would be his executioner.

That night, a few minutes after midnight, Perkins, dressed entirely in black in balaclava, with gloves and wellington boots, face smeared with black boot polish, moved stealthily across a ploughed field at the back of his grandfather's house. There was a full moon and an owl hooted away in the distance sending shivers down his spine knowing it was hunting prey as he was hunting his grandfather. Perkins used a torch to see his way and had walked three miles over fields and through a wood from the convent of the Sisters of Mercy to reach his grandfather's house. When he was within a hundred yards of the house he switched off the torch and slipped it away into his pocket.

The landscape was poorly illuminated by moonlight but there was enough light to see. He came to a barbwire fence at the edge of a field and taking hold of the top strand of wire forced it down as far as it would go and stepped astride the wire, slipped and lost his grip. The barbwire acting like a trampoline sprang up between his legs snagging his genitals. The pain was agonizing and there was a

27

ripping sound as a gaping hole appeared in his trousers. Down he went sitting astride the wire which instantly sprang up and down in rapid succession with Perkins suppressing an urgent need to scream. On his tenth upward bounce he managed to roll sideways off the barbwire to land in the lane behind his grandfather's house. Traumatized and panicked he knelt and nervously felt between his legs fearful the barbwire had cost him that which he held most dear, and sighed with relief to find everything was safely dangling in its rightful place.

Perkins entered his grandfather's house and using a plumber's rubber sink plunger positioned over a pane of glass in the French windows, scored around the plunger with a glasscutter on his Swiss army knife, and lifted away glass circle. He reached through the hole and unbolted the door bolt and opened the French windows. Inside the living room he took out the torch and switched it on and saw the door leading to the hallway was half open and closed it. Kneeling he wedged strips of paper from his pocket under the door sealing the gap. Going to the gas-fire he loosened the gas pipe at the back of the gas fire with an adjustable spanner and gas flowed into the room. Satisfied with his handiwork he quickly went out through the French window and covered the fist-sized hole in the pane of glass with a piece of cardboard held in place with sticky tape to prevent gas escaping. Happy with his endeavours he returned to the convent.

George Oliver Perkins rose from his bed at his usual time of 6.30am, woken by the cockerel's crowing from the farmyard down the lane. Yawning, he stretched himself and farted, then went to the toilet for his usual prolonged sit down to get his bowels open and moving while reading a few pages of 'War and Peace,' which he kept especially for the purpose in the toilet helping him to pass time needed for his bowls to function successfully. Dressed in threadbare candy-stripped pajamas, shabby grey dressing gown and grubby carpet slippers, he went downstairs to prepare his breakfast. Putting a dab of lard in the frying pan he placed it on the electric cooker and switched on the hotplate and fried a slice of bread, two eggs with three slices of bacon, a sausage and half-a-dozen mushrooms with a tomato. He ate from off the frying-pan while standing in the kitchen with a fork to save do the washing up.

When he finished eating he took out his pipe and filled the bowl with tobacco, then went to the door of the living room thinking to go in and listen to the BBC news on the radio. It briefly crossed his mind when he saw the door closed that when he retired to bed the night before he had left it open to keep the room aired. Taking a box of matches from his dressing gown pocket he struck a match to light his pipe and opened the door. There was a mighty explosion heard at the convent of the Sisters of Mercy three miles away. The house disintegrated showering rubble over a radius of five hundred yards. The largest object that was found by the emergency services was George Oliver Perkins pipe.

When Perkins returned to the Convent after his murderous visit to his grandfather and panicked seeing a single tulip laying on his pillow. Sister Tulip had entered his bedroom while he away committing murder and knew he was absence from the Convent when the explosion took place. He worried she might tell the Mother Superior, an intelligent woman, who might put two and two together and call the police who would check on his identity and find he was an impostor. Sister Tulip was a serious threat. He sat gloomily on the bed wrestling with his conscience then finally decided on what must be done, and muttered bleakly, "I've no choice but to murder a nun."

Sister Tulip was found the next morning by novice nuns on their way to chapel for morning prayers, floating face down in the goldfish pound at the north end of the cloisters. Foul play was not suspected because she was old and rickety with arthritis and it was thought she had been feeding the goldfish and slipped and drowned.

Sister Tulip was buried in the convent cemetery. The Reverend Jonathan Reed was asked to take the committal service but declined saying he had a sore throat. He feared with his ignorance of church services would reveal he was a fraud. He did, however, send a reef of tulips for the nun he murdered and replaced the five goldfish she crushed while he was drowning her.

Chapter Four

It came as a tremendous shock and huge disappointment for Perkins to learn his grandfather's house was a council house and not owned by the old man, and his life savings amounted to a paltry £150. George Oliver Perkins lived in miserly poverty and died in miserly poverty. The shortage of funds from his grandfather's legacy drastically changed Perkin's plans for raising money he needed for placing his bets on the sinking of the Oxford boat. When his grandfather's solicitors handed over the £150 to his mother, he asked her if he could have the money to buy law books needed for his University law course. She readily agreed and he used the money to place £10 bets instead of the £50 bets he originally planned.

With less than three weeks to go to the boat race Perkins still had not come up with a feasible plan for sinking the Oxford boat, but had placed all his £10 bets. The bookies, he knew, would not pay out on a deliberate sinking so it had to look as if it was an accident.

The four-mile boat race course on the day would be thronged with crowds along the riverbanks. Perkins visited London twice to reconnoiter the route of the boat race on the river Thames, after travelling from Oxford University by coach then walking from Putney Bridge to Chiswick Bridge. There was one bridge which caught his interest which did not allow public access, Barnes Railway Bridge, which he thought would provide him with the privacy he needed for sinking the Oxford boat.

Barnes Railway Bridge was half-a-mile from the finish of the race, and Perkins took a train from Barnes station on the south side of the river crossing the bridge to Chiswick station on the north side to see the layout of the bridge. The bridge deserted except for two railway workers in donkey jackets and yellow hard hats who were checking on the spikes in the sleepers on the down-track coming from Chiswick station, tapping at them with long handled hammers. It was these two men who blended in almost unnoticed into the background of the bridge that gave Perkins the answer needed to move about the bridge without causing suspicion. Who would look twice at a railway worker in donkey jacket and yellow hard hat checking railway tracks?

The next morning at first light Perkins climbed over a six-foot-high wire-netting fence gaining access to the bridge, and entered a trackside hut where he found a donkey jacket with a yellow hard hat and variety of tools. Minutes later, disguised as a railway worker with false black moustache, wearing a donkey jacket and yellow hard hat, he stepped briskly onto the railway track leading to Barnes Railway Bridge. He began to walk the length of the bridge carrying a long-handled hammer found in the hut, stopping every few yards to tap gently at the railway track as if testing for metal fatigue. He had been on the bridge less than half-an-hour when the method for sinking the boat came to him. He would drop a slab of masonry on the boat identical to the grey stone used for building the bridge. The slab would smash through the boat's flimsy hull sinking it. The police would think a chunk of crumpling masonry broke loose and fell from the bridge. Satisfied with his plan he smiled happily thinking the Oxford boat crew could all swim so there should be no loss of life, unless one of them had the misfortune to be sitting where the slab landed on the boat.

There was a clear view from the bridge to Chiswick steps a mile away, and through binoculars on the day of the race he would see the Oxford and Cambridge boats come sweeping around the bend, giving him nine minutes to prepare for the sinking depending on weather conditions and flow of the tide, and then determine which archway the Oxford boat would pass under. With his reconnoitering of the bridge done and plan made he returned the donkey jacket and yellow hard hat with hammer to the trackside hut, and climbed back over the six-foot high wire fence and returned to Braddock Towers where he was staying near Victoria coach station. He had booked into the hotel the previous day posing as an American tourist visiting London to see the sights, a disguise he successfully used for previous visits.

He stopped on the way to the hotel to visit a public toilet where he shaved with a battery-operated shaver, splashed on aftershave lotion, knowing most American men were keen on personal hygiene, and thinking it was a clever part of his disguise for fooling the Hotel staff. He concealed his clothes behind the cistern in a cubicle, the clothes disheveled and ripped from climbing the fence. He would pose as an early morning runner for the hotel staff, and wearing only boxer shorts and a vest, socks and shoes, he ran at a steady jog from the toilet.

When he entered the hotel lobby he nodded amicably to Allan Hawes the gangly desk clerk. Hawes, twenty-two, pale skinned with protruding eyes and a squint, ginger-haired with bushy eyebrows meeting in the middle of a domed forehead, which his mother insisted was the sign of genius. His mother had been frightened when visiting London Zoo when five months pregnant carrying him by a filthy minded male orangutan swinging from bars by one paw while doing unspeakable things with a banana with the other paw. This was thought to be the reason for her son's gangly appearance and squint, but the truth was it was the gangly ginger haired milkman, Arthur Bywaters, with protruding eyes and a squint who was responsible. Arthur had regularly been presenting Hawes's mother with more than a daily pint of milk with a smile and his trousers down. Indeed, his milk round which spanned thirty-three-years until he retired produced an abundance of ginger haired children born with protruding eyes and a squint.

Hawes sat behind the reception desk in the lobby reading a detective novel, 'Murder by the Score,' by Mary Grace Dicker. Crime fighting Hawes great passion and ambition to be a private detective, a brilliant private detective equal to the exploits of his hero the great Sherlock Holmes and his medical sidekick Dr Watson. He tried on his eighteenth birthday to join the Metropolitan police but failed on medical grounds because of flat feet and a squint.

Hawes was frustrated with his job as hotel desk clerk and was desperate for the excitement and challenge of crime busting in his flat-footed eye twitching life. He took out a year's subscription for the 'Private Detective Magazine' to learn the business and purchased a magnifying glass to look for clues. He was considering when he became a private detective to buy a bloodhound to be called Dirty Bertie until house trained, and when house trained just Bertie. Being an avid fan of Sherlock Holmes, he had read many times every story written by Conan Doyle of the adventures of the famous fictitious detective, and was convinced he could do better as a detective than the great man. The gangly desk clerk yearned to solve crimes that baffled Scotland Yard's best detectives, and was saving from his wages to set himself up as a private detective. He would take rooms in Bakery Street and have a delightful rotund jolly cockney housekeeper, and an assistant with a medical degree to record for posterity all his crime fighting triumphs for posterity.

Hawes glanced with bemused look at Perkins over the top of his detective novel as he entered the hotel lobby, and was not surprised to see him looking like an early morning runner. Indeed, most of the American male hotel guests of a certain age went running first thing in the morning to keep fit. "Any mail for me?" called out Perkins brightly in the Texan drawl he learnt from watching cowboy films on TV. His cover story for the hotel staff was that he was American tourist Roger Shepherd the third from Houston, Texas, with wealthy parents, who having just graduated from college travelled to Britain on a gap year to sightsee in Europe before beginning a career in his father's oil business.

"No mail for you this morning, Mister Shepherd," called back Hawes who liked Americans because they were good tippers, and especially so when told with a beaming smile how wonderful it must be living the American dream with an abundance of hotdogs and Kentucky fried chicken on sale day and night throughout the United States.

Perkins, pretending to wheeze for breath after having a strenuous run jogged over to the reception desk. "I was wondering," he began with a weak smile between wheezes, "If you could direct me after breakfast to the Tower of London. My mother would love to have a photo of me with a real Beefeater. It would impress her knitting circle no end and also the overweight ladies of her slimming club 'Fatties in Decline.'

"Of course, Sir."

"I was also wondering what are the chances for me meeting the Queen and have her pose for a photo with me?"

"The Queen pose with you?" echoed Hawes, appalled an American tourist had the audacity to think he could ask the Queen to pose with him for a photograph. He struggled to keep smiling not wanting to give a scornful retort and upset the American and so lose a tip when he ended his stay at the hotel. American guests always gave hotel staff a big tip upon leaving.

"Sure, buddy, I'd love to meet her and shake her hand," replied Perkins carried away by his impersonation of an American starry-eyed over British royalty. "I'd wish her well and ask after her corgi dogs and if they chase the footmen and bite their ankles. Are they house trained?"

"The footmen?"

"No, the dogs."

"Her Majesty's too busy to meet tourists. She spends most of her time attending garden parties or going away on holiday to Scotland."

"So, there's no chance to meet the Queen?"

"None Mister Shepherd, and anyway the royal family are not in London. They're in the Highlands of Scotland stalking deer and shooting pheasants."

"Shooting peasants? But that's no way to treat the poor. In America we give them food stamps."

"Not peasants but pheasants, birds specially reared by gamekeepers for British gentry to shoot who are stuffed with parsley and sage and eaten."

"Can I have the key to my room? I'd like to get out of these running clothes and to take a shower before breakfast."

Hawes handed over the key. It was only after Perkins had gone up to his room did the thought enter the young desk clerk's inquisitive suspicious mind that if the American had been out jogging as he claimed, then why was he wearing black polished shoes and not running shoes? And why was he looking fresh as a daisy and was clean shaven and smelt of aftershave? Do early morning joggers shave and put on aftershave before going on a run? He doubted it, and what about the shorts that looked suspiciously like boxer shorts? Now, he decided to take more than a passing interest in Roger Shepherd the third and treat him as being a possible suspect, but a suspect for what he was yet to discover. The American was, as the police would say, a person of great interest, and taking a notebook from his pocket Hawes wrote at the top of the first page 'Case of the running American,' and smiling and pleased with himself he closed the notebook and returned it to his pocket. "Aha, my first case," he muttered wistfully, then picking up the detective novel continued reading.

Three weeks later with an hour to go to the start of the Oxford and Cambridge boat race, Perkins with false black moustache and an eye-patch to confuse facial identification, with a heavy backpack, climbed over the six-foot-high wire-netting fence sixty yards from Barnes Railway Bridge. He entered the trackside hut and put on a donkey jacket found hanging on a peg with a yellow hard hat, then advanced along the railway track towards the bridge. Inside the backpack a heavy slab of sandstone size of a football.

Trains clattered back and forth over the bridge rattling and rolling as they came and went with the drivers peering ahead through cabin windows, eyes focused on the tracks ahead alert for red signals warning of danger. They took no notice of the solitary railway worker walking across the bridge, Perkins blending in with the landscape. He stopped halfway across the bridge and slipped off the backpack to rest briefly, the heavy slab of sandstone making his shoulders ache. He had gone to a great deal of trouble finding the right sandstone, a sandstone matching the masonry of Barnes Railway Bridge, and found a quarry in East Sussex where he visited at midnight a week earlier. He surmised after sinking the Oxford boat it would be thought by the police a slab of sandstone broke loose from the bridge with trains rattling back and forth. The boat's crew would witness the tragedy and give statements saying it was an accident and the bookies pay Perkins his winnings without protest.

Perkins glanced at his pocket watch and saw there were thirty-nine minutes to go to the start of the boat race. With a clitter and a clatter a passenger train rattled towards him on the down-line and he stepped quickly aside off the tracks and gave the driver a thumbs up greeting. The driver, a harassed looking young man with brown hair and staring eyes, was too busy concentrating on the signals ahead and did notice the workman standing beside the track with his thumb raised in greeting.

There was one big weakness in Perkins plan for sinking the Oxford boat he needed to know beforehand which archway the Oxford boat would pass under to drop the slab of sandstone. He studied the river through binoculars up to Chiswick steps and saw the riverbanks were thronged with people. "Hi, you there," called a man's deep baritone voice speaking with a Welsh accent. "What are you doing?"

Startled, Perkins looked towards the sound of the voice and saw a big thickset man dressed in a donkey jacket and a yellow hard hat striding towards him. The man carried a 4ft long spanner for tightening nuts on railway sleepers. "I didn't know anyone else was working on the bridge this morning," replied Perkins apologetically, speaking with a Cornish accent, panicked and knowing he could not drop the slab of sandstone on the Oxford boat with the man watching him.

"Who are you?" asked the man eyeing Perkins suspiciously and noticing his hands were smooth and soft and not rough and covered with calluses like a railway workman's hands would be, which led him to conclude Perkins was not a railway worker and had no business to be on the bridge. He was a trespasser up to no good.

"I'm checking the rails on bridge," declared Perkins, carried away with his portrayal of being a Cornishman, his Cornish accent intermingled with a bit of Scottish and a touch of Irish with some Welsh thrown in. "I used to work on the Looe railway in Cornwall before moving to London," he said brightly with a smile. "Aye, and what a windy place Looe could be especially with a westerly wind was blowing. I miss working on Cornwall railways where my wife's daily pride was seeing my lunchbox was well-filled."

"Lunchbox?" echoed the man, startled, and thinking Perkins was talking to what was tucked away inside his underpants knowing some men and women referred to a man's bulging genitals bunched in a pair of Y-fronts underpants as his lunchbox.

"Yes, with Cornish pasty and small bottle of Scrumpy."

"Scrumpy?" The man took a step back from Perkins thinking he was either deranged or was suffering with a bizarre fetish for stuffing Cornish pasties down his underpants with a bottle of cider.

"In your underpants?"

"No, that would be a mad thing to do, it was my lunchbox prepared by my wife with bottle of scrumpy," replied Perkins with a smile, "the best cider made from apples, a drink that can blister paintwork, a real man's drink that puts hairs on the chest and that's why women won't drink it."

"I'm not a drinking man," retorted the man with a grimace, relieved it was a real lunchbox referred to and not a man's underpants. "I haven't had a drop of alcohol pass my lips since my wedding night when I was drunk and my wife made me take the pledge before allowing me into bed with her."

Perkins decided try and empathize with the man and to hopefully gain his sympathy so he would let him go thinking a little humour would add to his deception, and said although he was not married, "When my wife arrived at the altar rail for our wedding ceremony she raised her veil and the vicar took one horrified look at her then asked me in a shocked voice, "Are you sure?"

The man stared blankly at Perkins. He was not amused.

"What's your name?" asked Perkins, hoping by using the man's Christian name it would ease the tension between them and he could charm his way out of a bad situation.

"David Penrose and I'm working on the bridge tightening loose nuts on the south going tracks. What are you doing here?"

"Working like you, David," smiled Perkins hoping to ingratiate himself with the man.

Penrose scowled. He did not like a stranger using his Christian name, and especially a stranger who he knew was up to no good and had lied to him. Only track workers based at Chiswick station were allowed on Barnes Railway Bridge and he knew each man personally because he was their foreman. This man speaking with a bizarre mixture of accents, Cornish, Scottish, and Welsh, with a little Irish creeping in, claiming to be a Cornishman was a fraud. Penrose suspected he was dealing with a possible terrorist and wondered what was in the backpack? Was it a bomb? He was working alone on Barnes Railway Bridge because his work crew had been given the morning off to go and see the boat race and were somewhere among the crowds thronging Chiswick steps.

"I was told by the Barnes station master to check on the northbound railway tracks," continued Perkins glibly. "He said train drivers were reporting bumpy rails."

"Really, what's the Barnes station master's name?"

"I'm new here and I don't yet know the names of the station staff."

"Ah, but you've met the station master, haven't you?"

"Yes, he was in his office drinking tea."

"Describe him?"

Perkins panicked, this was a disaster and beads of sweat formed on his forehead. He glanced at his wristwatch. The boat race had started and there was less than eighteen minutes before the two boats would pass under Barnes Bridge. "I've must go," he declared, and picking up the backpack set off running down the tracks crossing the bridge.

"Stop. I'm making a citizen's arrest," shouted Penrose after him, and taking a firm grip of his spanner he set off in pursuit of the fleeing Perkins.

Chapter Five

Police constable Edgar Briggs, nicknamed 'Lanky' by fellow officers because of his diminutive size, five foot five, had been attached to the river Thames police less than a month and now ashen-faced and terrified was crouched in the back of a speeding police launch clinging desperately to the side of the boat with both hands, knuckles white. Briggs, a non-swimmer with terror of water had lied to his superior officer, Chief Inspector Howard, after telling him that he could swim like a fish thinking attachment to the river police would improve his chance of promotion. So far, his police career had been one of being transferred from division to division authorized by exasperated superior officers who were desperate to be rid of him. They had all after only a brief period of having him under their command reached the conclusion he was without doubt the most incept officer serving in the Metropolitan police.

Briggs was transferred to the river police after a tempting offer was made offering him promotion to the rank of sergeant after serving three years on the river. The offer was made with no possibility of him ever being made sergeant. His superiors considered him too much of risk to be allowed to mingle with the general public. It was thought it would be safer for the reputation of the Metropolitan police having out on a launch mid-river away from the general public.

Briggs had been hastily transferred to the river police from the horse-riding diversion following an embarrassing incident at Buckingham Palace during a royal garden party, which involved a horse ridden by Briggs and a member of royalty. When he joined the police he had passed out of Hendon police academy with the lowest grade possible, and was attached to the horse diversion where it was soon found that he had no empathy with horses and no control whatsoever over a galloping horse. All the horses he rode, mare or stallion, galloped madly away neighing furiously the moment he swung up onto the saddle. The out-of-control galloping horses not only a disaster for Briggs but also for members of the public, with Briggs screaming hysterically gripping the reins, shouting frantically, "Wow, there, wow, horsy wow." The horse taking no notice wanting to be rid of its unwanted rider. Briggs galloping through London streets become a financial disaster for New Scotland Yard with irate citizens, mostly motorists with cars damaged by flying horse hooves, making claims for car repairs and compensation for a harrowing experience.

The end came for Briggs in the horse diversion when a horse he was riding bolted through the main gates of Buckingham Palace scattering guests attending a royal garden party. Over went the guests like skittles at a bowling alley with tables and chairs flying. The horse, a five-year-old mare called Dumpling, galloped wildly across the back lawn neighing while trying to unseat Briggs. Dumpling leapt a table throwing him off and he landed on the lap of overweight labour MP Sidney Smyth from south Wigan, with a fifteen-vote majority and sixty-eight-inch belly. Smyth's belly cushioned Briggs fall and he received a rousing cheer from the other guests seated at the table all thankful he had not landed on them. The unfortunate Sidney Smyth, delirious and babbling incoherently was rushed to hospital badly bruised with a lifelong fear of policemen landing on his belly.

Meanwhile, Dumpling continued to gallop until she came to a fishpond where she stopped and lowered her head and took a long refreshing drink. Seated three yards away with back turned towards Dumpling was Her Majesty the Queen having a scone cream tea with American Ambassador Joseph Lawrence the fifth. When Dumpling finished drinking she raised her tail high and emitted a loud resounding fart sounding like a pistol shot. "Get under the table, your Majesty," cried the Ambassador as he dived under the table thinking an assassin had taken a shot at the Queen.

"It's alright, Mister Ambassador," replied the Queen smiling and unruffled, her voice steady and calm, holding a cup of tea. "It was not a gunman."

"Not a gunman?" replied the Ambassador, much relieved and peering out from under the table and feeling he was now defiantly in need of a change of underpants.

"Merely a fart, Mister Ambassador."

"A fart, your Majesty?" replied the Ambassador bewildered as he crawled out from under the table.

"Oh, yes, I recognized it immediately and the smell confirmed it."

The Ambassador did not reply thinking, 'that she who smelt it must have delt it."

The Queen felt as reigning British monarch she should apologize for the horse farting, and with a smile said, "I'm awfully sorry, Mister Ambassador, whatever must you think of me?"

"Oh, think nothing of it, your Majesty," replied the Ambassador bowing his head reverently and thinking the Queen was owning up to making the fart. "It can happen to the best of us."

Briggs was hastily transferred after the incident of the horse's fart to the Police Dog Division where he lasted two months. The dogs kept trying to mate with his right leg which was embarrassing during training sessions but a disaster when out on patrol walking a dog in public. Chief Inspector Owen Mackey the officer commanding the Metropolitan Police Dog Division tried every dog in the police kennels to work with Briggs, even his wife's longhaired little Pekinese Chan Chong, but all the dogs made straight for Briggs's right leg the moment they were introduced to him and humped merrily away until manhandled away barking with frustration. There was something about Briggs right leg that excited dogs and aroused their mating instincts.

It was the morning of the Oxford and Cambridge boat race and police constable Briggs cowered terrified in the back of a speeding police launch, face sickly green, legs unsteady, and body swaying. He wore a peaked hat with chinstrap down preventing it being swept away by the buffering wind. The other police officer on board the launch and seated at the steering wheel was constable Robert McDougal, thirty-two, barrel-chested, broad-shouldered a six-foot tall Scotsman, with a passion for eating haggis and supporting Manchester City football team, and making love to his wife Linda five times a week. The police launch was two hundred yards behind the Oxford university boat and speeding towards Barnes Railway Bridge. The Cambridge boat less than a boat's length ahead of the Oxford boat. The police launch ready to rescue crews should there be an accident and also to keep the motor boats packed with TV crews and journalists from getting too close to the University boats.

There came a great bellowing roar from crowds thronging the riverbanks as the University boats swept passed with each boat jockeying for position to be first under the bridge. "Here we go, Lanky, hold on tight," shouted constable McDougal as he swung the wheel over to follow in the wake of the Oxford boat. Briggs groaned with fear as the police launch pitched and rolled and waves crashed against the bow, and seeing Barnes Railway Bridge looming ahead he was shocked to hear someone scream. The scream continued and he wished it would stop then realized it was himself who was screaming.

Meanwhile, on Barnes Bridge railway worker David Penrose had caught Perkins after a hundred-yard dash and was threatening him with the 4ft spanner. "Come quietly," he said grimly. "I'm making a citizen's arrest."

"Please," protested Perkins, "you're making a terrible mistake." He no longer spoke with a Cornish accent but in his normal posh English public-school accent. "I haven't done anything wrong."

"What about trespass? The bridge is private property and belongs to British Rail."

"How do you know I'm not authorized to be on the bridge?"

"Because I'm the man who authorizes track workers to work on the bridge, and they work in pairs never alone. You're coming with me to Chiswick station where I'm going to call the police."

"But I was only taking a shortcut across the bridge to see the boat race."

"Dressed as a railway worker? I don't think so. What's happened to your Cornish accent?"

Perkins smiled sheepishly. "It comes and goes," he explained ruefully. "I've been living in London so long that sometimes I misplace my Cornish accent."

"What's in the backpack? Have you got a bomb?"

"Bomb? Why would I have a bomb?"

"So, you can blow up the bridge."

"That's ridiculous," replied Perkins indignantly. "I'm not a terrorist."

"Then what's in the backpack?"

"Sandwiches, cheese and pickle, with a flask of tea."

"Heavy sandwiches by the look of it. Show me?"

Perkins unzipped the backpack and opened it to reveal the slab of sandstone. "There," he said, "as I said it isn't a bomb."

"No, and it isn't sandwiches with a flask of tea either!"

Perkins re-zipped the backpack and decided to try a bribe. "Can't you turn a blind eye and let me go? I'll make it worth your while."

"No, I'm making a citizen's arrest and you're coming with me."

Perkins picked up the backpack and holding it before him with both hands he began walking towards Chiswick Railway station, followed by Penrose holding the spanner ready to strike should he try to run. They had not gone far when Perkins suddenly spun round swinging the backpack striking Penrose on the chest a tremendous blow sending him sprawling. Perkins raced away carrying the backpack.

"Come back," shouted Penrose throwing the spanner at the fleeing Perkins hitting him a glancing blow and knocking off his yellow hard hat. With a groan Perkins fell between the railway tracks with blood seeping from a gash behind his left ear.

"I must keep going or I'll end up in prison," he thought, and getting to his feet staggered on between the railway tracks. Penrose ran after him and dived for his legs bringing him down in a rugby tackle. The backpack flew from Perkins hands to disappear over the side of the bridge.

Meanwhile, the police launch with constable McDougal at the wheel was passing beneath the bridge following in the wake of the Oxford University boat. The backpack dropped on the constable's head killing him instantly. In the back of the launch Briggs, traumatized witnessing McDougal's death fainted as the launch with a dead man's hands on the wheel, body slumped over the throttles keeping them open, continued to race forward narrowly missing the Oxford University boat by inches.

Half-a-mile downriver the launch ran aground on a bend near Mortlake with bow embedded in soft squelchy mud. Police recovered the blood-stained backpack with the slab of sandstone. Briggs survived without injury. The Metropolitan Police forensic laboratory found fingerprints on both backpack and the sandstone. Scotland Yard and launched the biggest murder hunt since Jack the Ripper. The case file of a murdered policeman never closed until the murderer has been apprehended. The hunt was on for 'The Backpack Killer.

Perkins watched the backpack slide over the side of the bridge and thought it would splash harmlessly into the river below. He lay between railway tracks with legs gripped by Penrose who was determined to make his citizen's arrest. Perkins to evade arrest rained blows with both fists onto Penrose's hard hat trying to render him unconscious. Penrose fought back and they rolled backwards and citizen's arrest. The fight lasted only a few minutes before

Perkins the youngest and fittest of the two managed to get to his feet. Penrose reached out to grab Perkins and caught hold of his false moustache and held it gripped tightly in his hand. Perkins punched him on the nose and Penrose crumpled to the ground momentarily stunned. Glancing up he saw the fleeing figure of Perkins scurrying away across the bridge and getting to his feet gave chase. He tripped on a wooden sleeper and fell striking his head on a railway track and bleeding profusely and unconscious lay dying.

Next day in the mortuary the false black moustache Penrose ripped from Perkins face was found clenched in his right hand and bagged as evidence for DNA testing. The police mistakenly believing David Penrose had been murdered, and with him murdered on top of the bridge and police constable Robert McDougal murdered under the bridge, concluded they were seeking a serial killer with a liking for bridges and boats.

Perkins head throbbed painfully where he was struck by Penrose's spanner as he escaped from the bridge and fled back to his hotel. But in desperation to escape and suffering with mild concussion he forgot to change out of his donkey jacket disguise. He reached Braddock Towers holding a bloody handkerchief to an egg-sized lump behind his left ear, and staggered disheveled through the revolving glass doors into the hotel lobby.

Desk clerk Allan Hawes was on duty at the reception desk and glanced up as Perkins entered the lobby and was shocked and intrigued to see the filthy state of the man he thought was Roger Shepherd the Third. This for Hawes, a budding private detective, made the American even more of an interest as a possible suspect for committing some crime, with him bizarrely dressed in a donkey jacket and holding a bloody handkerchief to his ear.

Perkins moved unsteadily across the lobby towards the open lift doors to go to his room. "Mister Shepherd," called out Hawes, wanting to question him about the donkey jacket and bloody handkerchief. "What's happened to you?" Hawes had been reading an article in the Detective Monthly magazine about conmen and how they pretended to be somebody else to carry out their dastardly crime. Was this why Roger Shepherd the Third was dressed in a donkey jacket? Had he been pretending to be workman to commit a crime, and why was he trying to enter the lift without collecting his room key at the reception desk? This was very suspicious behaviour indeed, and Hawes was determined to question him and make notes for the case file he was keeping on him.

Perkins paused about to step into the lift and turned to face the desk clerk. "Ah, good afternoon," he called forcing a weak smile and forgetting in his panic to speak in the Texan drawl he had used when talking to hotel staff. "Any mail for me today?" he asked, speaking in his normal posh English public-school voice.

Hawes hearing the English accent believed his suspicions confirmed and the man defiantly was a criminal. "What's happened to your American accent?" he called out experiencing one of his famous hunches telling him villainy was a foot.

Perkins quickly reverted back to his Texan drawl, and replied, "Ah, so you've noticed, have you? Well, I've been practicing for when I go home to the States. Americans love hearing the English accent and I thought it would delight my friends if I did it for them as my party piece."

"How interesting," replied Hawes, not believing a word of it, conmen according to the article were expert liars and could convince victims that black was white and the moon was made of cheese. He took a room key from the board on the wall behind him and hurried across the lobby to join Perkins. "Have you got a moment?" he asked politely.

"Sorry, but I'm in a hurry. I've things to do," retorted Perkins stepping into the lift. He reached out to press the button for his floor and the doors began to slide shut.

"What about your key?" asked Hawes holding up the key and putting his right foot into the lift stopping the from doors closing, "You won't get in your room without your key."

"Thanks, I'd be forgetting my head next," muttered Perkins apologetically with a weak smile, taking the key. "Please remove your foot so I can go to my room."

Hawes did not remove his foot. "Just a few moments of your time before you go. It's important."

"I'm tired and need to take a shower."

"The manager wants your passport," lied Hawes, in an effort to keep Perkins talking and the lift door open. If there was as he suspected no American passport in the name of Roger Shepherd the Third then his hunch was right and the man was a criminal pretending to be an American tourist.

"Passport? But why? I don't understand?"

"It's only a formality, all foreign tourists must hand over their passports when staying at Braddock Towers. It's Home Office regulations."

"My passport? But I've stayed here three times in the last six weeks and never been asked for my passport."

"It must have been overlooked, Sir. Passports from overseas guests have to be handed in at the reception desk when they sign in."

"Alright, I'll get it for you."

"Thank you, Sir," replied Hawes removing his foot from jamming the lift doors. "I'll be waiting for you at my desk." Perkins closed the lift door and pressed the button for his floor, the fifth floor, and the lift shot upwards.

Hawes, pleased with his questioning, thought it was good practice for when he was a real private detective. He strode cheerfully back to the reception desk with a smile on his face. The man who called himself Roger Shepherd Third was a criminal and he would prove it. Sitting at the desk he wrote in his notebook the conversation he had with Perkins, and when he finished writing glanced up at the wall clock and saw half-an-hour had passed and the man still had not returned with his passport. "He's up in his room trying to think up a plausible excuse for not producing his passport," thought Hawes with a knowing chuckle. He switched on the radio on his desk to listen to the BBC news and was shocked to hear the announcer say the Oxford and Cambridge boat race had been abandoned because of a double murder, a river policeman and a railway worker. The news reader said the police were seeking a man dressed in a donkey jacket who was seen climbing over a six-foot high wire fence at Barnes Railway Bridge at the time of the murders.

Hawes switched off the radio, heart beating faster with excitement believing the man calling himself Roger Shepherd the Third was the man the police were seeking. Picking up the telephone he dialed 999 and when the woman operator asked which emergency service he required, replied, "Police. I've a suspected murderer to report."

Meanwhile, Perkins lost no time when he reached his hotel room making his escape from the hotel, and he clambered out of a window and down a fire escape. In a side street behind the hotel, flagged down a passing taxi and was taken to Victoria coach station, and thirty minutes later was seated in a coach heading for home.

Chapter Six

Chief Superintendent Sydney Masher of New Scotland Yard sat at his desk reading a report from a bulky red file. An enormously fat man, so fat his office chair has been widened and reinforced three times in four years to take his ever-increasing blubbery bulk. Called 'Fatty Bum," by colleagues behind his back, and 'Lardy Arse' to his face by his wife's parents who never liked him. Sydney Masher, fifty-three, married with four grown-up children, wearing thick pebble lensed glasses that magnify his eyes giving him a frog-like appearance. There is a timid knock on the door. "Enter," called out Masher in a squeaky voice because his hemorrhoids were misbehaving again.

The door opened and police constable Edgar 'Lanky' Briggs entered and standing to attention he saluted. "You sent for me, Sir," he said removing his peaked hat and placing it under his right arm.

The Chief Superintendent sighed and returned the report to the red file and closed it, adjusted his glasses and studied the constable standing before him. He had been reading with growing dismay the latest escapade of the constable which caused chaos and questions asked in Parliament. The bulky file was full of stories of horses galloping out of control damaging cars, a farting horse upsetting royalty and frightening the American Ambassador, dogs attempting to have sex with the constable's right leg in public places. "Do you know why I've sent for you, Briggs?" he asked coldly, eyeing the constable contemptuously. Masher had been instructed by superiors to convince the hapless Edgar Briggs to take an early retirement and save the Metropolitan police from any more embarrassment with his incept chaotic deplorable activities.

"My promotion, Sir," replied Briggs with a smile.

"Promotion?"

"Thank you, Sir, I won't let you down. I'll be a credit to the force."

"What are you thanking me for?"

"My promotion to sergeant, Sir."

"Blithering idiot. I wouldn't promote you to sergeant not if my life depended on it. God knows what would happen if you were made a sergeant. We can't have an inmate running the asylum."

"Oh, then I'm not being promoted, Sir?"

"I'd rather stick my head up an elephant's arse than promote you, Briggs."

"I was wondering . . ."

"Wondering what?" interrupted Masher. He wanted the interview with Briggs over as quickly as possible so he could rush away and be head of the dinner queue in the dining room for streak and kidney pudding. If he was late and ended-up at the back of the queue then there might be no steak and kidney pudding left and it was his favourite.

"Well, I was thinking, Sir, it would have to be a really big elephant like an African elephant."

"What are you talking about?"

"For you to put your head up its arse, Sir."

"Are you mad?"

"No, Sir, I've got my National Service discharge papers to prove it."

"What did you do during your National Service?"

"I was a cook's assistant at Pirebright barracks, Sir. The sergeant cook said I was performing a most important service for the regiment."

"Important service?"

"Yes, Sir, an important service."

"You peeled potatoes, didn't you?"

Briggs nodded. "Yes, someone had to do it and at my best I could peel half-a-ton in a day. Might I ask why you've sent for me, Sir?"

"Ah, yes, I'd forgotten with all your nonsense. I want to talk to you about your future with the police."

"My future, Sir?"

"Yes, I thought you might not be happy being a policeman after all that's happened to you, and you might be thinking that you're in the wrong job, you know like a round peg in a square hole. I can help find you a more suitable job. Something you'd be good at doing and I'd give you a glowing reference. You like wearing a uniform, I know that, so how why not join the fire service?"

"When I was in the boy scouts, I made fires, Sir, my scout leader said I was the best scout in the troop for making fires."

"Well, there you are, Briggs, you like fires. What about putting them out as a fireman?"

"My scout master thought the same, Sir, about me liking fires. I kept setting fire to the scout hut when I was trying for my camp fire lighting badge!"

"How long were you a boy scout?"

"Five months, Sir."

"How many times did you set fire to the scout hut?"

"Five, Sir."

"That's why you left the scouts? You burnt down the scout hut?"

"Yes, Sir, the scout master said he couldn't hold any more troop meetings without a hut."

"How did you feel about that?"

"Really bad, Sir, the scout master refused to give me my fire lighting badge."

Masher took out a handkerchief and mopped his sweating brow. "So, you insist staying a policeman?" he asked, resigned the hapless Briggs was determined to remain in the police force.

Briggs smiled and nodded his head. "Yes, Sir, it's the only career for me. "

"I read in your service file that you've been transferred four times in the last year, Briggs, and haven't made a single arrest."

"It's not my fault, Sir, people and animals don't like me."

"Ah, but dogs like you, don't they?"

"Only my right leg, Sir."

"Would you consider taking early retirement with an enhanced pension?"

Briggs shook his head. "No, Sir, I'm happy being a policeman. It's what I always wanted to be."

"Is there nothing I can say to make you change your mind?"

"No, sir, I'm needed in the force."

"Very well, Briggs, then I'm going to transfer you to CID with immediate effect in the hope when you're on duty in plain clothes members of the public won't know that you're a police officer."

"Thank you, sir, I'll do my best. Can I take my truncheon and whistle with me?"

Twelve years have passed and Perkins is now a solicitor with Williams, Williams, Williams, and Pritchard, in Purely, Surrey, where he deals with shoplifting, illegal parking, flashing and dropping litter. He has prospered with his secret pastime of murdering for hire, and is engaged to Hilary Doors, a widow, well-endowed, a woman keen on pot plants and being adventurous in bed. They plan to marry at the church of St Freda's the Eveready in

Bumstead-on-the-Wold on their return from a holiday in Greece.

Perkins hired a yacht to cruise the Greek islands and four days into the cruise as night was falling with Hilary Doors up on deck at the wheel, with him below decks preparing dinner, a mist descended with visibility down to three feet in any direction. Hilary Doors heard a splash coming from the stern of the yacht and hurried to investigate and leaning over the rail slipped and toppled into the sea. The yacht continued sailing. Half-an-hour later Perkins appeared on deck and called out, "Dinner's ready, Hilary." He was pleased with the leg of lamb he prepared with roast potatoes, carrots all set peas, with mint sauce, to be followed with a sherry fruit trifle, all set out below on a candle lit table. There was no response from Hilary and panicked he searched the boat from stem to stern then realized to his horror she had fallen overboard. He turned the yacht around to look for her and called out her name into the darkness, "Hilary, Hilary."

Hilary Doors had been kept afloat by her huge buoyant breasts acting as water-wings, and two hours after falling over board she heard Perkins calling her name away in the darkness. Cupping her hands to her mouth she was about to answer him when up from the depths below with jaws open came a gigantic hungry white shark, who with a one snap of its jaws dragged her down into the deep.

Perkins returned to England a broken man and sold his cottage. Hilary left everything to him in her will including her cottage. He retired from being a solicitor and with the money kept in a Swiss bank account, the money earned for murder for hire, he purchased a manor house five miles south of the village of Bumstead-on-the-Wold. He moved in with his mother Hetty telling her and the villagers he had won the lottery. Grieving for Hilary he threw himself into his murder for hire business to keep himself occupied and expanded it to cover the world, going away on trips abroad to murder for wealthy clients. But made it a rule never to murder more than three people in a calendar year.

Posing as Japanese tourist Wun Hun Low with three cameras dangling from his neck, Perkins was in Yellow Stone Park, Wyoming, America, engaged in conversation with wealthy American banker Melvin Rose and his wife Gloria. The couple stood hand in hand admiring a hot spring waiting for it to spout up again with boiling water over fifty feet in the air, which happened every five minutes. "You likee me takee picture?" asked Perkins with a bow of his head with a bad Japanese accent, smiling broadly showing his false buck teeth.

"Oh, let's, Melvin," cried Gloria looking at her husband, "it'll be such a lovely memento of our visit here."

Melvin Rose handed Perkins his camera. "Thanks, it's good of you."

Perkins looked through the viewfinder on the camera. "You standee closee together," he said, and Melvin Rose put his arm lovingly round his wife's waist and she put her arm round his waist. "Steppy backee pleese so both in picture," continued Perkins. The Roses took a backwards step looking at the camera. "No, still steppee backee more pleese," encouraged Perkins. The Roses took another step backwards. "One more steppee pleese," called Perkins. The Roses stepped back to stand over the hole of the spring. "Smile pleese," called Perkins. The Roses smiled and a jet of boiling water burst up from the hole shooting them fifty feet in the air boiling them alive. Perkins hurried away leaving the bodies to be found by park rangers. The contact for their deaths had been made by their twenty-three-year-old daughter Monica, who was impatient to inherit their wealth.

Four months later, Perkins disguised as Frenchman Marcelle Frieral, with false beard and false Roman nose, was employed as assistant elephant keeper to be close to his intended victim at Lyon Zoo, in France. He was assisting the head elephant keeper, Jules Dupier, washing Nancy an African female elephant with mops and buckets of soapy water. Perkins had been working at the zoo for three days, and Nancy was a rescued circus elephant who was trained to sit on her haunches when offered a bunch of bananas. The head keeper stood at the rear of Nancy busily washing away at her rear end when Perkins, standing by her swinging trunk, offered the elephant a bunch of bananas. Nancy promptly sat down on the head keeper who disappeared headfirst up her fundament with only his feet showing. He suffocated before hauled out by Perkins with the help of two other assistant keepers and a rope. The client for the head keeper's murder was his wife Brigitte who received his life insurance with substantial compensation from the zoo. Perkins was given an added bonus for a job well done, and Nancy the elephant banned from eating bananas.

Thirteen years and thirty-one murders later and Perkins is a multi-millionaire living in luxury in his mansion with his mother and girlfriend, the supple luscious athletic Miss Melody Austin, who was half his age, blonde, beautiful, and loved spending his money. The mansion has a staff of eight including Cobblers the butler, an Australian cook called Shorty, six foot six inches tall, who plays the didgeridoo badly and with himself when nobody is looking, two maids, a chauffeur, four gardeners, and a stable girl called Dilly Potter who looks after the three thoroughbred horses in the stables, two mares and a stallion. Perkins with Melody regularly ride with the local foxhunt 'The Bumstead Hunt.' Master of the hunt the pompous blustering Colonel Ivor Biggan late of the Suffolk Fifth Artillery, a regiment who performed without distinction in the North African desert campaign during World War Two, where they terrified the Germans and thrilled Arab women when showing them their enormous artillery pieces.

Edgar 'Lanky' Briggs career had blossomed over the years and he had become a Chief Inspector in CID, the result of a typing error by a short-sighted typist. He was determined to track down the double killer of the Barnes Bridge murders, and kept the murder file on his desk should new evidence become available. There was the sighting of a man dressed in a donkey jacket seen climbing over a fence at Barnes Railway Bridge, and the DNA sample taken from the false black moustache found clasped within railway worker David Penrose's dead fist. Blood found on the long-handed spanner on the bridge did not match with David Penrose's blood, which was Rhesus Positive.

The DNA taken from the false moustache and the long-handled spanner Rhesus Negative belonging to the killer. There was also a statement made by hotel desk clerk Allan Hawes reporting a mysterious hotel guest staying at Braddock Towers claiming to be Roger Shepherd the Third from Dallas, Texas, who disappeared immediately following the murders without trace. Scotland Yard had sought help from Interpol who contacted the CIA in America who confirmed no passport was issued to Roger Shepherd the Third from Dallas, Texas. Fingerprints found in the bogus Roger Shepherd's hotel room in Braddock Towers matched with those found on the backpack and on the sandstone that fell on policer constable Robert McDougal's head crushing it like an egg shell.

New Scotland Yard believed the man they were seeking was an educated Englishman with public-school background, this was because when pretending to be Roger Shepherd the Third he made the mistake of speaking briefly with a posh English public-school accent to Allan Hawes before reverting back to a Texan drawl, when challenged in the hotel lounge wearing a donkey jacket. Briggs vowed at police constable Robert McDougal's funeral, a watery one with weighted coffin tipped into the river Thames estuary from off the back of a speeding police launch, that only his death or retirement would prevent him tracking down and arresting the killer responsible.

Chapter Seven

Sir Rupert Slattery, knight of the British theatre, thespian of world-renowned, founder member of the Watford Shakespearean players, advanced slowly and majestically towards the glaring footlights and his adoring audience. He looked resplendent alone on stage, a theatre legend within the bright spotlight, magnificent in white tights with bejeweled encrusted glittering codpiece. The codpiece thrice the normal size to invoke the delight and interest of female members of the audience and make men feel dreadfully inadequate. The bold knight playing the lead role in Shakespeare's Richard the Third with an artificial hump beneath an ermine trimmed red jacket limping as if one leg was shorter than the other, advancing towards the footlights he began his opening speech. The audience are spellbound listening to the great thespian's booming baritone voice. Sir Rupert at the peak of his acting career, the darling of London and Broadway critics, who recently was offered a supporting role in a Sterling Spellberger western film starring cowboy Dusty Jones, with Sir Rupert Slattery playing his trusty grisly old sidekick Gabby Winkle in 'My Horse Henrietta."

Sir Rupert, fifty-seven, married to fellow thespian lady Doris Slattery with four grown-up children; all girls who had followed their parents into the theatre and were sitting in the front row eating popcorn. In the darkness under the stage Perkins dressed entirely in black crept forward in the darkness guided by a slender beam of light from a small torch. Above him he heard the shuffling steps of the great actor. "Now is the winter of my discontent," boomed the theatrical knight in his clarion voice as he waved his right hand above his head bringing shocked gasps from the audience. He was giving them the one-finger gesture by mistake.

"Now is the time for you to go," muttered Perkins grimly as he slid back the two bolts holding the stage trap door in place, "either straight to heaven or straight to Hell."

"Made glorious summer by this son of York . . ." continued Sir Rupert as he took the fateful step onto the trap door which promptly gave way beneath him. With startled anguished cry he vanished from sight down the open the trap door. The audience expecting to see Sir Rupert's own brilliant interpretation of the role of Richard the Third, a portrayal that will astound the critics thought he had devised the fall himself through the stage door as part of the play. What a stupendous opening of the play seeing the bold knight in his well-padded codpiece disappear down the stage trapdoor. Such a theatrical feat never performed before not even on Broadway. Sir Rupert Slattery was thought to be a genius of the theatre with his interpretations of the Shakespearean roles he played with gusto and imagination. The audience were in no doubt that they were witnessing his most brilliant portrayal so far, a triumphant of live theatre and as one they stood up from their seats and gave a standing ovation calling for the vanished thespian.

Meanwhile, below the stage in darkness the theatre knight lay in a crumpled agonized heap having twisted his right ankle. He glanced up to see a shadowy figure holding a torch approaching him. It was Perkins. "Ah, tis a stage hand come to help," muttered Sir Rupert, and hearing the thunderous applause of the audience calling his name coming down the open trap door, beamed with pride. "Oh, but listen to my audience," he cried joyfully momentarily forgetting his painful ankle, "they call for me." He wiped away a teardrop from both cheeks with the index finger of his right hand.

Perkins gazed down at the knight of the theatre, disappointed he was still alive having hoped the fall would have broken his neck. Now, he would have to finish off the thespian for which he had been most handsomely paid. "Oh, but how they cheer for me, the dear hearts," proclaimed the tearful knight carried away by his own rhetoric. "How can I let my audience down? Come, my friend," he called to Perkins, "help me to my feet. I shall astound my audience and continue to play Richard from a wheelchair. I'll be the first to do so on stage and it will amaze the critics."

Perkins wondering how to finish off Slattery shone his torch beam directly onto his face. The actor smiled broadly showing his teeth. The light for him was but another slender spotlight with an audience behind it even if the audience was only a stagehand to enjoy his performance. He turned his head to the left to present his best profile within the small pool of light. "There'll be no wheelchair," declared Perkins grimly.

"No? Why not? How can I perform without it?"
"Because you won't need it."
"Then how will I move about on stage?"
"You'll not be moving anywhere."

"I don't understand. What are you saying?"

"You'll be gone."

"Gone? Where to? Are you talking about taking me to hospital? No, my dear fellow, I refuse to go. The play must go on. I'll suffer for my audience. I can't disappoint them. They want to see the whole play and I must have my curtain calls at the end. I had six curtain calls in the pantomime Cinderella last season in Brighton when I played Dame Twankey. It was a great success although that dreadful theatre critic Joselin Howie of 'The Sunday Bugle' said in his review that I was more Wankey than Twankey."

"This is your final curtain call, Sir Rupert," replied Perkins grimly, as he swung a claw hammer shattering the knight's head with a single blow. He wanted the thespian's death to look as if he had fallen headfirst through the trapdoor onto his head.

Sir Rupert's body was found three minutes later crumpled and bloody on the floor under the open trapdoor by two stagehands. The police recorded it as accidental death.

Sir Cedric Royston, knight of the British theatre, well-known thespian and TV talk show bore, sat at a small table in the corner of a dimly lit south London pub in the pub bar. The public house sixteenth century with low oak beams and called 'The Queen's Headaches,' after Queen Elizabeth the First and her legendary headaches when she kept refusing to have sex and died a virgin queen who never spread her legs except for riding a horse.

Sir Cedric Royston, thin and bony, talks in hushed tones to a woman, rotund, middle-aged. with blue-rinsed-hair gathered at the back in a bun, dressed in green tweed jacket and skirt, wide brimmed white hat. The woman is Perkins in his favourite disguise as the overweight middle-aged Miss Marion Pringle, which he uses for meeting clients for his murder for hire business to conceal his true identity. He has a duck feather filled pillow stuffed up the back of the tweed skirt giving the appearance of prominent buttocks, with a cotton wool filled extra-large bra. The face heavily made up with lipstick, rouge and powder. Miss Pringle's character portrayed brilliantly by Perkins as a middle-aged countryside loving spinster with passion for horses and riding to hounds.

Sir Cedric Royston had come to pay the final half payment he owed for the murder of his archival of the theatre Sir Rupert Slattery. The two great thespians had been rivals in both the theatre and affairs of the heart. Sir Rupert having married the woman who Sir Royston loved, cherished and desired, his childhood sweetheart Nelly Lilly King. Both men born in the same year on the same month on the same day under the star sign of the rutting ram. They met as young teenagers when they started their theatre careers at The Betty Boo Stage School in south Catford, where Rupert Slattery was star pupil who took to acting and tap dancing in tights like a duck takes to water, while Cedric Royston, suffering with severe stage fright and especially so when wearing tights, took to acting and tap-dancing like an ostrich takes to flying. But he persevered in his chosen career determined to succeed because he was born into a theatrical family with his father assistant stage manager of the Hippodrome puppet theatre in south Norwood and mother selling ice creams during the interval, with sister Doreen the usherette showing people to their seats and sweeping up afterwards.

Rupert Slattery was a born actor with poise and great delivery, the delivery learnt when he delivered letters and parcels as a postman between acting jobs. After leaving stage school at the age of eighteen with a passion for wearing tights, he was soon playing major Shakespearean roles such as Hamlet, King Leer, and Bottom in Midnight Summer's Dream. Meanwhile, Cedric Royston who was racked with jealousy against his arch-rival played only minor roles such as the third or fourth spear carrier in Shakespearean productions, performed in Glasgow theatres where men in tights were not welcome. Cedric Royston did not get a major starring role until he played Bottom in Shakespeare's Midnight Summer's Dream at a rundown seedy theatre in Lower Watford next door to Fred's greasy spoon café. He was thirty-one-years-old and implored family, friends and neighbours, some bribed, to come and see his Bottom, declaring with pride, "It's the best Bottom in tights you'll ever see on stage!"

This claim was endorsed by Courtney Howler the theatre critic of the Sunday News, a gay man who praised Cedric Royston's bottom in his weekly column saying it was truly magnificent and made him think of a delicious hot-cross bun. However, Cedric Royston's doctor, Gordon Spence, who became a doctor for the opportunity for seeing naked women without having to pay for the privilege, disagreed with the theatre critic, and said he had seen Cedric Royston's bottom many times in his surgery and on more than one occasion called in a colleague for a second opinion.

Sir Cedric Royston nervously eyed the plump woman in green tweeds sitting opposite him. There was something strangely unfeminine about Miss Monica Pringle and he could not put his finger on it, and indeed had he known what it was then most certainly he would not have put a finger on it. Taking a quick swallow of whiskey on the rocks to steady his nerves he said in a whisper, keeping his voice low so he would not be overheard by people sitting at nearby tables "I read Sir Rupert Slattery's obituary in 'The Times' and it said his Hamlet was superior to mine. I'm appalled and upset about it. My Hamlet was more superior than his and I've had more curtain calls in my career than him. I commanded the stage like a colossus with my Hamlet making the audience gasp with amazement. Tell me, dear lady, have you seen my Hamlet?"

"Why? Are your flies undone?"

"No, I mean Hamlet the Prince of Denmark, Shakespeare's play."

"Do you want him murdered? I can offer you special rates for a second murder. Shall we say twenty per cent off my usual fee. What do you say?"

Sir Cedric Royston shook his head and took another swallow of whiskey to steady himself. Since employing Miss Pringle, he had been drinking more than was good for him. The woman terrified and unnerved him. "No, thank you, dear lady," he muttered, "one murder is enough for me, but thank you for the offer."

"Well, keep it in mind."

"I've the rest of your fee here. I must go now. I've a train to catch and time's pressing. I'm performing tonight."

"Shakespeare?"

"No, in bed with the wife. It's her birthday treat and I always make a special effort for her birthday. I know how much she looks forward to it all year." He reached into his inside jacket pocket and took out a thick brown envelope and handed it to Perkins. "It's all in used bank notes as you requested, Miss Pringle."

"Thank you, Sir Royston. I hope you'll keep my services in mind. Old customers as I said get a discount for a second murder."

"Thank you, Miss Pringle. You've done a good job with the demise of Sir Rupert Slattery."

"Pleased to have been of service."

"How that bastard Slattery had the nerve to call himself the greatest Shakespearean actor of the age I'll never know, everyone who loves Shakespeare knows my Bottom is in a class of its own,

57

supreme and majestic as I trod the stage in tights."

"With Sir Slattery dead there isn't any doubt that you're the greatest Shakespearean actor of the age."

Sir Royston smiled and nodded; eyes moist with tears. "Yes, that's true, dear lady, I'm the greatest. But I shall be humble and wonderful for my next season at Stratford-upon-Avon where I shall perform King Lear. My King Lear will astound the critics and I shall be proclaimed a genius in tights as I was with my Bottom."

Perkins smiling took the brown envelope and slipped it into a black handbag on the table in front of him. "Yes," he agreed, "a genius in tights," thinking the thespian was over-rating his Bottom.

"That bastard Slattery, Miss Pringle, tell me, dear lady, was he any good in his last role as Richard the Third?"

"What do you mean was he any good?"

"Did he have any curtain calls?"

"No, dear lady, he went without any curtain calls."

"Went?"

"Yes, disappeared suddenly from the stage."

"Was it a good performance up to then?"

"No, he corpsed at the beginning of the first act."

Chapter Eight

Doctor Albert Windrush MD was visiting the home of his best friend and fellow criminologist super sleuth Allan Hawes, residing at 202B Bakery Street. The doctor a semi-retired consultant employed three days a week at St Thomas's hospital in Cheam, Surrey, where he specialized in flatulent disorders, persistent piles and floppy penises. The doctor, grey haired, tall and distinguished looking with high cheekbones, bristling bushy moustache with sideburns, long spindly legs, who wears a monocle for important social occasions. He considers himself to be a gentleman with clean habits and good intentions who daily wears freshly laundered underpants ironed by his mother. He is a bachelor living with his elderly mother Glenda, an arthritic widow with passion for ironing and knitting gloves and scarfs, in a four-bedroom detached house in Chelsea. The doctor is immensely proud of his regular daily bowel movements which he believes a sign of good health and clean living, and likes to bring them into conversation whenever possible. He is a martyr to gout which effects the joints of both big toes, and also to the constant nagging from his mother who thinks at the age of forty-six he should be married and have given her grandchildren to spoil.

The doctor wears a navy-blue three-piece suit with pale blue tie, with pink carnation in the buttonhole, with a stethoscope dangling from the left jacket pocket to show he is a medical man. He sits at a table eating breakfast spreading butter over a slice of toast.

Standing at the open French window and posed dramatically with the morning breeze gently fluttering the floral curtains stands the imposing figure of the great detective himself, Allan Hawes. The detective wearing a purple silk smoking jacket with gold piping, light grey trousers with sharp creases and red-carpet slippers. His eyes are closed and there is a look of rapture on his face as he lovingly plays a violin, moving the bow more rapidly over taught strings as the music reaches a crescendo. With a shrill a gasp of pain a finger catches in the strings and muttering a foul oath he places the violin and bow with a clatter onto a table. The music continues to play. The detective walks over to a record player on a sideboard and switches it off and the music stops playing.

"My dear chap," cried the doctor, alarmed and leaping to his feet.

"Are you in need of my medical services? Have you hurt your finger ain?"

"It's only a finger, Doctor. I must learn to take pain without complaint and concentrate my thoughts on defeating crime."

"How I admire your courage and resolve."

"Thank you, Doctor."

"I know what'll cheer you up. I experienced a most excellent bowel movement this morning before leaving home."

"Why tell me this, Doctor? I've no interest whatsoever in your bowel movements be they good or bad. Indeed, I can't think of a less interesting topic for conversation."

"I thought it might take your mind off your finger."

"Well, it hasn't, and it still hurts. I'm sure that a lesser man than myself would have fainted."

"Sorry, Hawes."

"Apology accepted, old chap."

There came a knocking on the door and a woman's bright cockney voice called out, "You've got a visitor, Mister Hawes. Don't panic it's a lady, Mrs Mabel Frogmorton, and not the rent collector come again demanding his money."

"Please show her in Mrs Gooseberry," exclaimed the super sleuth brightly as he stepped quickly to stand in front of the fireplace knowing that first impressions count especially in the private detective business. He liked to pose himself standing before the fireplace for visitors to 202B Bakery Street. The door opened and a small robust roly-poly woman in her late fifties, rosy red apple cheeks, wearing a white apron with matching frilly cap, came bustling into the room, Mrs Brenda Gooseberry the housekeeper. She has been a widow for eight years. Her late husband, Clive Gooseberry, an alcoholic and Crystal Palace football supporter, had been returning home late one night drunk with his friend Gilbert Parker, equally drunk, both singing and supporting each other from the Dog and Duck public house. Giggling and hardly able to stand they lifted a manhole cover in the Edgeware Road saying they were going in for a swim and jumped down into the sewer never to be seen again.

Mrs Gooseberry in her grief turned to her hobbies of knitting willy warmers for Crystal Palace football supporters and collecting Victorian glassware when shop assistants were not looking. She is the epitome of a cheerful cockney landlady, born within the sound of

London's Bow Bells with a passion for pie and mash and jellied eels, and like all cheerful cockneys smiles at adversity while insisting on making cups of sweet tea as remedy for all ills and misfortunes.

Following close on Mrs Gooseberry's heels a petite beautiful woman in her early thirties with a pale face. She has a haughty contemptuous expression and expensively dressed in the latest abstraction of wealthy bad taste, clearly showing she has either a wealthy husband without much sense or a wealthy lover without much sense. She wears a pale blue silk dress with a white mink stole draped over her slim alabaster shoulders and a double rope of South Sea pearls round her neck, and advances confidently into the room with head held high. On each finger of her black velvet gloved hands sparkles rings, each ring set with a precious stone. Her nose is deliberately raised high as if there is a nasty smell in the room. "Mrs Mabel Frogmorton," declared Mrs Gooseberry introducing her to Allan Hawes, as the lady in question swept passed her like an old sailing ship in full sail.

Mabel Frogmorton is the fourth and youngest daughter of an improvised Welsh landowner, and she married for money in expectation of her husband being knighted with her having the grand title of Lady Frogmorton. She married multi-millionaire George Frogmorton, sixty-three, who started work at fourteen selling fruit and vegetables off a street-market barrow and ended up owning a chain of supermarkets.

Doctor Windrush, seeing Mrs Mabel Frogmorton enter the room, leapt to his feet with a half-eaten slice of toast and marmalade in his hand. He instantly recognized her. Three months earlier he had treated her husband for persistent piles and a floppy penis. "Ah, Mrs Frogmorton," he exclaimed as he stepped out from behind the table. "It's good seeing you again." He forgot in his haste the slice of toast in his hand as he offered his hand, and she, not seeing the slice of toast shook the toast instead of his hand. Marmalade oozed between the fingers of her black velvet glove. "Oh, I'm awfully sorry," spluttered the doctor acutely embarrassed.

"Have a cup of tea, Doctor," suggested Mrs Gooseberry sympathetically seeing his distress.

"No, thank you, Mrs Gooseberry," muttered the doctor thinking the last thing he needed was to have a cup of tea, but a whiskey would be ideal. "That's your answer to all of life's ills, isn't it?" he replied looking at the housekeeper, "have a cup of tea. If a fellow breaks an arm or a leg you'd offer him a cup of tea. It's rubbish I tell you; tea doesn't cheer a fellow up, no, actually it does the opposite and especially so if he doesn't like tea."

"I know what'll cheer you up, Doctor," proclaimed Mrs Gooseberry brightly, "laughter always helps in adversary I find."

"Oh, no," cried Hawes appalled and knowing she was about to tell another one of her ripe cockney jokes. The housekeeper's humour was at best crude and extremely rude. "Not another of your jokes, Mrs Gooseberry, please, not in front of a lady!"

"Have you heard the one about the flasher who wanted to retire," continued Mrs Gooseberry unabashed and not to be stopped, "who decided to stick it out for one more year?"

Mrs Frogmorton, with a look of disgust, turned to Hawes and declared indignantly, "I haven't come to hear cheap music hall jokes but to hire your services because I've heard you're the best private detective in Great Britain if not the world, and you're very discreet in your work."

"Yes, Hawes is most certainly the best detective in the world," agreed the doctor proudly. "I can vouch for that."

"You can rely on my discretion, Mrs Frogmorton," added Hawes, beaming with pride with the praise, then looking at Mrs Gooseberry wondered if she had been at the cooking sherry again. "Mrs Gooseberry," he declared with a grimace, "there's a time and place for your bawdy humour and it isn't here in front of this lady whose come seeking my help."

Meanwhile, Mrs Frogmorton had removed her marmalade-covered glove and slipped it discreetly away into her handbag out of sight with the rings. She took a deep breath to steady herself wishing she had bought her smelling salts. "Mrs Frogmorton," called out the doctor, "don't you remember me? I'm the consultant at St Thomas's who treated your husband for piles and his penile problem. Surely you remember me? Doctor Albert Windrush?"

Mrs Frogmorton stared incredulously at the doctor and shook her head. Doctors in her world were the same as tradesmen who used the backdoor when visiting her palatial home. "I'm sorry but I don't recall you," she replied haughtily, "you look like any other tradesman to me."

"Tradesman?" exclaimed the doctor aghast and insulted. He prided himself on his friendly relationships with his wealthy clientele thinking they in turn took equal pride in knowing him. How could she have forgotten him? "But surely, Mrs Frogmorton," he continued determined to jog her memory, "you must remember me? I was the doctor who corrected with surgery and a small battery power pack your husband's failure to rise and remain upstanding during your intimate occasions together." Mrs Frogmorton's husband George had been fitted with a remote control to produce an erection when required within seconds of the button on the remote control pressed, and as an added bonus the hospital had given the penis erecting device a five-year guarantee of providing an upstanding service whenever required.

"Intimate occasions? I don't understand. What are talking about?" asked Mrs Frogmorton indignantly.

"I mean when you and your husband unite bodies to express your love, Mrs Frogmorton."

"Have you lost your wits? My husband expresses his love by buying me expensive jewelry and clothes."

"But I inserted a penis corrector on your husband to help him produce an heir, Mrs Frogmorton," declared the doctor bluntly, "all he had to do to perform was press the red button on the remote control to produce a fully erect serviceable penis."

"Oh, yes, I know you now, doctor Windrush," snapped Mrs Mabel Frogmorton angrily, face red with anger, "with your inadequate handiwork on my poor unhappy husband."

The doctor could hardly believe his ears. "Inadequate handiwork?" he exclaimed indignantly. "But I don't understand, Mrs Frogmorton, the patented penile corrector I implanted worked perfectly. I know because I tested it in the operating theatre by making it rise and fall several times to amuse the nurses."

"The penile corrector was a dangerous menace," retorted Mrs Frogmorton, "operating when it should have remained dormant."

"But how? I don't understand."

"Whenever I pressed the electric bell in my drawing room to summon my housemaid my husband's trouser front extended by several inches."

"But Mrs Frogmorton that's . . ."

"My housemaid Hilda was badly traumatized," interrupted Mrs Frogmorton getting into her stride. "She had been with me ten years and gave in her notice on the spot. She entered the drawing room in answer to my bell-press summons for cucumber sandwiches and a pot of tea to find my husband trying to unextend his trousers. She fainted when he thrust both hands down the front of his trousers trying to correct the malfunction of your handiwork, Doctor, and in doing so he suffered an electric shock to his private parts with a complete loss of pubic hair."

"Loss of pubic hair?"

"Yes, doctor, the contraption caught fire."

"Oh, what a dreadful story," declared Mrs Gooseberry sympathetically, "men with their extended trousers can never be trusted and I should know."

"Please Mrs Gooseberry enough of that kind of talk," declared Hawes, cheeks flushed with anger, "please leave us. I'm sure there must be things for you to do in the kitchen."

"I've had some cheeky encounters with men with extended trousers," continued Mrs Gooseberry looking directly at Mrs Frogmorton and feeling they had something in common, a fear of men with extended trousers. "There was this man on the circle line who . . ." she began with gusto.

"Mrs Gooseberry, no, stop at once," interrupted Allan Hawes. "I'm sure Mrs Frogmorton doesn't want to hear about your encounter on the circle line."

"But . . . "

"Please return to your kitchen at once."

Mrs Gooseberry muttering under her breath about not being appreciated went out the door and slammed it behind her showing her annoyance with the detective.

"Well, there goes us having Spotted Dick for dessert tonight, Hawes," sighed the doctor wistfully, "she won't be bothering now she's in a bad mood."

"Spotted Dick?" shrieked Mrs Frogmorton repulsed by the image that entered her mind of a penis covered in spots.

"It's quite delicious covered with custard," added the doctor licking his lips.

Mrs Frogmorton gasped, shocked, and swayed and almost fainted, the image of a man's spotted penis covered with custard too much for her.

"It's only a suet pudding, dear lady," explained Hawes hastily as he grabbed her right arm to steady her. "Sit down and calm yourself."

Mrs Frogmorton sat down on the sofa in a swoon, face white as a sheet. "Thank you, Mister Hawes, you're most kind," she muttered, her voice hardly audible as she dabbed at her eyes with a handkerchief."

"Would you like a glass of water?" asked the doctor.

"No, thank you," responded Mrs Frogmorton fanning herself with a hand, "I'll be all right in a moment."

"Would you like me to loosen your clothing?"

"No, I wouldn't like you to loosen my clothing, Doctor. I'm not that sort of woman."

"Good gracious, dear lady, I wasn't implying you were. I'm a medical man and I've seen it all before."

"I've no doubt you have, Doctor, but you haven't seen mine and you're not going to see it now!"

"You misunderstand me. I wasn't . . ."

"Finish your breakfast, old chap," said Hawes kindly, knowing his friend's pride as a professional medical man had been hurt. "Mrs Frogmorton doesn't need your medical attention."

Doctor Windrush returned to the table and sat down and began to butter a slice of toast. "As you say, my dear Hawes," he muttered glumly. Women were a great mystery to him and the more he learnt about the fair sex the more he was convinced they were minefields of emotions ready to explode at the slightest comment they did not like or understood.

"Now, Mrs Frogmorton," said the detective taking up a regal pose standing in front of the fireplace and turning his profile towards the lady in question with right elbow resting on the mantelpiece. "How might I be of service to you?"

"You're the renowned private detective Allan Hawes are you not?" she asked, eyeing him suspiciously.

"Indeed, I am, Mrs Frogmorton."

"The same private detective who retrieved the Duchess of Ditchwater's stolen diamond necklace and lady Montcalm's missing poodle Sweetie Pie?"

"Yes, I've the honour of being that man, Mrs Frogmorton."

"There are so many Allan Hawes listed in the phone book and I must be certain I'm talking to the right one."

"You are. What can I do for you?"

"I want to employ you on a matter of great importance, Mister Hawes, not only for myself and my family but also for Great Britain. If you accept I'll double your usual fee."

"Double my usual fee? That's very tempting but I think not."

"No?"

"For such money being offered there must be great danger involved."

"But I thought . . ."

"That I'd accept any case if the money was tempting enough?" She nodded. "Well, I don't take just any case, Mrs Frogmorton. No, I'm very selective about my clients and of any danger that might be involved."

"Please, Mister Hawes, reconsider. It's a matter of life and death and my family's honour. Oh, but the disgrace should you fail me. I feel quite faint thinking about it."

"Are you sure you don't want me to loosen your clothes?" asked the doctor getting to his feet ready to rush to the lady's side and start unbuttoning her clothing.

"Sit down, Doctor," exclaimed Hawes, voice stern as if he was telling a misbehaving dog to sit. The doctor meekly sat down. "You should know, Mrs Frogmorton," continued Hawes looking at the lady directly, "I only accept cases that will stretch my intellect and further my knowledge of the criminal mind. Indeed, I revel in pitting my superior intellect against criminal minds of genius, engaging them in a turbulent game of mental chess, out-thinking them at every move and bringing their evil twisted careers to checkmate in a prison cell."

"My case will surely stimulate your intellect to the very limit and beyond, Mister Hawes."

"Really Mrs Frogmorton, I'm intrigued. Come, tell me more, as you can see, I'm all ears."

"Not your ears again, Hawes," exclaimed the doctor. "I've told you before I can get them radically reduced by plastic surgery? I know a good plastic surgeon in Harley Street. You don't have to have ears that flap in the wind if you don't want them."

"What I told you about my ears was in strict confidence, Doctor, between patient and doctor and not to be blurted out in my sitting room in front of a client."

"Sorry, Hawes, I wasn't thinking. It won't happen again."

"Alright, Doctor, but please do think before you speak. I'm trying to have a serious conversation with Mrs Frogmorton."

"Of course, Hawes, I won't say another word. My lips are sealed."

Hawes turned to Mrs Frogmorton, "Please continue, Mrs Frogmorton," he said with a faint smile. "We won't be interrupted again."

"Would murder be stimulating enough for you, Mister Hawes?" asked Mrs Frogmorton.

The detective felt a shiver of excitement run through him. He had never had a murder case to solve. "Murder," he gasped, "and most foul you say?"

"Yes, murder, Mister Hawes."

"Murder at last to investigate. But are you sure, Mrs Frogmorton?"

"Yes, I'm sure. Are you interested?"

"But I haven't read of any murder in the papers."

"The victim isn't dead yet, Mister Hawes."

"Isn't dead? Then how can there be a murder without a dead body?"

"There's going to be a murder."

"I don't understand, Mrs Frogmorton, please explain yourself."

"I overheard my husband speaking on the telephone yesterday afternoon. He was in his study with the door locked. I know it was locked because when I tried to peer through the keyhole the key was still in the lock and I couldn't see anything. I happened, by accident you'll understand, to pick up the extension phone in the hall and overheard him talking to a woman who . . ."

"Ah, so he's got a mistress, the cad," interrupted the doctor.

"No, there's no mistress, not with my husband's penile problem. Sex is the last thing on his mind which I can vouch for being his wife."

"Then who is the mystery woman?" asked Hawes. "Did she give her name?"

"She did, Mister Hawes. I heard her say her name, Miss Marion Pringle, and she's the go between for a professional killer. My husband hired through her so a foul murder can be committed."

"Fowl? Are chickens involved?" asked the doctor incredulously.

"No, chickens aren't involved, Doctor," retorted Mrs Frogmorton glaring at him and thinking him a stupid simplistic man, and wondered why such a brilliant detective as Allan Hawes had him as his companion and biographer.

"Murder? Murder who?" asked Hawes. "I need to know the intended victim's name."

"The one person my husband despises most in all the world."

"Your mother?" asked the doctor brightly.

"No, Doctor," replied Mrs Frogmorton, "not my mother but someone who failed him."

"Ah, so it's you then," declared the doctor, delighted he had solved the identity of the murder victim before Hawes.

Mrs Frogmorton glowered at the doctor and shook her head.

"Not you?" exclaimed the doctor, disappointed. "Well, I'm surprised I must say."

"The man my husband wants murdered is the man who he holds responsible for leaving his name off the Queen's honours list for three years running. The same man, Mister Hawes, he blames for not rewarding him with a knighthood for all the donations he has given to the Tory party."

"Not the Prime Minister?"

"Yes, Mister Hawes, the Prime Minister Sir Anthony Dingle is the man to be murdered."

"Mrs Frogmorton, I'll take the case."

Chapter Nine

The Reverend Peter Catchpole, twenty-five, dashingly handsome, blond hair and blue eyed, timid and bashful, the new curate at the little sixteenth century parish church of St Freda the Eveready in the village of Bumstead-on-the-Wold, was making his first pastoral home visit without having the vicar with him for support. With cassock flying in the wind and trousers tucked into grey socks, he rode the vicar's wife's rickety old bicycle down a twisting leafy lane. The young cleric, nervous and apprehensive, was having serious doubts about his pastoral skills. The vicar, the Reverend Sidney Bloom, had advised before sending him off on
the visit, "This is an important day for you, Peter, visiting a parishioner without me. But I know you'll make me proud. I've chosen Rodney Perkins for your visit because he's the richest man in the parish and a friend who plays the organ for me in cold weather when my organist Miss Jessica Kemble can't play with her arthritic fingers. Now, do your best and get a big donation from him. There's a good fellow. We need bells for the bell tower."

The curate nodded and gave a weak smile. He knew the vicar would report back to the bishop his success or failure and the visit must be a success.

"Rodney Briggs isn't too keen on clergymen who talk too much shop, Peter, so talk about his hobbies and praise them, and don't dwell on your parish duties. He plays a good game of golf and chess, and he can complete the Times crossword at one sitting in under an hour. Oh, and he's a decent horseman with a good seat who rides regularly with the Bumstead-on-the-Wold fox hunt."

"I don't like blood sports and I can't play golf or chess and have never completed a crossword in my life. I think, Sidney, that my first solo pastoral visit would be better served if made to a sweet little church going old lady who doesn't do crosswords nor rides a horse."

"Nonsense, of course you should visit him. It's good practice for you to use the parochial skills you learnt at Theology College, and you need to impress the bishop. Now, away with you there's a good fellow, Peter, and get a donation for St Freda's the Eveready."

It was a sweltering hot summer's afternoon and the curate's brow was covered with beads of sweat before he cycled less than a mile. He was not a countryside loving man seeing no poetical romance in birds chirping among the hedgerows nor in clouds of buzzing biting midges. Indeed, for him the countryside was a place with piles of manure, mostly from cows littering fields and meadows, and farmyards, like minefields waiting for unwary folk like himself to step into them. He was not dressed for cycling on such a hot summer's day but wore a heavy wool cassock with a tight clerical collar. He should have cycled in shorts and a vest as the vicar's wife suggested who wanted a glimpse of his thighs. But felt as a priest he should advertise his vocation to the world which meant wearing a cassock with clerical collar on all occasions and in all-weather. He wanted parishioners to see him as a young priest of a quiet and serious disposition, a dedicated pious Christian with clean habits and underwear, a man with a bookcase that was full of cookery books, cooking being his hobby. Indeed, his most prized cookery book was 'Cooking with Nuns,' a collection of recipes by nuns of the order of St Sybil the Cook; a religious order of fast-food cooking nuns renowned for their toad in the hole, toad out of the hole, and toad without any hole at all.

Peter Catchpole had led a sheltered childhood growing up in Hastings, Sussex, in the old fishing town cared for by two elderly maiden aunts, twin sisters Mavis and Doris Fundy. The spinsters had a dread of sex and of seeing men naked and had raised their nephew with the same perspective.

Peter Catchpole cycled up the long gravel driveway towards the residence of Rodney Perkins and was impressed by the huge red-brick mansion surrounded with acres of garden, immaculately trimmed lawns and hedges, flowerbeds a multitude of colours. There were orchards of fruit trees, apple, pear and cherry, and on the front lawn pranced a haughty male peacock displaying fanned out rainbow tail feathers hoping to attract a mate.

The curate cycled on towards the main door of the manor. He leant the bike against a wall then walked up stone steps to the front door and rang the bell. The door opened and there stood a squat rotund man with an abundance of nose hair, wearing black tails and a bow tie, the butler Cobblers. "May I help you, Sir?" he asked in the monotonous tone's butlers use to sound humble and servile.

"I've come to see Mister Perkins," replied the curate.

"Are you expected, Sir?"

The curate shook his head. "No, but I'm sure he'll see me."

"Whom do I say is calling, Sir?"

"Reverend Peter Catchpole, the curate of St. Freda the Eveready church in Bumstead-on-the-Wold."

"Very good, Sir, if you'll follow me."

The curate followed the butler through the house into the kitchen and out into the back garden. There was a heart-shaped swimming pool in which a beautiful young woman in revealing skimpy white bikini floated on her back on an airbed. The sun shimmered brightly on the water like a thousand tiny lights. "Reverend Peter Catchpole to see you, Madam," announced the butler loudly from the side of the pool.

The woman appeared to be in her mid-twenties, and she was as lovely as any Hollywood film star with long black cascading hair and pouting red lips. She looked at the curate and smiled sweetly. "Oh, how nice to have a visitor," she called out gaily and swam over to the side of the pool and climbed slowly up a ladder with water dripping from her luscious body. The curate gasped having never seen such a beautiful woman with body so clearly displayed and felt a familiar stirring beneath his cassock, his penis beginning to stir. "Melody," she said brightly, holding out her hand for him to shake.

"No, not Melody, my name's Peter," he replied, confused, and trying not to stare at her breasts but was transfixed and finding it impossible. They were the most exciting breasts he had ever seen, and his penis stirred again which worried him.

She noticed his interest and laughed, the laughter sounding like soft tinkling bells. "Melody Austin's my name, silly boy," she said enjoying the effect she knew she was having on him beneath his cassock by his blushing cheeks. "But you can call me Mel, all my friends do."

"Thank you, Mel, I'd like that."

The butler appeared at the woman's side holding a white bath towel which she took and began to dry her hair using both hands making her breasts jiggle and bounce,
which delighted and thrilled

the curate making his penis stir even more. He gazed astonished and transfixed at her loveliness, heart beating faster than normal. The tips of his ears turned crimson and he realized he was hopelessly in lust with the gorgeous woman standing before him. She was for him the personification of feminine loveliness and he desired her with a yearning he had never known before. No one warned him that a beautiful near naked woman would have such an amazing effect on him and on his misbehaving penis.

"Would you like a cool drink? You must be hot in your cassock?" asked Melody, voice suddenly husky, "lemonade with ice?" She felt attracted to the young cleric finding his naive innocence and handsome face alluring and felt her passions rising.

"Thank you," muttered the curate gratefully as he took a handkerchief from his cassock pocket and mopped his sweating bow. He tried to look away from her breasts but could not. He was like a helpless mouse hypnotized by a snake about to strike.

Melody turned to the butler, and said, "Get the Father a lemonade, Cobblers, with ice cubs, please."

"Certainly, Madam," replied the butler, and turning away he walked quickly into the house to fetch the lemonade.

"I think there's been a mistake, Mel," muttered the curate weakly still staring at her breasts. "I'm not a Father."

"You're not? But I thought all priests were fathers."

"Not in the Church of England unless they're married with children."

She laughed heartily showing her sparkling white teeth, every tooth expensively whitened by a Harley Street dentist. "Sorry, I was thinking of Catholic priests. They're called Father but don't have children? How curious and bizarre don't you think?"

The curate nodded "Are you a Roman Catholic, Mel?"

"No, but I was once a musical hall act before becoming a pole dancer to earn money to pay my way through University. I was a fully paid-up card holder of 'The Snake Dancers Union' and voted Liberal at the last election."

"Snake dancer?"

"Oh, yes, Peter, I had a fifteen-foot anaconda called Brian. We used to perform on Saturday nights and I was the star turn in the Leeds and Cockfosters Working Men's club performing a striptease while Brian crawled between my breasts and thighs as I danced."

"Oh, goodness gracious me," gasped the startled curate, the image of a naked Melody with a fifteen-foot Brian moving between her thighs corrupting his mind and making his penis twitch under his cassock.

"Are you alright, Peter, you've gone a funny colour."

"It's the heat, it's making me feel faint."

Clobbers the butler returned carrying a silver tray on which stood a tall single glass of lemonade with ice cubes floating on the top. He walked up to the curate, bowed his head slightly, and offered him the tray, "Lemonade, Sir," he said humbly.

The curate took the glass. It felt cool in his hand. "Thank you," he said gratefully and took a sip of the refreshing drink.

"I'd better go and change out of my wet costume," exclaimed Melody gaily. "I'll be catching my death of cold if I stand here much longer in just a bikini. Finish your drink, Peter. Cobblers will show you to the sitting room and I'll join you for a cup of tea when I've changed into something that's more formal for a clergyman's eyes."

Peter Catchpole sat on a sofa in the sitting room waiting with growing impatience for the lovely Melody to make her appearance. He had been waiting almost an hour not understanding being single without the experience of having a girlfriend that women like to take three to four times longer than men in getting ready for social company. There was a silver-framed photograph on a coffee table showing a smiling man in his early fifties with his arm around Melody's shoulders. Both sun-tanned and obviously happy to be in each other's company. The curate supposed the man was Rodney Perkins and Melody his daughter. But where was Rodney Perkins? After all it was to see him for a donation he had been sent by the vicar. The butler Cobblers came and went replenishing the teapot with hot water. "Madam doesn't like cold tea," he explained on his fifth visit, "and she's very partial for having a sponge finger with a gentleman."

"The gentleman in the picture," asked the curate pointing at the silver frame photograph on the coffee table, "is he Rodney Perkins?"

"Yes, Sir, that's the Master, Mister Perkins."

The door opened and Melody came gliding in wearing a skin tight white leather trousers, low-cut pale blue blouse, and red high heel shoes. The curate gasped at her stunning beauty her magnetism and her overwhelming sexual appeal, and watched open-mouthed as she moved gracefully towards him like a young gazelle on the great African Plains. "Sorry I took so long, Peter," she apologized as she sat down on the sofa next to him, and taking his hand gently squeezed it, "but I couldn't decide on what to wear to please you. I've a huge collection of clothes and wanted to look my best. It's not every day a handsome young vicar comes to call."

"I'm not a vicar, Melody, only a humble curate."

She picked up the teapot and looked him steadily in the eyes. "Shall I be mother?" she asked coyly.

"Oh, yes, please, I'd love making you a mother," he blurted out without thinking, staring transfixed at her breasts, and then acutely embarrassed at what he said, blushed deeply, and averted his eyes feeling ashamed, "Oh, I'm so sorry. What must you think of me?"

She poured the tea smiling. "That you're a sweet mischievous boy," she giggled, "with such naughty intriguing thoughts."

"Will that be all, Madam?" asked the butler eyeing the curate with disdain.

"Yes, thank you, Cobblers, you may go."

The butler left the room and closed the door behind him.

"I was wondering about your father, Melody," began the curate, desperate to make conversation and to stop thinking about her breasts. "I'd like to meet him. Is he home?"

"My father?"

"Yes, Melody, your father."

"Well, that would be rather difficult, Peter."

"Surely not. Tell him the curate has come to see him. My vicar wants me to meet all the prominent people in the village and he's top of my list."

"Sorry, but it can't be done, Peter."

"Why not?"

"Because I never knew my father."

The curate looked stunned. "Never knew your father?"

"No, my mother is a lesbian and daddy a sperm donor. I was conceived by mummy's girlfriend using a turkey baster on a kitchen table.. On my birth certificate where the father's name and occupation should have been the midwife wrote, 'Wanker."

Shocked, the curate could not speak for a moment, then regaining his composure he pointed to the silver-framed photograph. "Then who is that gentleman?"

"Ronnie, my benefactor."

"Your husband?"

"Oh, no, we're not married."

"But he looks too old to be your . . ."

"Lover," interrupted Melody with a giggle.

He nodded and forced a weak smile.

"I'm always truthful with people I like, and I like you very much indeed. You're a beautiful young man with potential. My relationship with Ronnie isn't one of love on my part. I know he loves me and he provides me with the luxury I need. He's sweet, kind, gentle and generous, a dear man, who gives me everything I want and in return I give him what he wants."

"Which is?"

"Having me naked in bed for sex whenever he wants it."

"That's must be nice for him," muttered the curate sheepishly, thinking of her naked on a bed, his penis straining and trying to bust free from the restriction of his Y-fronts. Desperately he tried thinking of an iceberg to lose his erection. He had been using the visualizes of an iceberg as remedy for deflating unwanted erections since entering Theological College.

"What's nice for Ronnie?" asked Melody with a mischievous glint in her eyes, delighted with the effect she was having on the curate and loving it, "the thought of me naked or with me spending his money?"

"Eh, both . . . I suppose," he replied, finding it impossible to lose his erection no matter how hard he visualized an iceberg with her delectable breasts in such close proximity. When he returned to the vicarage he would take an ice-cold shower, then seek the vicar's advice about his passionate feelings for the lovely Melody Austin and her responses to him. The vicar was happily married and understood sex and the complexities of a woman's mind.

"Another cup of tea, Peter?"

"No, thank you, Mel."

"Cake?"

"No, thank you. I don't want to spoil my dinner."

"Silly boy, you won't spoil anything."

"Where is Mister Perkins? I'd like to meet him."

"Ronnie's in London for a few days with his mother for her birthday treat. They're planning to see a West End show then to do some shopping to buy her an expensive gift, a ring, bracelet or necklace, made with rubies, red her favorite colour. They'll be coming home late Friday night."

"Might l call back on Saturday, Mel?"

"Of course, you may, Peter. I'd love to see you again." He blushed and stood up facing her and to his surprise she kissed him on the lips, and holding the kiss plunged her tongue deep into his mouth. He felt a hand deftly unbutton his cassock over his groin area and slip inside to rest lightly over his trousers, fingers gently squeezing the outline of his erection. He almost fainted with the wave of pleasure that swept over him. "I thought so," she whispered, and removed her hand and stepped back from him smiling, "but I needed to be sure."

"It would be nice to see you in church on Sunday morning," he muttered, his penis stiffer than it had ever been and out of control.

"Church going isn't my scene, Peter, but knowing how you feel about me, well, I'll definitely be attending church to see more of you."

"I'd love seeing more of you, Melody, I really would."

She giggled. "Naughty boy."

"I didn't mean . . ."

"I know, darling, but I did."

"What about Mister Perkins?"

"Don't worry about Ronnie. What he doesn't know can't harm him."

"How did you meet him?"

"Through a dating agency. It was love at first sight for him and lots of money to spend for me."

"He must be very rich to own such a big manor house with a heart-shaped swimming pool."

"Very rich, Peter. He was a solicitor until he won the lottery and now has a private business as a hobby specializing in removals world-wide for wealthy clients."

"Removals?"

"Transporting priceless paintings and antique furniture. He never discusses the business with me saying he can't break a customer's confidentiality, and two or three times a year he'll return from a trip abroad with a suitcase full of money."

Chapter Ten

The train pulled slowly out of London Bridge railway station and sitting in a first-class compartment were Rodney Perkins with his mother Hetty, returning home to Bumstead-on-the-Wold after a three day stay at the five-star Ritz hotel near the British War Museum, after celebrating Hetty's seventy-fifth birthday. Her birthday treat to see 'The Mousetrap,' a play she wanted to see for many years, with Perkins then taking her shopping to buy a ruby necklace with matching earrings. But he also used the London trip as his cover for committing murder carried out while his mother sat in the third row in the theatre watching the 'Mouse Trap,' eating a box of milk chocolates. She thought her son had popped out to make an important overseas phone call but he was away committing murder.

The murdered man, Giovanni Congui, handsome and flamboyant, a charming young Italian diplomat adored by the ladies, who especially enjoyed the thrill and danger of seducing married ladies. He worked at the Italian Embassy in London after making the fatal mistake of having an affair with the wife of a French Cabinet Minister when he worked in Paris. The Minister, suspecting there was something amiss something when his wife kept pleading headaches when he wanted to make love, searched her handbag and found incriminating letters from Giovanni Congui with a packet of condoms. He never used condoms himself having had a vasectomy six years earlier.

The Minister never revealed to his wife he knew about her affair, and wanting Congui punished asked the Italian Ambassador, a family friend, for help. Congui was transferred to London. But that was not enough punishment for the cuckolded French Minister, for him it was a matter of honour to be avenged in blood. The services of Miss Monica Pringle were discreetly employed.

Giovanni Congui liked to gamble and made regular visits to a casino in North London travelling there by tube train on the circle line. One evening he was discreetly followed by Perkins disguised as Miss Monica Pringle, in blue-rinsed wig and green tweeds jacket and skirt. The station platform crowded with people waiting for a tube train to arrive. When the train came rattling out of the tunnel Miss Monica Pringle stepped briskly forward and pushed Giovanni

Congui under the crunching wheels of the train, then stepped back into the crowd and was quickly lost to sight.

"Blimey, what a ghastly sight," exclaimed a horrified porter as he peered under the train at the mangled remains of Giovanni Congui. "There's a mangled body down there looking like a squashed tomato. We'll need a bucket and spade to scrap it all up."

Within fifty minutes of the murder Ronald Perkins had changed out of his Miss Monica Pringle disguise and dressed in dinner jacket and bow sat with his mother in the third row of the theatre watching the Mousetrap. She was still eating milk chocolates as the curtain came down for the halftime interval.

The train leaving London Bridge gathered speed as it pitched and rolled clattering down the tracks. Hetty Perkins sat opposite to her son reading a newspaper 'The Evening News,' holding the newspaper spread out while reading an article on the woman's page 'Women's Elusive G Spot." The article written by feminist novelist Sue Fender; an ardent explorer of her own G spot who claimed to have finally located it on her twenty-fourth birthday while sitting in a bath scrubbing herself with a loofah. She was famous for burning her kickers outside the Houses of Parliament but forgot to remove them in her excitement with the Press being there, and badly singed her assets. Hetty was amazed and intrigued by the article having never known before there was such a hidden delight to be found in a woman's body as the elusive G spot, and made a mental note to ask her doctor if she could have her own G spot located on the National Health.

Splashed across the front page of the newspaper was the banner headline: "ITALIAN DIPLOMAT COMMITS SUICIDE." Ronald Perkins read the headline with professional satisfaction. It was another successful murder to add to his impressive list. With the money received for killing Giovanni Congui he would buy a sea-going motor launch, having dreamt of owning such a craft with toilet, shower, galley, radio and navigation equipment, with a double bunk for making love to Melody. He would moor the launch for holidays in the harbour of Cape Croisette in the South of France, a beautiful holiday paradise. His plan to retire at fifty and buy a villa with a vineyard in the hills overlooking the sea and make his own wine.

Three days earlier Perkins and his mother left Bumstead-on-the-

Wold for their London trip, he had made contact with a client for murder arranged through his box number in an upmarket woman's magazine 'Feminist Women on The March,' in answer to his advert placed in the magazine. It was so worded only people wanting to hire a killer would understand the coded meaning.

DISCREET SPEACAL REMOVALS.

Fast reliable service of removal of a serious problem. Half payment when hired to remove, and second half paid on completion of removal of annoyance. Satisfaction guaranteed or money refunded. Reply Box No.3951.

The editor, Miss Linda Finch, an Australian and licensed didgeridoo player, did not understand the real meaning of the advert and run it for ten years in her magazine. Initial contact made between Perkins and a client was a letter sent to Perkin's box number at the magazine's editorial offices with the client's phone number. All future communications made by telephone from Perkins to the client's home number calling from a public call box. There would be one face to face meetings in a south London dimly-lit pub of Perkins choice to establish the identity of the victim to be murdered from a photo, with arrangement made for the first half payment paid into a Swiss bank account. The final payment made when the job was completed. Perkins had spoken to a new client before leaving for London with his mother, and the money offered was too tempting to be refused, and would buy him the villa he wanted in the south of France.

The new client hired him to murder the British Prime Minister Sir Anthony Dingle, a task that would take all his masterly skills, intellect and cunning, and a challenge he could not refuse and would cap his murder for hire career. "I'm going away on business next month," he told his mother as they sat in the train as it left Victoria station. He lit a Havana cigar with a silver cigarette lighter, a Christmas present from the gorgeous Melody.

Hetty never liked her son to smoke worried it would damage his lungs and stunt his growth, and make the house smell. She scowled disapprovingly at him over the top of her newspaper. The years had not been kind to her and she had become embittered with false teeth, bad breath, with plenty of attitude. Her life was focused on her son's happiness with Ronald both sun and moon in her small Universe. "Oh, no, you're not going to leave me with Melody again, are you?" she snapped angrily, "You know despise her. I don't know what you see in her."

"That's because you're not a man, Mother."

"Whenever you go away on one of your jaunts, Ronnie, I have to put up with her endless silly chatter about her designer clothes, jewels and expensive make-up. She thinks my clothes are drab and wants me to use more make-up with an expensive French perfume to mask my natural smell, which she says is rank like an old wet dog."

"Melody thinks you've let yourself go a little bit, Mother, and you could do with her guidance and spend time in a ladies saloon, and buy a new wardrobe of clothes." He blew a cloud of blue smoke at his mother and smiled to see her struggle not to cough. "Melody's all right, it's just that you don't understand her. She's a sweet girl with a heart of gold."

"I've known her for two years and despise her more now than I did when I first met her, and as for understanding her, Ronnie, well, I understand her well enough. Money's all she wants and thinks about. She'll take you for every penny you've got before she's done, you see if I'm not right."

"Oh, come now, Mother, Melody has her good points."

"Yes, and I know what you think they are, Ronnie, her breasts!"

"Please, Mother, don't be crude. I love Melody."

"What use is she? She can't cook or sew and she's lazy and lolls about in the swimming pool all day, and likes nothing better than spending your money."

"As I've said, Mother, I love Melody."

"I don't like the way she parades around the house in her skimpy clothes showing off her womanly bits," continued Hetty bitterly. "The postman has started calling more often without any post, and I've seen him on his knees peering through the letterbox trying to get a glimpse of her."

"I wish you and Melody would be friends."

"Pigs will fly first, Ronnie."

The compartment door slid open and an overweight red-faced man with a bristling grey handlebar moustache stood on the threshold, immaculately dressed in smart navy-blue blazer with five glittering brass buttons, Royal Air Force Association badge displayed on the left breast pocket, with a cravat of air force blue, and white trousers with sharp creases. On his head a white fedora hat. Group Captain Huey Luey Lampton DSO SFC, WC, retired, widower, pompous, bombastic, returning home after spending the day at the Oval cricket ground watching England take a beating from the Australians and losing the ashes, and being patriotic was in a foul mood.

The Group Captain studied the only two occupants of the first-class compartment with disdain. He always travelled first class and never liked to rub shoulders or even converse with those he considered to be ill-bred loutish people. When he was a boy between the two World Wars it was safe to leave houses unlocked, but now thieves would take anything that was not nailed down, and street crime was on the increase. The Group Captain wanted petty criminals and persistent illegal parkers flogged, especially the bastards who parked outside his house blocking the driveway. Indeed, he had written to the police nine times demanding the swine blocking his driveway be arrested but received no reply.

The Group Captain did not like the look of the drab elderly woman sitting in the first-class compartment. She looked like a common ill-bred person who lived on a housing estate on social security benefits. He was suspicious Hetty had a second-class ticket with no right to be seated in a first-class compartment, but was somewhat relieved to see Perkins was dressed in a smart grey three-piece suit with polished shoes. But angered that he was smoking a cigar in a non-smoking compartment. "Buggering swine, he ought to be flogged," thought the Group Captain with a snort of rage making his jowls wobble. He would put a stop to such brazen contempt for the no-smoking sign displayed on the railway compartment wall. Smoking was a filthy disgusting habit and anti-smoking was another of his campaigns next to complaining repeatedly to the council about his next-door neighbours for throwing rubbish over his garden fence. He had written nine times to the Council demanding his neighbour be flogged but received no reply.

The Group Captain purchased a first-class ticket and this was a first-class compartment on a corridor train and was the only first-class compartment with empty seats. It was either stand for the entire journey in a cold drafty corridor or to occupy a vacant seat in a warm compartment. He strode into the compartment and sat down next to Hetty and being a gentleman raised his hat. "Madam," he said, then turned to Perkins and glowered at him to show his displeasure and contempt for his blatant cigar smoking, and exclaimed angrily, "Do you mind, Sir?"

"Pardon?" said Perkins, blowing smoke at the Group Captain.

"The cigar, Sir, the cigar."

Perkins took out his silver cigar case and opened it with a flourish and offered a cigar to the Group Captain. "Would you like one?" he asked, "from Havana, the best money can buy. I'm told each one was rolled on a young beautiful woman's naked thigh."

"No, sir, I don't want a ghastly cancer stick. This is a non-smoking apartment. Can't you read?" The Group Captain pointed a quivering finger at a non-smoking sign on the wall. Perkins shrugged his shoulders and made no reply. He had seen the non-smoking signs but was not going to give up the pleasure of smoking his daily cigar. Indeed, he had been looking forward to it all day. The Group Captain coughed pretending the cigar smoke was affecting him. Perkins took no notice and continued puffing away on his cigar believing a cigar was like a good woman in bed to be enjoyed at one's leisure while making the pleasure last as long as possible.

The Group Captain coughed again louder than before and Perkins blew a small cloud of blue smoke that drifted up to the ceiling of the carriage. The Group Captain coughed a third time, a long spluttering cough, so there could be no mistaking his repulsion to the cigar smoke. "Somebody needs cough syrup," said Perkins enjoying himself, as he winked an eye at his mother, who not wanting to get involved pretended to read her newspaper although she was watching events closely. The Group Captain's face turned purple with rage and he coughed a fourth time, a racking cough that echoed around the small confinement of the railway compartment. "What do your stars in the paper say for you today, Mother?" asked Perkins taking no notice and addressing his mother directly. "Are you going to meet a tall dark stranger who'll sweep you off your feet?" His mother, embarrassed, continued reading her newspaper and gave no reply.

"Sir, I find your cigar most offensive," declared the Group Captain glaring at Perkins.

"And I find you rude and offensive trying to ruin my smoking pleasure."

"Are you going to put out your cigar, Sir?"

"No, not until I've finished smoking it."

"I'll have you know I'm Group Captain Huey Lampton, Sir. Will you do me the curtsey of informing me to whom am I speaking?"

"The man smoking a cigar and who isn't going to put it out."

"Give me your name, Sir? I demand to know your name."

"Just call me Smokey."

The Group Captain leapt to his feet, eyes almost popping from his head with rage his patience gone. "I flew Spitfires against the Hun during the Second World War, Sir," he spluttered the vein on his forehead throbbing, "and I'll have you know that you're dealing with a man who's not afraid to stand up and be counted when his country needs him."

"Sit down, you're making a fool of yourself."

"How dare you, Sir."

"Sit down, and mind your own business."

"You wouldn't have lasted two minutes flying Spitfires. They needed real men to be pilots and not ill-mannered cigar smoking types like you." Perkins, losing his temper, leapt to his feet and thrust his face within a few inches of the Group Captain's crimson face and blew a cloud of smoke at him. "How dare you, Sir," spluttered the Group Captain coughing this time for real. "If you were under my command in the RAF during the war I would have had you inside the guardhouse in double quick time. Your feet wouldn't have touched the ground."

"Oh, be quiet, you're hurting my ears with your nonsense."

"You're asking for a lesson in fisticuffs, Sir."

"Oh, don't tell me you were a boxer as well as a spitfire pilot?"

"I was a boxing champion three years running at University and a Cambridge blue."

"What did you box? Apples or oranges?"

The Group Captain's moustache bristled and his top lip trembled and a red mist descended upon him,. "Filthy buggering lout," he spluttered, "you should be locked up with the key thrown away."

"I've had enough of your baloney," declared Perkins grimly. "Let's take this outside into the corridor."

The Group Captain face turned white as a sheet with his bluff being called and the cigar smoking lout wanting to fight him. He had been a practicing coward since losing his nerve flying a Spitfire into a tree on take-off, his one and only flight in Fighter Command, then grounded for the rest of his service in the RAF. "Alright, I accept your apology," he mumbled taking a hasty step back from Perkins afraid that he was about to strike him.

"But I haven't apologized."

"Hit me and I'll report you to the guard."

"Oh, for God's sake it's only a cigar!"

"That was Hitler's attitude before he invaded Poland. He said it was only Poland then invaded the rest of Europe."

"Sit down," retorted Perkins angrily, prodding the Group Captain in the chest with a finger, "before I knock you down."

"That does it. I'm going to report you to the guard," spluttered the Group Captain as he slid open the compartment door and stepped out into the corridor. He wanted to get away from Perkins as quickly as possible. There was a hostile glint in Perkins eyes that sent icy shivers up and down his spine. "We'll see what the guard has to say about you smoking in a non-smoking compartment. You'll end up in court and be fined and hopefully flogged." He closed the door and walked rapidly away down the corridor towards the guard's van at the rear of the train.

"Oh, Ronnie," cried Hetty stifling a sob, "what have you done? He's right and you'll go to court and it'll be in all the papers. Oh, what a disgrace. I won't be able to hold my head up again in Bumstead-on-the-Wold."

"It's all right mother, don't go upsetting yourself. I'll sort it out."

Perkins hurried after the Group Captain following him down the corridor of the pitching rolling train. The last thing he wanted was to have his name and address taken by the guard. What if the guard was not satisfied with his explanation and called the police and they opened his suitcase that was full of money? How could he explain it? The police would visit his manor house with a search warrant and find his notebooks detailing his murders with payments made for doing them. He quickened his pace to catch the Group Captain before he reached the guard's van. With cigar clenched between his teeth he grabbed him from behind in a stranglehold and pulled him backwards and down the corridor. The terrified Group Captain struggled for breath with pressure tightening on his windpipe choking him as he was manhandled towards the nearest door.

"Out with you," hissed Perkins in his ear, opening the door.

"Are you trying to kill me?"

"Not trying I have killed you," retorted Perkins as he pushed the Group Captain out the door.

"Noooooooo," screamed the Group Captain hysterically as he made a desperate grab at Perkins to save himself and grabbed hold of the cigar. Holding the cigar clenched in his hand he fell away into the darkness to fall down a steep railway embankment and land in a ploughed field. Perkins closed the door. He was annoyed with himself for having lost his temper and having murdered without being paid to do it. He waited a few minutes to regain his composure then walked back to join his mother.

"What happened to the man?" asked his mother as he entered the compartment and sat down. "Did he report you to the guard, Ronnie?"

Perkins shook his head. "No, Mother, we came to an agreement."

"I'm pleased to hear it. Will he be joining us?"

"No, Mother, he found another compartment further up the train."

"And he's happy there?"

"But of course, Mother, I even opened the door for him and closed it after him."

Chapter Eleven

Group Captain Huey Luey Lampton's body was found early the next morning by cowman Clive Mitchell as he was walking to work and mistook the body for being a badly stuffed scarecrow. The Group Captain, stiff as a board with rigor mortise, stood upright buried up to the knees in a half-ploughed field below a steep railway embankment. Mitchell was late for milking thought the farmer had put up the scarecrow as he hurried up the lane to the milking shed, "Strange to put up a scarecrow when the field hasn't yet been fully ploughed or seeded."

An hour later the farmer, Burt Wilson, a tall gangly bearded man, found the body and called the police. He had driven into the field on his tractor pulling a plough to finish the ploughing and dropped the blades of the plough to begin cutting farrows. He was surprised to see the scarecrow at the top of the field below the railway line and drove up to investigate and stepping down from the tractor with the engine running, muttered, "Well, bugger me silly with a feather," staring in amazement at the Group Captain, "if that isn't the ugliest looking scarecrow I've ever seen." He walked up to the scarecrow and prodded it gingerly with his right hand and the head moved slightly revealing the dead glazed eyes of the Group Captain. "Hell's bells it's a human body," exclaimed the traumatized farmer, and within seconds he was back on the tractor and racing at full throttle back to the farmhouse to call the police. In his panic he drove out through the open field gate and up the lane forgetting he was towing the plough with blades down. The lane ripped up with four neat furrows all the way to farmhouse.

Detective Chief Inspector Edgar 'Lanky' Briggs of the Metropolitan CID walked from the police car across the half-ploughed field towards the body of the Group Captain, and at his side his new sergeant, Jenny Hopper. It was her first day working with the Chief Inspector and CID. Both officers in plain clothes, grey mackintoshes and wellington boots, the mackintoshes because rain was forecast and the wellington boots because of the muddy field.

Jenny Hopper, twenty-five, beautiful, brunette, hazel eyes, a Cambridge University graduate with a master's degree in

Criminology and Applied Feminism, marked by superiors at New Scotland Yard for rapid promotion, considered a rising star with her passing out top of her class at Hendon Training College. Career minded; she has put her bright future before marriage and children. "There'll be time enough for a husband and babies when I'm an officer of command rank," she told her parents who persisted in asking her with every time she visit them to bring a nice young man for tea and to get married and have babies.

She was transferred to CID for work experience in readiness to be promoted to the rank of Inspector. Her new boss, Detective Chief Inspector Edgar 'Lanky' Briggs, promoted through a series of typing errors by a short-sight secretary.

"Now, Sergeant," said Briggs brightly to Jenny Hopper as they squelched across the muddy field in wellington boots, "you've been sent to me to be trained in the skills of detection and be a good CID officer. I want you to think of yourself as being a lump of pliable clay for me to shape and mold."

She glanced at her superior officer with a bemused look on her face. "Yes, Sir, like a lump of clay."

"You'll be thinking, Sergeant," continued Briggs, "I've got a wise head on my shoulders and exceptionally good at my job, otherwise I wouldn't hold the rank of Chief Inspector in CID. Well, that's all true of course, so listen to me and learn and you won't go wrong."

"Yes, Sir, I won't go wrong."

"Do you know, Sergeant, what's the most important tool for being a good detective?"

"An inquisitive mind, Sir."

"Of course, Sergeant, that goes without saying, but even more important for a detective is to have a good nose, an experienced nose, a reliable nose for crime solving."

"A reliable nose, Sir," echoed the sergeant, thinking it was the silliest thing she had ever heard about being a detective and for solving crime.

"Yes, Sergeant, a nose for sniffing out clues and for tracking criminals. I'm an old-fashioned cop and I pride myself on having such a nose, and hope that by the time you leave CID you'll also have such a nose."

The sergeant forced a weak smiled. The stories she had heard in the police canteen about Briggs were now being confirmed. He was indeed a buffoon. "Thank you, Sir," she said, and stifling a giggle she took out a handkerchief to blow her nose to hide it.

"My job as your superior officer is teaching you to have a good nose and how to use it to sniff out clues."

"Yes, thank you, Sir," she replied, and loudly blew her nose to stifle another giggle.

Police Pathologist Arthur Dean, thirty-eight, tall and slender, divorced with a teenage daughter, dressed in a white plastic zip-up jump suit used by police at crime scenes, stood looking at the body of Group Captain Huey Luey Lampton with a quizzical look on his face. He heard voices and saw Chief Inspector Briggs and sergeant Hopper approaching across the field towards him, and sighed deeply and grimaced, then muttered under his breath, "Oh, not Lanky." He had hoped Scotland Yard would be putting a skilled officer in charge of the case and not the idiot of the force.

"Good morning, Doctor Dean," called out the Chief Inspector jovially. "Nice day for a visit to the countryside."

"Yes, but not for the corpse, Chief Inspector."

"What do we have here?" asked Briggs going up to the body of the Group Captain and peering closely at it, "not a scarecrow as the farmer first thought I see," he chuckled, thinking he was being witty.

"No, and not a man whose waiting for a bus either," replied the doctor impatiently.

"What? I didn't know there's a bus route near here," replied Briggs amazed. "Make a note of that, Sergeant. This could be an important clue on how the body got here. The deceased came by bus."

"There isn't a bus route near here, Sir," explained the sergeant trying to keep a straight face. "The doctor's being sardonic."

"Sardonic? What has Sardinia got to do with the dead body?"

"It hasn't, Chief Inspector," replied the doctor with a sigh, thinking with Briggs in charge and the dead man murdered, the murderer would never be caught unless there was a signed confession found in the victim's pocket.

"Then why did my sergeant say Sardinia?"

"She didn't. She said I was being sardonic, which means I was being sarcastic."

"Sarcastic?"

"Mocking you."

Briggs thought for a moment then his face went red with embarrassment, looking at the doctor he retorted angrily. "Let's keep to the known facts, Doctor. I haven't time for sarcastic remarks. I've got a death to investigate."

"Alright, then these are the known facts, Chief Inspector. The body's stiff as a board and beginning to smell of decay."

"Aha, yes, so that explains the smell," replied the Chief Inspector and turning to Sergeant Jenny Hopper he gently tapped twice on the end of his nose with a finger. "Now you understand, Sergeant, what I meant when I told you that a detective needs a good nose when investigating." Briggs turned back to the doctor. "Have you examined the body?"

"Only a preliminary examination. I'll be carrying out a full post-mortem tomorrow afternoon at the mortuary. But I can tell you this for now the deceased is male, white, aged between sixty and sixty-five, was a member of the Royal Air Force Association, drove a Bentley, and is a non-smoker and a cricket supporter."

"Cricket supporter? But isn't that worn by men protecting their genitals when they bat during a game of cricket," replied Briggs, thinking his knowledge of the game would impress the doctor who he knew played cricket. "Is the deceased wearing one?"

"No. I was saying he's a cricket fan not that he's wearing a cricket support."

Briggs scowled feeling foolish. "How do you know all these things about the deceased?" he asked.

"Because I found the dead man's wallet in his coat pocket. The deceased is Group Captain Huey Luey Lampton."

"His wallet?" replied Briggs brightly. "Now, there's an important clue, Sergeant. Please take notes."

"Yes, Sir." Jenny Hopper took out her notepad and pen and began to write.

"Inside the wallet," continued the doctor. "I found a driving licence with a car insurance certificate for a Bentley, and a day ticket for the Oval cricket ground. Oh, and a membership card for 'The British Anti-Smoking League. The man's wearing a blazer with the Royal Air Force Association badge on the breast pocket."

"Which means what?" asked Briggs.

"He served in the RAF."

"Cause of death? Natural causes?

"Well, he fell from a train and down the railway embankment. There are marks on the embankment showing where he tumbled down into the field. Death, I would say at this point without examining the body at the mortuary death was caused by a broken neck."

"Ah, so it wasn't a heart attack?"

"No, it wasn't a heart attack."

"Might it have been suicide?"

"That's possible I suppose, he came off a train and might have jumped to his death. But I think the death far more sinister."

"Then these are the known facts of the case," said Briggs with a smile hoping to impress his sergeant, "We've a dead man who came off a train, drove a Bentley and has a connection with the RAF and likes cricket."

"And doesn't like smokers," added the sergeant.

"What makes you say that, Sergeant?" asked Briggs.

"The membership card for the British Anti-Smokers League found in the dead man's wallet, Sir."

"Quite so, Sergeant, quite so, I was about to point that out myself," lied Briggs.

"Yes, Sir, I'm sure you were."

"Now, Sergeant," continued Briggs hoping to show her he was a compassionate man. "I don't want the family of the deceased to be told the body was used as a scarecrow, as police officers we must be sympathetic and sensitive to their feelings of grief and loss. I wouldn't be happy myself if told a loved had been propped up in a field and used as a scarecrow."

"Might I take a closer look at the body, Sir?" asked the sergeant.

"But of course," replied Briggs, thinking all clues had been gathered by the doctor and she could no harm by looking at the body.

"Thank you, Sir," replied the sergeant and she went to the corpse and peered at it for a moment then bent forward and pried open the rigor mortised fingers of the tightly clenched right hand.

"What are you doing?" demanded the horrified Briggs thinking she was going to shake hands with the corpse.

"I was looking for this, Sir," replied the sergeant, holding up a three-inch long Cuban cigar butt. "It's a vital clue, isn't it?"

"Is it?"

"Yes, Sir. We need to know why a non-smoker had a cigar butt clenched in his dead hand when we know that he was a non-smoker!"

"Why do you think, Sergeant?"

"I think he was murdered, Sir."

"Murdered," gasped Briggs shocked.

"That's when life is taken forcibly by a second party" explained the doctor impatiently.

"I know what murder is, Doctor," retorted Briggs indignantly. "I'm a detective in CID and catching murderers is my daily bread and butter. I wasn't asking what murder is, no, I was merely agreeing with my sergeant's assessment of the facts regarding the cigar butt. But I must ask myself if this is really murder?"

"Most defiantly, Sir, it's murder without a doubt," replied the sergeant.

"Give me the cigar butt, Sergeant," said Briggs. She handed him the cigar butt. He held it to his nose and sniffed deeply and sighed wistfully. "Ah, yes, it's one of the better Cuban cigars. Now, Sergeant, remember what I told you about having an experienced copper's nose?" She nodded. "Well, I can tell you this is a Havana cigar . . ."

"It says so on the cigar band you've just read," interrupted the doctor, frustrated and fed-up with Briggs stupidity.

"Yes, and one of the best cigar's money can buy," replied Briggs, as he slipped the cigar butt into his coat pocket. "I'll smoke it later."

"You can't do that, Sir," exclaimed the sergeant.

"Why not, Sergeant, I don't mind smoking someone else's thrown-away cigar butt, not if it's a Cuban cigar."

"The cigar's evidence in a murder case, Chief Inspector," declared the doctor curtly, "and must go into an evidence bag. The killer's DNA might be on it."

The Chief Inspector reluctantly took the cigar butt from his pocket and handed it back to the sergeant. "Pop it into an evidence bag, Sergeant," he said glibly, "but I think it's a waste not to smoke it." She took the cigar butt and popped it into a plastic evidence bag.

Next morning at 11am Sergeant Jenny Hopper sat in the CID office of her boss at New Scotland Yard waiting for Briggs to arrive at work. The last thing he said to her the night before as she left for home was, "We've a murderer to catch, Sergeant, and so we'll start bright and early in the morning. It's the early bird who catches the worm." She arrived at 7.30am at New Scotland Yard wanting to impress him with her keenest to work in CID, and five hours later was still waiting. Bored and fed-up she had read every notice and bulletin pinned on the office notice boards then turned her attention to a red cardboard file lying on his desk, written on the cover 'Barnes Railway Bridge Murders.' The file made riveting reading with all the statements and police reports on the murders of railway employee David Penrose and river policeman Robert McDougal.

The murders happening twenty-five years earlier and they intrigued and challenged her. There was, she thought, a strong similarity between them and the death of Group Captain Huey Luey Lampton with fake black moustache found clenched in the railway worker's right hand, and in the Group Captain right hand a cigar butt. Was this too much of a coincidence? Both men clutching a vital murder clue in their right hands? Group Captain Huey Luey Lampton's cigar butt had been sent to forensics for tests but what of the fake moustache found clutched in David Penrose's hand twenty-five years earlier? Perhaps laboratory tests today would reveal DNA evidence taken from the spirit gum used to attach it to the murderer's face? "I hope the moustache hasn't been destroyed," she thought, "and is still kept in the evidence box. She picked up the phone and when the woman switchboard operator answered told her, "I want the department where old cases are stored."

"Suitcases?"

"No, murder files still open for investigation."

"How old?"

"I'm twenty-eight."

"Not you. The murder files!"

"Twenty-five years, double murder case that's never been closed."

"Putting you through now."

The evidence gathered for the 'Barnes Railway Bridge Murders,' was a backpack and football sized slab of sandstone with blood samples and fingerprints, and a fake moustache, stored in cardboard boxes in the vaults of New Scotland Yard. Jenny Hopper asked for the blood samples and the fake moustache to be sent to forensics for DNA testing. She had only just put the phone down when it began to ring and picking it up, she said brightly, "CID, Sergeant Jenny Hopper speaking."

"Doctor Dean here, Sergeant. I'm at the morgue calling about Chief Inspector Briggs."

An icy shiver of foreboding ran through the sergeant, was Chief Inspector Edgar 'Lanky' Briggs dead and stretched out cold on a slab in the mortuary? Was that why he had not turned up for work? "Oh, no," she muttered, "he's there with you, isn't he?"

"Yes, I'm afraid he is."

"Oh God, how awful."

"I know, and he's driving me crazy with all his silly nonsense."

"Driving you crazy? But how can a dead man drive you crazy?"

"He's not dead, Sergeant, only fainted when I started the post mortem on the Group Captain Huey Luey Lampton and cut into the body. I need you to come and collect him."

"The Group Captain?"

"No, the Chief Inspector."

"I was wondering what happened to him. I've been here all morning waiting for him."

"He did say when he arrived for the post-mortem that he would be seeing you later at New Scotland Yard."

"Well, he didn't tell me he was attending a post-mortem this morning. I thought you were doing it this afternoon?"

"Yes, so did I, Sergeant, but he wanted it done first thing this morning. He rang me at home last night saying, "It's the early bird who catches the worm. Please come and collect him. He's slumped in a chair and is making the place look untidy."

"I'll be right over, Doctor."

"Oh, and that reminds me now. I have you on the phone and we can talk privately without being overheard. I've a personal question that I'd like to ask you. Will you have dinner with me?"

There was a moment's hesitation then the sergeant replied, "I'm flattered, Doctor, but I never mix work with pleasure."

"We can talk about pathology in police work. It would be a learning experience for you and a delight for me to enjoy your company."

"That's nice of you to say."

"Have dinner with me. I can book a table at my favourite Italian restaurant. You'll love the food."

"Let me think about it, Doctor. "

"Call me Arthur."

"Arthur."

"May I call you Jenny, it's such a sweet name."

"Yes, I'd like that, Arthur."

"Have dinner with me, Jenny, please. It'll make me so happy."

"I said I'll think about it."

"Thank you. Now, is there anything else that I can do for you, Jenny?"

"Yes, when can a family member of the deceased see the Group Captain's body at the mortuary? We need to have a family member make an identification for police records."

The pompous blustering master of the Bumstead-on-the-Wold foxhunt, Colonel Ivor Biggan, rode at a canter exercising his stallion Horsy, riding along the edge of Grime-Dyke woods when something caught his eye. There was something moving among the swaying grass two hundred yards ahead of him under an oak tree. "Wow, there Horsy, wow," he called out reining in the horse, and shading his eyes against the glare of the sun was startled to see it was a man lying on his stomach. "Damn poacher," he muttered angrily. "Well, the bugger's in for a nasty surprise." Dismounting the Colonel moved quietly forward leading the horse by the reins and when he was hundred yards from the man he was shocked to see the man was naked from the waist down, trousers and underpants around his ankles, buttocks rising and falling in a steady rhythm. The Colonel recognized the missionary position for sexual intercourse. It was the position which he had once favoured himself when enjoying a fortnightly session of sexual intercourse lasting between three to five minutes with his wife. "The damn bugger's fucking," he gasped enraged with jealousy. He had not had sexual intercourse since his wife took up flower arranging six years earlier saying she found it a more satisfying activity. Gritting his teeth, he gripped his riding crop tightly and without thinking in fury brought it hard down on his right thigh making him wince with pain.

The man actively engaged in sexual intercourse lifted his head, face distorted with pleasure, then he kissed the woman laying beneath him passionately on the lips. The Colonel recognized the man and was so flabbergasted he could hardly believe his eyes, he was the new curate Peter Catchpole coupled in missionary position with cassock pulled above the waist and skinny buttocks rising and falling like a steam hammer. Under him and writhing in ecstasy Miss Melody Austin. The couple sweating and breathing heavily and oblivious to anything happening around them, both lost among the waves of pleasure that were overwhelming them.

The Colonel watched for a few moments then led Horsy quietly away. "This is going to put the cat among the pigeons," he thought mischievously with a smile as he mounted the horse and rode home to tell his wife what he had seen. "You should have seen the new curate, the filthy young blighter," he told her gleefully, "there he was mounted firmly upon Melody Austin's saddle and was riding her for all he was worth. It's our duty as church wardens to write an anonymous letter to the bishop."

"Are you sure it was the curate and Miss Austin, Ivor?" asked his wife who wanted to be certain before putting pen to paper to write to the bishop before giving the identity of the fornicating couple, and then have the delight of spreading the damaging gossip around the village. There could be serious repercussions if she named the wrong man as she had done previously when she had accused the village postman, Albert Figg, of putting more than letters through letterboxes when it was a door-to-door salesman selling loofahs who had been demonstrating the size of his product.

"There's no doubt, dear, he wore a cassock and dog collar, and the buttocks were too skinny to be those of the vicar who has a fat bum, and anyway I saw his face."

"Well, as long as you're sure it was the new curate."

"What about Ronald Perkins? Shouldn't he also be getting a letter like the bishop? It was his girlfriend having sex with the curate."

"Yes, Ivor, we'll send him an anonymous letter too. It's our duty to let him know what's been going on in Grime-Dyke woods with his girlfriend Melody Austin with her legs spread wide."

"Yes," agreed the Colonel with a smirk, "and who was giving her one!"

They both laughed heartily.

Group Captain Huey Luey Lampton's body was identified by his sister Mrs Annie Quemby, a roly-poly red-faced elderly woman who smelt of whiskey. She had travelled down from Edinburgh with her husband Jock, a haggis wholesaler and importer of bagpipe flutes, who on Burns Night wore his sporran under his kilt back to front to tickle his fancy. They stood looking at the body of Huey Luey Lampton laid out in the mortuary's chapel of rest in the presence of doctor Arthur Dean and Sergeant Jean Hopper.

Mrs Quemby, moist of eye, gazed at her brother for a long time before speaking then observed with a wistful sigh, "Ah, but he looks so much better dead than he ever did alive. Do you think I could have a photograph for the family album?"

"I'll ask the undertaker," replied the doctor sympathetically. "I'm sure he won't mind taking a snap before the coffin lid is screwed down."

"That's kind of you," muttered the tearful Mrs Quemby dabbing at her eyes with a handkerchief. "My dear brother was always unlucky. When he was a twenty he was told by a gypsy woman fortune teller at a fair that he was going to die. Now, forty-three-years later the prediction has come true. Spooky, isn't it?"

"Yes," agreed her husband with a fearful look who believed in ghosts and did not want to remain longer than was necessary in the presence of a dead body. He never liked his brother-in-law Huey Luey and feared he might do something to scare him from beyond the great abyss.

"Death comes knocking for us all," muttered Mrs Quemby dolefully, "coming like a thief to steal us away." She turned to her husband. "Soon it'll be my time to step into the great unknown, Jock. When I die don't cremate me. I've a terror of consuming fire which leaves nothing but ashes. I don't want to end up as ashes in an urn."

"Ashes in an urn? Are you drunk, woman?" he demanded, eyeing her suspiciously, and wondering if she had found the whiskey bottle hidden in his suitcase back at the hotel where they were staying.

Only with grief," responded Mrs Quemby dabbing her eyes with a handkerchief.

"Grief my eye, woman, you've been at the bottle again, haven't you? You couldn't keep off the booze long enough to make a sober identification of your brother Huey Luey? You ought to be ashamed of yourself."

"Ashamed? It isn't me whose carried home on Saturday nights from the pub," retorted Mrs Quemby angrily, glaring accusingly at her husband.

"There you go, woman, embroidering the truth again when it's you they carry home not me, and more than once in a wheelbarrow."

"FLUUUMPH." There was a loud raspberry-sounding fart, a clarion-call of a fart. Mrs Quemby panicked, and fearing she would be blamed she rounded on her husband hoping to establish her innocence, exclaiming loudly while pointing an accusing finger at him. "Go outside and shake yourself, Jock. Whatever will the doctor and sergeant think?"

"It wasn't me, woman," retorted her husband ashen faced with fear, thinking the fart came from Huey Luey with his ghost trying to make contact. "Unlike you I fart only when I've had a curry."

"FLUUUMPH." There was a second rip-snorting fart and all eyes with the exception of the late Group Captain turned to sergeant Jenny Hopper. "I didn't do it," she protested meekly holding up her hands, "When I fart, they're dainty with hardly any sound."

"FLUUUMPH." There came a third rattling fart that echoed round the mortuary.

"Don't panic," declared doctor Dean pointing at the late Group Captain. "It's only wind coming from the corpse."

"What? A dead man farting!" exclaimed Jock Quemby with a look of terror on his face convinced his dead brother-in-law was making ghostly farts to frighten him.

"Dead bodies often expel wind from their bowels after death," explained the doctor in a calm soothing voice, "the undertaker has forgotten to insert a plug of cotton wool before you viewed the body."

"Gracious me but my late brother certainly can fart, can't he?" beamed Mrs Quemby proudly, much relieved the culprit had been found and she was no longer a suspect. "Huey Luey suffered with flatulence most of his life. His nickname in the RAF was 'Stinker.'"

"Must have been hell for the aircrews who flew with him in bomber command," replied her husband grimly. "Wasn't that the reason he was transferred to fighter command? Aircrews in bombers refused to share a plane with him in a confined space?"

"We never talk about it, Jock, not outside the family," replied Mrs Quemby, blushing with embarrassment. "Show respect for Huey Luey now he's dead. "

"I'd like to know how much money he's left us in his will."

"Please, Jock, not in front of the body. We'll know soon enough what we'll be getting when we visit the solicitor tomorrow for the reading of the will."

"I don't know about you, woman, but I've thirst on me that Negara Falls wouldn't satisfy. I'm away to the nearest pub for a few pints, and a few pints more, replied Jock as he hurried towards the mortuary door. "There's still five hours left before closing time."

"Wait for me, Jock," cried his wife running after him.

Chapter twelve

The Metropolitan police launched the biggest murder investigation second only to the Jack the Ripper case to find the murderer of Group Captain Huey Luey Lampton. The case file titled, 'Cigar Butt Murder.' Forensics completed DNA tests on the cigar butt found clenched in the Group Captain's hand and on the fake moustache clenched in David Penrose's hand, and football sized slab of sandstone. There was a definite DNA link to both murders committed twenty-five years apart, and the police knew they were hunting a serial killer with three known murders to his or her credit.

Chief Inspector Briggs sat at his desk drinking coffee from a plastic cup, reading the forensic report handed to him by sergeant Jenny Hopper. "As you see, Sir," she said glibly, "the report states that DNA found on the false moustache matches with DNA found on the cigar butt. This means the moustache was worn with cigar smoked and slab of sandstone handled by the same man or woman, the murderer."

"Then with all this DNA evidence we'll soon have the killer under lock and key, Sergeant, isn't that so?"

"The killer's been on the loose killing for twenty-five-years, Sir, perhaps even longer. We're dealing with a clever, devious and cunning individual. Yes, we've got the murderer's DNA which is useless without having the murderer to match it with. We must be cleverer and out think the murderer."

"Do you think I'm cleverer than the murderer, Sergeant?"

She did not reply and prudently kept her thoughts to herself.

The Right Reverend Charles Ashley, bishop of the diocese of Portland and Penge, sat in his office desk reading for the eighth time with dismay the letter he had received anonymously denouncing one of his vicars for having unbridled lust in a wood. It was a complaint which he had to investigate. The bishop, a leading light in the Church of England, theologian and popular with his clergy, and bishop elect for the post of Archbishopric of Canterbury, in red cassock and clerical collar, with large silver cross dangling from a blue cord from around his neck, with soft white fluffy slippers to ease his feet. The bishop suffers with gout and is a martyr to bunions and chilblains. Small of stature and thin as a beanpole, an oval pie-dish of a face with perpetual smile, and an enormous passion for his overtly fat wife, Melinda, who he adores. He is what the Americans call a 'chubby-chaser,' having married the fattest woman he could find during his three years at Oxford University as a young student.

There came a knock on the bishop's study door. "Enter," called out the bishop brightly thinking it was his wife bringing him a cup of tea and a jam doughnut. The door opened and Peter Catchpole the curate of St Freda the Eveready entered looking sheepish, ushered in by Henry Davenport the bishop's chaplain, a pale faced individual with permanent grimace which made him look as if he had just swallowed a mouthful of vinegar.

"Peter has finally arrived, my Lord," explained the chaplain curtly looking with distain at the curate. There was an unpleasant smell which made the bishop reach for a handkerchief and hold it to his nose. "He thumbed a lift down from Scotland in the back of a truck carrying pigs," continued the chaplain. Peter Catchpole was two days late for his appointment with the bishop. In his haste not to be late he caught by mistake a non-stop express to Edinburgh from King's Cross station, a six-hour journey. He should have caught the train stopping at every station to Brighton, one hour's journey from London.

"Thank you, Henry," replied the bishop realizing the unpleasant smell, identified as pigs by the chaplain, came from Peter Catchpole, and decided that as a practicing Christian he must suffer it without complain. With forced smile he returned the handkerchief to his pocket. "I'll ring the bell if I need you." Henry Davenport nodded and left the room closing the door behind him.

Peter Catchpole, in black suit with clerical collar, suit badly crumpled and looking as if he had slept in it which indeed he had. The bishop stood up and held out his hand in greeting. "Well, here you are at last, Peter," he said brightly, "I was wondering what had happened to you." The men shook hands.

"I'm sorry, my Lord. I didn't know the train I caught from Victoria station was non-stop to Scotland."

"But of course, you didn't. Well, you're here now and that's what counts."

"I didn't have enough money to buy a ticket back to London and so, hitch-hiked from Scotland, my Lord. Sorry about the smell. The truck that gave me a lift carried pigs to market. I had to sit in the back with them for six hours. There was a large boar with a big snout who took a most unwanted amorous interest in me and I had to keep beating him off with my prayer book."

"Well, that explains the unfortunate smell, Peter. Now, come and sit down and rest yourself." The bishop led the way to two brown leather armchairs in front of a roaring log fire. The bishop sat down and gestured to the other chair with his right hand. The curate sat down. He was worried having no idea why the bishop sent for him except it was on a very serious matter.

"Peter, is there something you'd like to tell me?"

"Tell you, my Lord?"

"Something that's troubling you?"

"Can't think of anything, my Lord."

"Confession is good for the soul. Think deeply, is there something that you need to tell me as your bishop but are finding it difficult to do so?" The curate shook his head. "Oh, dear, you're not making this easy for me, so I'll have to come straight out with it. I've received a letter."

"Letter, my Lord," echoed the curate, wondering what a letter to bishop had to do with him.

"Yes, Peter, a letter. What have you got to say about that?"

"The Post Office did a good job delivering it, my Lord!"

The bishop sighed deeply. The interview was proving harder than he supposed it would be. "The letter was written anonymously, Peter. Surely, you must have thoughts on that?"

The curate thought for a moment then nodded. "Yes, my Lord, the letter writer forgot to sign the letter."

"No, no, Peter, the letter writer wanted to remain anonymous so nobody would know who he or she is to hide their identity. The envelope had a Bumstead-on-the-Wold postmark which means the letter writer is a member of your own congregation. Serious allegations were made against you, very serious indeed."

"Allegations, my lord. What allegations, my Lord?"

"Concerning a young lady. Does the name Melody Austin mean anything to you?"

"Yes, I know the lady, my Lord. She's a member of my congregation."

"The letter claims you know her intimately and on more than one occasion."

"Intimately, my Lord? What do you mean intimately?"

"In the biblical sense."

"Oh, I see." The curate's face went bright red with embarrassment. The bishop knew of his affair with Melody and he wondered if he had broken some Church law by being her lover? But she was not married and nor was he and so they could not be accused of committing adultery. But had he disgraced himself as a budding curate in the eyes of bishop by raising his cassock when he should have kept it lowered. The affair started a month earlier when Melody invited him to tea and crumpet a week after his first visit to see her. She was at home alone and ended up drinking hardly any tea while enjoying an abundance of crumpet with his cassock raised.

"What have you got to say for yourself, Peter?" asked the bishop impatiently.

"It's true, my Lord, Melody and I are lovers. "

"I was afraid you'd say that, Peter. You understand how serious this is for you don't you? You could be unfrocked."

"Oh, no, not unfrocked. What a chilly experience that would be especially on a cold day."

"It means your license to preach and administer the sacraments would be revoked and you'd have to hand in your clerical collar. My lawyers tell me the Church can be sued by Melody's husband because you took advantage of her when you should have been the good shepherd and guiding a lost ewe back into the fold."

"Melody isn't married, my Lord."

"Not married. Well, that puts a different light on things. If adultery wasn't committed then you won't be unfrocked."

"What about Melody, my Lord?"

"She can remove her own frock whenever she likes. Now tell me, Peter, are you in love with Melody or were you giving into the temptation of the flesh?"

"I'd never slept with a woman before Melody and so I don't know the difference between love and lust. She's my first and only lover and I do think of her most of the time."

"Which means you love her, Peter."

"Oh, thank you, my Lord. I wasn't sure but now you've confirmed it for me."

"Can you give her up?"

"I don't know, my Lord."

"What about the priesthood? Can you give that up?"

"Never, my Lord, not my calling."

"Good man, now I can now see a light glimmering at the end of a long dark tunnel. If you want to remain in the priesthood, Peter, then you must do what I tell you."

"But of course, my Lord. Whatever you say."

"You're not to return to the parish of St Freda the Eveready. I want you to take a break from clerical duties, a short holiday away on a religious retreat to revitalize your spiritual batteries and to sort out your feelings for Melody."

"Yes, my Lord, a short holiday."

"Somewhere quiet and peaceful so you can reflect prayerfully on your future in the Church. I'd like to send you on a month's retreat to the Convent of the Sisters of Mercy, an enclosed order of nuns. I know the Mother Superior sister Rosebud who's a dear friend of mine. But I must insist you have no contact with Melody until after the retreat. Do you promise, Peter?"

"I do, my Lord, I promise."

"Good man, and if at the end of the retreat if you decide you still have a vocation as a priest then I'll arrange for a new parish for you, a fresh start with exciting challenges, an inner-city parish. What do you say? Shall I arrange for the retreat with Sister Rosebud?"

The curate nodded thinking sadly there would be no more tea with an abundance of lovely crumpet with his cassock raised with the beautiful Melody. He did not mind missing the tea but was desolate about missing the lovely crumpet and lifting up his cassock.

Perkins opened the anonymous letter the postman delivered with the morning post. He was having breakfast with Melody, dressed in white silk pyjamas, red dressing gown with matching slippers. She sat opposite to him sucking orange juice through a straw from a tall glass, she was on a diet trying to reduce a few inches from off her thighs and buttocks wanting to look as desirable as possible for her curate lover. Her dressing gown slightly open exposing her cleavage to please Perkins, who was a breast man and had a pet names for each of her breasts, Pinky and Perky. Since beginning her romance with the young curate and when having sex with Perkins she closed her eyes and fantasying it was the dashingly handsome young Peter Catchpole who was thrusting merrily away between her thighs.

Perkins was in a good mood when he began reading the two-page letter, but after reading the first few lines his face turned red with anger. The anonymous letter was far more sexually explicit than the letter sent to the bishop. When he finished reading the letter he gave a choking gasping sound as if struggling for breath. Melody the love of his life had betrayed him with a man in a clerical collar in Grim-Dyke woods. "Are you alright, Ronnie?" asked Melody, alarmed by the sudden redness of his face and hearing him gasp for breath fearing he was having a heart attack. "Shall I call a doctor?"

He took a deep breath to control his fury and managed to compose himself. "There's no need for a doctor. I've swallowed a bit of toast that went down the wrong way," he said giving a little cough to illustrate the fact then folding up the letter slipped it away into his dressing gown pocket. He would need time to think. Was his beloved Melody having an affair with the curate as the poison pen letter writer alleged? He would need proof before punishing the guilty.

"Oh, thank goodness, Ronnie," said Melody with a smile relieved he was not having a heart attack. "You scared me for a moment."

"I'd like us to attend church on Sunday morning for the family service," he replied forcing a smile, "I've heard good things about the new curate and the sermons he preaches." He wanted to see Peter Catchpole and size him up as his possible love rival for Melody's hand. When he saw them together he would be able to tell if they were lovers by the way they looked and spoke to each other.

"Yes, he preaches a good sermon," agreed Melody, then added quickly, "so I've heard," not wanting Perkins to know she had been visiting the church secretly to meet the curate in the bell tower with the door locked, then engaging in strenuous sexual activities with him.

"Ah, so you've met the curate?"

"Once," she lied, "when he came here to see you. But you were in London with your mother for her birthday treat. I told you about it."

"Oh, yes, what a pity I missed him, but never mind I'll be meeting him on Sunday."

Melody did not reply, there was something about Perkins eyes and the way he looked at her that sent a cold shiver through her.

On Sunday morning the Reverend Sydney Bloom, vicar of St Freda the Eveready, was in the bell-tower supervising the pealing of the bell summoning the faithful of Bumstead-on-the-Wold to the family service. Jake Turner, verger and gravedigger, forty-three, a squat slow-witted swarthy fellow dressed in dark blue polo-neck sweater, baggy blue dungarees, pulling half-heartily on the bell rope with both hands. When he finished tolling the bell the vicar said to him, "I've had a complaint from Rawlings and Sons the Undertakers about the grave that you dug for them last Thursday. They've requested that in future would you check with them on the size of the coffin before you dig the grave. The grave you dug was three inches too short to take the coffin and they said at the burial you leapt up and down on the coffin lid trying to force the coffin down into the grave, shouting 'Get down, you bastard, get down.' The family of the deceased are very upset about it and say the deceased was not a bastard. His parents were married four years before he was born."

"Sorry, Vicar, it won't happen again."

"See it doesn't there's a good fellow. Now I need you to be my server for this morning service. Charlie Smith's wife phoned to say he's in bed with a cold and can't serve this morning. Now, be off with you and light the altar candles. I've put out a cassock and a surplice for you in the vestry. Put them on before you prepare the altar and side table."

"Couldn't the curate assist you at the altar, Vicar?" Wearing a cassock and surplice always troubled Jake Turner who thought it made him look like a badly shaped woman with broad shoulders and big feet. This was because when he looked in the vestry mirror when wearing a cassock and surplice he resembled his aunt Mavis, and nobody not even aunt Mavis wanted to look like aunt Mavis.

"The curate's left us, Jake, sadly he's gone from the parish."

"Gone, Vicar? "

"Never to return according to the bishop."

"Not dead, Vicar?"

"No, not dead but moved on to another parish."

"I thought he was settling in nicely. He asked me to bring him fresh vegetables from my allotment to make a stew, Vicar. I've got a marrow, lettuce, tomatoes, with some King Edward potatoes, carrots and onions in a carrier bag."

"Pity to waste them, Jake, I'll take them home to the wife."

"Why did the curate leave us? I thought he liked it here."

"The bishop said it was expedient for him to go."

"Ah, so there's a woman involved?"

"My lips are sealed, Jake, it's confidential."

"I've heard village gossip. It seems the curate and Melody Austin had been . . ."

"Please, Jake," interrupted the vicar, "no gossip in church please."

Perkins sat with Melody on a front pew in church directly under the pulpit. The vicar preaching with gusto a sermon on the theme 'Let he who is without sin cast the first stone,' and as he spoke he kept glancing down at the faces of the congregation looking for guilty faces so he would know who had written the anonymous letter to the bishop. The faces of his two churchwardens Colonel Ivor Biggan and his wife Gloria flushed bright red and they quickly looked away whenever he caught their eye unable to meet his accusing glances.

After the service the vicar stood at the church doors shaking hands as the congregation left to go home. The last couple to leave were Perkins and Melody. "How nice to see new faces at the family service," beamed the vicar shaking Melody's hand warmly, "I hope we'll see more of you?" Perkins forced a smile, thinking the curate already might have been seen more of her than he should have done, and wondered where he was.

Melody smiled and nodded, "That would nice, Vicar. I enjoyed the service and your sermon."

"I was hoping to meet the new curate," said Perkins.

"Peter's gone I'm afraid. It was very sudden and took us by surprise."

"Dead?" gasped Melody, ashen-faced with shock.

"Dead?" echoed the vicar, wondering why she thought that. With a groan Melody fainted collapsing into the arms of Perkins. "Peter's not dead, my dear young lady," exclaimed the vicar bending over her and fanning her face with his prayer book. "He's gone away on religious retreat for a month to the Convent of the Sisters of Mercy. But sadly, he won't be returning to us afterwards. The bishop is sending him to an inner-city parish."

"Sisters of Mercy," muttered Perkins. The name was familiar but where had he heard it before? Then he remembered his visit to the Convent of the Sisters of Mercy twenty-five years earlier when he was disguised as the Reverend Jonathan Needham and murdered his grandfather and the elderly nun sister Tulip.

Next day, after much thought, Perkins decided to hire a private detective to visit the Convent of the Sisters of Mercy to question the curate without arousing his suspicion. He wanted answers, and if Melody and the curate were lovers then he would punish curate.

Chapter Thirteen

Mrs Brenda Gooseberry, robust middle-aged cockney housekeeper of private detective Allan Hawes at 202B Bakery Street, opened the front door to be confronted by an imposing man with grey goatee beard, immaculately dressed in evening dress with neat black bow tie and top hat. Draped over his shoulders a black opera cloak lined with sky blue silk lining, and held in his right hand a silver-topped gentleman's cane. The image one of a wealthy gentleman who enjoyed the opera and travelled first class on British rail. The man was Perkins in disguise. He raised his hat respectfully, "Good afternoon, Madam, is Mister Hawes the detective at home?" he asked. "I've come seeking his help."

"Mister Hawes is at home, Sir, but too busy working on a case of international importance to see anyone."

"I'll pay him three times his usual rate with expenses. It's a matter of the heart, a heart that might or might not have been cruelly betrayed. Only Mister Hawes can discover the truth for me."

"Heart cruelly betrayed," echoed the housekeeper, eyes becoming moist for she too had known heartbreak. Her late husband jilted her four times at the altar before she managed to get him drunk and into a registry office and married before he sobered up.

"I believe the love of my life has betrayed me."

"Oh, you poor man. I'm sure Mister Hawes will see you when he knows about your heartbreak. He's a sympathetic man who understands sorrow. Please follow me, Sir." Mrs Gooseberry led Perkins down a hallway and up a winding staircase leading to the detective's rooms. As they neared the top of the stairs the sound of a violin beautifully played wafted to his ears. Mrs Gooseberry paused for a moment to listen with a look of rapture on her face. "That's Mister Hawes," she said wistfully, "he likes an occasional fiddle about to give himself a smile." She proceeded up the stairs. The first door on the landing was open and the resplendent figure of the private detective Allan Hawes could be seen standing inside the room with eyes closed playing a violin with concentration and gusto. He wore a purple smoking jacket and blue carpet slippers.

"There's a gentleman here to see you, Mister Hawes," called out Mrs Gooseberry gaily, dabbing at her eyes with a handkerchief overwhelmed by the beautiful music.

The detective stopped playing the violin and held the bow poised above the strings and the music continued playing. "What gentleman might that be?" he asked anxiously with a frown worried it was the rent collector calling again for the back rent and wondering if there was time to hide behind the sofa.

"He says he wants to employ your services."

"But I'm already engaged on a case of international importance."

"I've told him that, Mister Hawes, but he says he'll pay three times your usual fee with expenses."

"Show the gentleman in, Mrs Gooseberry."

Doctor Albert Windrush sat on a sofa with an open notebook on his lap busily writing. He glanced up as Perkins entered the room. Hawes switched off the record player and the violin music ceased abruptly. He put the violin and bow on the table and stepped forward to shake Perkins hand. "Allan Hawes," he said introducing himself.

"Freddy Basilweight," replied Perkins, shaking the detective's hand.

Hawes turned to Mrs Gooseberry. "What about a cup of tea and a biscuit for our visitor, Mrs Gooseberry?"

"But of course, Mister Hawes. Shall I take the gentleman's hat and cloak?"

"Only if you promise to return them," smiled the detective hoping to impress his visitor with his ready wit and humour.

Perkins removed his hat and cloak and handed them to Mrs Gooseberry.

"Thank you, Mrs Gooseberry," said the detective, "that'll do for now. Please return to your kitchen where I think you'll find there's a steak and kidney pudding waiting your attention to be popped into the oven."

"Goodness gracious me, Mister Hawes, how could you possibly know that?" cried Mrs Gooseberry, greatly impressed. "It's true, I'm making a steak and kidney pie for you and the doctor's dinner."

"Brilliant, my dear Hawes, utterly brilliant," exclaimed the doctor, who never ceased to be amazed by the detective's logic and amazing assumptions.

Allan Hawes smiled, a self-knowing smile, not revealing that twenty minutes earlier he slipped down to the kitchen for a glass of milk and had seen the steak and kidney pie on the kitchen table. Mrs Gooseberry turned to go. "Don't forget the tea and biscuit for our visitor, Mrs Gooseberry," he called out after her.

The doctor, smiling broadly, shook Perkins hand. "Doctor Albert Windrush at your service, Sir," he said, "both in medicine and in detecting crime."

"Good to meet you, Doctor," responded Perkins. "I've heard good things about Mister Hawes trusted companion and biographer."

"I don't know about biographer," replied the doctor humbly, delighted his writing talents were finally being recognized and praised. He had thirty-three notebooks full of the exploits of Allan Hawes but only one exploit had been published 'The Case of The Screaming Scotsman,' about a Highland marathon runner called Jock who had run with nothing under his kilt screaming through a three feet high field of thistles, which is a stingingly good read.

Hawes studied his visitor as he shook hands with the doctor. There was something familiar about the face and he knew they had met before but where and when? The great detective liked to think he had a good memory for faces but could not place the man. What Hawes was struggling to remember was meeting Perkins twenty-five-years earlier when he worked as a desk clerk at the Braddock Towers Hotel with Perkins disguised as wealthy American tourist Roger Shepherd the Third. "Please be seated, Mister Basilweight," said Hawes gesturing towards an armchair.

Perkins sat down feeling uneasy with the inquisitive look the detective gave him wondering if his flies were open, but a quick glance down at his groin confirmed all was well and safely zipped in.

"Now, down to business," said Hawes, as he sat on a sofa and was joined by the doctor. "How might I be of service to you, Mister Basilweight?"

"Well, it's a delicate matter concerning the Church of England."

"Not the Archbishop of Canterbury again?" gasped the doctor looking shocked. Hawes sighed. The doctor had an obsession with the archbishop of Canterbury. "Why do you always think the Archbishop of Canterbury is to blame whenever we get a case involving the Church of England, doctor?" asked Hawes glowering at him.

"He's top fellow, isn't he? The buck always stops with the top fellow, don't you know."

"Be quiet, Doctor and make notes. Let me do the thinking."

"Of course, my dear Hawes. I can always add the guilt of the

Archbishop of Canterbury to my notes later."

Hawes frowned and shook his head. "Please continue, Mister Basilweight. Does your wife know you're seeking my help?"

"I'm not married . . ." began Perkins.

"Nor are we," interrupted the doctor brightly. There was a long-embarrassed silence, then the doctor mumbled, "I mean we're just good friends and not . . ."

"Oh, be quiet, Doctor," snapped Hawes angrily, "another outburst and you'll have to leave the room."

"It's all right, Mister Hawes, I quite understand," said Perkins sympathetically, "it's not for me to judge your friendship with doctor Windrush. I had an uncle living in Ireland who called himself Auntie Clara and wore lipstick, high heels, and dresses. Sadly, he took up river dancing and drowned."

"My relationship with doctor Windrush is strictly a working one," retorted Hawes indignantly. "We're good friends and nothing more, isn't that so, Doctor?"

"Yes, quite so Hawes" agreed the doctor speaking in a deliberate deep baritone to emphasis his masculinity, "we like the ladies don't we Hawes?"

"I really do like women," insisted Hawes, glaring furiously at the doctor hoping to cower him into silence.

"Please, gentlemen, you don't have to explain yourselves to me," said Perkins, "each man to his own taste I say, and as long as it doesn't bother anyone else or frighten the horses then why not follow your preference for a same sex partner?"

"I'm not gay, Mister Basilweight," insisted Hawes indignantly, "I'm happy at times but never gay. Please continue with your reason for coming to see me."

"I think my girlfriend has been sleeping with a Church of England clergyman . . ."

"The Archbishop of Canterbury," interrupted the doctor triumphantly.

"No, not the archbishop of Canterbury," retorted Perkins, "but a young curate called Peter Catchpole."

"What makes you think they've been sleeping together?" asked Hawes.

"I received an anonymous letter detailing a sexual rendezvous they supposedly had in a local wood, and on Sunday at church my girlfriend fainted when told the curate was gone."

"Not dead?" asked Hawes.

"No, Mister Hawes, not dead merely gone. He has left the parish for good. The vicar said the bishop sent the curate away on a religious retreat to the Convent of the Sisters of Mercy. What I need from you is evidence to prove or disprove the curate's guilt."

"And if guilty I hope you're not thinking of taking justice into your own hands?"

Perkins shook his head. "No, Mister Hawes, I wouldn't hurt a fly. My intention should you find the curate guilty will be to write a strong worded letter of complaint to the Archbishop of Canterbury demanding he be unfrocked."

"The Archbishop of Canterbury?" asked the doctor.

"No, the curate Peter Catchpole."

"If the curate is on a religious retreat, then how can I gather evidence?" asked Hawes. "I need to catch him with your girlfriend actively engaged having sex and take photographs. But if they're not together it can't be done."

"I want you to go to the Convent on a religious retreat, Mister Hawes, and find Peter Catchpole and get him to confide in you."

"You'll pay money for this?"

"Name your fee, Mister Hawes."

"Alright I'll do it, but I can only spend one day on it before having to return to London to continue working on the case I'm presently engaged upon of international importance. I can't tell you anymore about it without breaking the official secrets act and the confidences of persons highly placed in Government."

"Thank you, Mister Hawes."

"Doctor, get out the yellow pages book from the bookcase," cried Hawes getting to his feet, "we've a religious retreat to arrange with the Sisters of Mercy."

Next morning Sister Rosebud the Mother Superior walked from the Convent gatehouse towards the main building with two men. Her sweet lilting Irish accent melodious as ever, with hair hidden under her wimple having turned snowy white. She walks slower with a faltering step aided with a walking stick. One of the men wears a deerstalker hat and the other man has a stethoscope dangling from his jacket pocket. "Are you gentlemen Church of England?" asked the Mother Superior as they walked up the gravel path toward the front door of the main building. "Not that it matters for your retreat but you should know that we take our bible readings from the King James Bible."

"We're both Church of England," replied Hawes, "baptized and confirmed."

"And booked for a weekend retreat of prayer and meditation," replied the nun with a smile."

"Reflecting on our spiritual life, Mother Superior, "responded Hawes, smiling back at her. "I was wondering how many nuns there are at the mother house?"

"Sadly, numbers have declined in recent years and we're down to a third of the sisters that we had ten years ago. Women aren't entering the religious life like they used to. They don't want to get up in the dark at 5am and take an icy cold shower before spending three hours on their knees praying in a freezing chapel."

"Have you any men on retreat beside us, Mother Superior?" asked Hawes.

"Yes, there's one gentleman, a young curate, Reverend Peter Catchpole, but you won't see much of him. He spends most of his time on his knees in the chapel wrestling with a deeply troubled conscience."

"What troubles him?" asked the doctor.

"I don't know," replied the Mother Superior, "but the bishop said he's in spiritual crisis and for me to do all I can to support him and see he gets a chocolate biscuit with his cup of cocoa at bedtime."

"That's very good of you," said Hawes.

"Our sins always catch us out in the end," said the nun looking at the doctor, who blushed deeply, wondering if she had read his mind and knew about his stack of girlie magazines under his bed at home and what he used them for. But she knew nothing about them and was merely making a general observation about sin.

"Could the curate's trouble be an affair of the heart, Mother Superior?" asked Hawes.

"You mean had he been doing that which he ought not to have been doing in the first place?"

"Pardon?" asked the doctor, confused by the nun's answer.

"Getting his leg over," she smiled sweetly.

"Precisely," agreed Hawes shocked by the nun's crudeness.

"But that's mere speculation on my part," replied the nun, "even If I did know there had been hanky-panky I wouldn't tell you. We keep our guest's confidentiality here."

"Oh, what a pity," replied the doctor, disappointed, "it would have made your discussion group so much more interesting."

Peter Catchpole came out of the Convent chapel after a long prayer session with knees sore. He had been reflecting on his love for Melody and having the strength not to see her again with cassock raised. Waiting outside the chapel door was a man wearing a deerstalker hat. "Peter Catchpole?" asked Hawes with a smile.

"Yes."

"Might I have a word with you? We've a common interest."

"We do? And what might that be?"

"Miss Melody Austin."

"Did she send you?"

"No, I've been sent by somebody else who has both your interests at heart."

"My mother?"

"No, but a good friend of you both. Do you love Melody?"

The curate nodded, "Yes, I love her."

"And you were lovers?"

"Yes, but no more."

"Then it's over?"

"Yes, like the poor unfortunate Dodo bird. There was an anonymous letter sent to the bishop telling him about Melody and myself, and he arranged for me to come here on retreat to sort out my future and make a decision on my vocation. I've decided my priesthood comes before having an affair with another's man's fiancée. This good friend of whom you speak? Was it Ronald Perkins?"

Hawes shook his head. "No, it wasn't Ronald Perkins," he said. "I can't tell you anymore but trust me when I say I'm here to help you." He glanced at his wristwatch. "Oh, no, is that the time. I'm late for my appointment with the Mother Superior." He turned and strode quickly away down the corridor.

"Who are you?" called the curate after him.

When Allan Hawes returned home to 202B Bakery Street he rang his client Freddy Basilweight to tell him of his conversation with Peter Catchpole outside the Convent chapel. "The details described in the anonymous letter are true," he confided, "your girlfriend has been playing away with the curate and he was regularly scoring in the back of her net."

"You mean?"

"She and the curate were at it like rabbits."

"You're in no doubt about it, Mister Hawes?"

"No doubt whatsoever, but you've nothing to worry about with the curate. He assured me the affair is over and he won't be seeing Melody again."

"Thank you, Mister Hawes, your cheque will be in the post."

The next day a clergyman arrived at the gatehouse of the Convent of the Sisters of Mercy and rang the bell. Perkins disguised as the Reverend Jonathan Needham, false moustache, horn-rimmed spectacles, white-haired wig. He had come on a hastily booked religious retreat. Perkins decided to give clerical promotion to the character he was portraying and promote him from vicar to Archdeacon, and he was wearing an Archdeacon's black gaiters.

Sister Buttercup, gatekeeper, oldest nun in the Convent, slid back the grill on the heavy oak door and peered out at Perkins. "Who's there?" she called out in a frail squeaky voice. "Are you the pizza delivery boy?"

"No, Sister, it's the Archdeacon. I've come on retreat."

"Speak up, I'm hard of hearing. Have you the cheese and tomato pizzas we ordered?"

"IT'S THE ARCHDECON," shouted Perkins, losing patience.

"What? Our pizza's been eaten by the Archdeacon?"

"I'M HERE ON RETREAT."

"What's wrong with your feet?"

"CAN I COME IN?"

"What's that about the bin? Are you the dustman? Why didn't you say so instead of going on about your feet?"

"IS THERE ANYBODY ELSE I CAN TALK TO?"

"What's that about Elise? We haven't got an Elise here."

"LET ME IN."

"Oh, so you want to come in." Sister Buttercup pulled back the bolts on door. "You'll have to push from your side because I'm too old and feeble to manage it by myself."

Perkins put his shoulder against the heavy oak door and pushed it slowly open. "THANK YOU," he shouted as he stepped inside the gatehouse.

"You want the loo?"

"NO. I'M ON RETREAT."

"I'm fed-up with hearing about your feet." She eyed him suspiciously. "You don't look like a dustman to me more like an Archdeacon in gaiters."

Perkins was given a bedroom five doors down the corridor from Peter Catchpole's bedroom, ideal for his planned visit to the curate during the night. At dinner he sat at table opposite Doctor Albert Windrush. Allan Hawes had returned to London to work on his case of international importance with the doctor remaining with the Sisters of Mercy for personal reasons. He wanted to discuss his obsession with the Archbishop of Canterbury.

The meal was toad-in-the-hole, mashed potatoes and sliced beans, followed by creamy rice pudding. The toad-in-the-hole mostly batter with hardly any toad, a tiny chipolata sausage. The Mother Superior sat at the head of the table. "I remember your last visit, Archdeacon, twenty-five-years ago when you were but a humble vicar and our dear Sister Tulip fell into the goldfish pond and drowned."

"Yes, a very sad business, indeed."

"Since Sister Tulip's death I've insisted on all my nuns taking swimming lessons."

"Haven't we met before, Archdeacon?" asked Doctor Windrush eyeing Perkins suspiciously. There was something about him that seemed familiar.

"No, we've not met, Doctor," replied Perkins nervously, worried the doctor had seen through his disguise. "I would have remembered you. I've a good memory for faces."

The convent tower clock struck the midnight hour as Perkins quietly opened his bedroom door and stepped out into the corridor. He wore pale blue pajamas, grey dressing gown and red slippers, and in his right hand held a syringe. Going down the corridor he reached Peter Catchpole's bedroom door and cautiously turned the door handle. The door was unlocked and he entered the room and from the light in the corridor he saw the curate was asleep in a bed. He advanced towards the bed thinking after the killing the post-mortem would never show the cause of death was from an air bubble being injected into a vein, with an injection of an air bubble leaving no trace and entering the heart to stop it and looking like a heart attack.

Perkins prodded the sleeping curate gently with a finger. There was no response. Peter Catchpole was a heavy sleeper. Perkins eased back the bedclothes uncovering the curate's left arm and paused briefly to see if his movements had woken him. The curate continued sleeping. Perkins looked for a vein in the crook of the curate's arm but it was too dark to see and he switched on the bedside lamp. The sharp prick of the needle in his arm woke the curate with a painful start and opening his eyes he was startled to see the Archdeacon bending over him. "What's happening?" he muttered, still half asleep.

"Go back to sleep," whispered Perkins soothingly as he pushed his thumb down on the syringe plunger. "You're dreaming." The lethal bubble of air entered into the curate's blood stream.

"Oooooh," gasped the curate as he felt a stabbing pain in his chest and reaching up he grabbed Perkins hair then went into convulsions, his fingers tightened on the hair and he yanked away strands of hair. The heart attack was mercifully short and twenty seconds after the air bubble injected the curate was dead. Perkins switched off the bedside table lamp and crept back to his bedroom and hide the syringe in his suitcase under two shirts, got into bed and went to sleep.

The next morning when the curate failed to appear for breakfast Sister Daisy the novice mistress was sent to his room to find him. She knocked timidly on the curate's door fearful of what she might see when the door opened, thinking there was nothing more disturbing for a cloistered nun than to see a man in bulging underpants. When there was no response, she knocked again and called out, "Reverend Catchpole." Still no reply and thinking he had overslept she opened the door and warily entered the room ready in an instant to cover her eyes with her wimple should the curate be in bulging underpants.

Peter Catchpole lay in bed in a twisted convulsed position with hands clutched at his heart, a terrible anguished look on his face with eyes open and glazed. Sister Daisy stared transfixed in horror knowing the curate was dead, then with piercing scream she fled from the room.

The Mother Superior summoned a doctor who declared the cause of death a heart-attack, and the body was taken by ambulance to a hospital mortuary for a post-mortem. Perkins watched the body loaded into the ambulance with satisfaction of a job well done. But he would not have been so pleased had he known a few strands of his hair tugged from his head were clutched within the dead fist of the curate's right hand.

The pathologist carrying out the post-mortem found the needle mark in the curate's arm and reported to the police a suspicious death. The post-mortem results were inconclusive. The curate died from a massive heart attack but according to his medical records he had undergone a full medical examination a week earlier for a life insurance policy where his heart was found to be in excellent condition. The strands of hair found in the curate's clenched fist were sent to forensics for tests and when the results came back a murder investigation was launched. The DNA found on the hair matched with the DNA found on the false moustache taken from railway worker David Penrose's dead hand who died on Barnes Railway Bridge, and also on the slab of sandstone, and DNA found on the cigar butt clenched within the dead hand of non-smoker Group Captain Huey Luey Lampton. They were murdered by the same killer.

Chief Inspector Edward 'Lanky' Briggs was put in charge of Peter Catchpole's murder investigation with case file titled, 'Curate's Murder.' "It's the same serial killer, Sergeant," he told Jenny Hopper, "and he or she has now killed four men."

"That we know of, Sir."

"What? Surely you don't think there could be more victims?"

"I do, Sir, there's been a twenty-five-year gap between the killings that we know about and that's a long time for a serial killer to stop killing. Serial killers are addicted to killing the same as a fat man is addicted to eating pies, cake and jam doughnuts. I think there are more victims."

"My detective nose agrees with you," replied Briggs glibly, wanting to impress the sergeant and wondering what a fat man with a liking for pies and doughnuts had to do with a serial killer. Did they both like pies and doughnuts?

Chapter Fourteen

After murdering the curate Perkins returned home to Bumstead-on-the-Wold to his mother and girlfriend Melody, with them both thinking he had been away for a few days on a business trip abroad. News of the curate's death was soon village gossip with Melody hearing of her lover's death when buying stamps from the village post office. Terribly distraught she put on a brave front before Perkins and his mother, and with heart-broken she wept copious tears for her lost lover walking alone in the garden so they would not know of her grief. "Buy yourself something nice, Melody," Perkins told her as they sat eating breakfast with his mother three days after she learnt of the curate's death, and smiling he handed her a credit card. "Treat yourself to something that's expensive. I haven't seen you smile since I got back from my trip and it's been worrying me."

Hetty scowled seething with jealousy. She had never been given free access to her son's credit card and enraged struck the top of her boiled egg with a teaspoon shattering the shell splashing yellow egg yolk over her fingers. Muttering angrily with dignity and composure gone she wiped her fingers on a serviette thinking how much she hated Melody, hating her with such intensity that it frightened her. Secretly in her bedroom she kept a small voodoo doll she had made from modelling clay and called Melody, and twice daily she gleefully thrust pins into the doll in places where she thought they would cause the most discomfort and pain on the real Melody. But so far, to her great disappointment there had been no signs of any discomfort or pain from Melody to show the voodoo doll was working. Melody with a smile took the credit card and slipped it away into her dressing-gown pocket. "Thank you, Ronnie, that's so very sweet and thoughtful of you," she said quietly, voice hardly above a whisper. "I'm sorry but I've not been myself recently and have been feeling depressed"

"You should see a doctor, Mel."

"No, I'm feeling much better now."

"You never spoil me with your credit card when I'm feeling off colour," muttered Hetty glaring at her son.

"Oh, come, Mother, you get plenty of treats I see to that."

"Yes, and so I should you should. I'm your mother and deserve treats, lots of treats. I was the one who carried you for nine months in my womb and gave birth after thirty-three hours of agony screaming my head off while struggling to expel you."

"I'm treating Mel, Mother, and that's an end of it," replied Perkins curtly, and then turning to Melody, said, "I love you, Mel."

Melody looked him in the eyes and was alarmed to see a coldness she had never seen before, a coldness that chilled and frightened her, and wondered momentarily if he had found out about her affair with the curate but quickly dismissed the thought thinking she and her lover had been too discreet to be discovered. "Yes, I know, Ronnie," she replied and lied, "and I love you, too, with all my heart."

Perkins reached across the table and placed his hand gently on her hand and gave it a gentle squeeze. "I know this isn't the time nor the place and that a woman wants to hear what I'm about to ask you in a more romantic setting than sitting at the breakfast table, but darling, will you marry me?"

Melody hesitated not wanting to upset Perkins any further and have him take back the credit card, and replied with a forced smile, "Yes, Ronnie, I'll marry you."

"And his money too," added Hetty bitterly seething with anger at the thought of Melody becoming her daughter-in-law. When she was only her son's girlfriend Melody could be thrown out of the house without a penny, but if she became his wife then she would have the legal right to half of everything he owned, and on his death would inherit everything. She knew Melody despised her as much she despised her and would kick her penniless out of the house if she could. Somehow, she must stop the wedding.

"Any thoughts on where we'll get married, Mel?" asked Perkins brightly. "Registry office or church?"

"I'd like to have a church wedding at St Freda's the Eveready in Bumstead-on-the-Wold in a lovely white dress with bridesmaids and the reception held in marquees here on the back lawn."

"Then that's what you shall have."

"When?" asked Melody, thinking that when they were married she could demand her own credit card and have her own bank account funded by him.

"Soon, Darling, very soon, but first I've an important business trip coming up, so let's say when I get back from the trip." The business trip to murder the British Prime Minister Sir Anthony Dingle and the client who paying for the assassination was supermarket tycoon Sydney Frogmorton. He wanted the Prime Minister murdered for not including his name on the honours list for a third year running. Sydney Frogmorton donated substantial vast sums of money to the Prime Minister's Party and had expected to be rewarded with a knighthood. Bribes were paid to smooth the way and each time his name was put forward it was crossed off the honours list by Sir Anthony Dingle.

"Could I have a diamond engagement ring, Ronnie?" asked Melody, smiling sweetly at him, her grief for the curate temporally set aside at the prospect of adding yet another expensive piece of jewelry to her growing collection. Indeed, jewelry was her insurance for old age when she hoped to be living in the south of Spain in a villa with a young muscular sexually rampant male, a Spanish gardener who would service both garden and herself whenever she felt the need. She knew beauty fades with the passing of the years but not the need for a woman like herself to be regularly and most reliably serviced.

"We'll go shopping this afternoon for a ring."

"Diamond ring?"

He nodded. "Diamond as big as a pigeon's egg."

Melody clapped her hands and smiled while Hetty scowled and thought dark thoughts of going to her bedroom and sticking more pins into the clay voodoo doll of Melody.

Doctor Albert Windrush had returned to London before the discovery of Peter Catchpole's body in the Convent bedroom, catching the early morning milk train after receiving a phone call from Allan Hawes requesting his urgent return. The detective wanted his loyal and trusted companion and biographer to be at his side making notes on his progress with the Sir Anthony Dingle case for posterity.

Hawes and the doctor sat eating breakfast at 202B Bakery Street, the great detective reading a newspaper and the column 'Your Stars' by gypsy fortune teller Ada Pickles, who claimed to be the seventh daughter of a seventh daughter, born on a housing estate in south Peckham at house number seven, at 7am on the seventh day of the seventh month. But really she was the only child of Fred and Daisy Pickles who ran together a greasy spoon café in South London and was born on the first of April, April fool's day.

Hawes read while eating cornflakes, his favourite breakfast cereal, and there was no sound in the room except for the munching and crunching of cornflakes. His star sign 'Taurus the Bull,' and the gypsy a week earlier predicted for his star sign, 'Beware of an unexpected downpour." The prediction spookily come true later that same day when dog strolled up to him as he stood at a bus stop and peed over his right leg. The encounter confirming for the detective his belief in the predictions made by the gypsy fortune teller.

In the newspaper there a report of the death of Peter Catchpole on page twelve, a small paragraph. Hawes and doctor Windrush had not seen the obituary and they were unaware of the untimely death of curate Peter Catchpole. When the detective finished his bowl of cornflakes he got to his feet and began to pace up and down pondering on his case of great international importance. How was he going to catch the assassin before Prime Minister Sir Anthony Dingle came to an untimely end? The case stretched his brilliant detecting brain and made him feel truly alive while trying to outwit a criminal genius who he believed was equal to his own genius, but his genius for solving crime and not breaking it.

He went over in his mind as he paced the room the facts he knew about the killer hoping to fit the pieces of the jigsaw together and bring the killer, man or a woman, to justice. The first piece of the jigsaw was the mysterious Miss Marion Pringle overheard discussing the murder contract on the telephone by Mrs Frogmorton. The second piece of the jigsaw Sydney Frogmorton who hired the killer through the mysterious Miss Marion Pringle, the woman who knew the identity of the killer. It would be through her that he would crack the case and find the killer. But first he must find the elusive Miss Marion Pringle.

Doctor Windrush sat on the sofa reading a car magazine. He was studying the classified columns looking for a suitable second-hand car that looked expensive to impress his patients and to show his medical practice was successful. But the car must be cheap as he was no longer carrying out as many penis correctors operations as he had been doing before the news of Sydney Frogmorton's misbehaving penile corrector catching fire with complete loss of public hair had spread among the country's wealthy floppy penis sufferers. The doctor's cash flow had fallen drastically and instead of performing two or three operations a week he was now performing one or two operations a month. "Aha, here's a car I like the look of, Hawes, old chap," he called out brightly, as the detective paced passed him for the tenth time, "it sounds it's a real magnet for the ladies. Driving such a car I'd have to ration myself with all the ladies all wanting me to give them a ride. Do you get it? Give them a ride?"

"I've got more important things on my mind, Doctor, than listening to your sex fantasies. I've a murdering fiend to catch before a dastardly crime of national importance is committed and the British Prime Minister slain."

"Shouldn't we inform the police?"

"My client, Mrs Frogmorton, wants complete confidentiality from us which means no police involvement."

"If the Prime Minister is to be murdered the police must be informed otherwise, we'll be considered accomplices before the fact."

"There isn't going to be a murder because we'll stop it from happening."

"But what if we can't stop it? Could you live with the Prime Minister's death on your conscience? I know I couldn't."

"Pull yourself together, Doctor, it won't happen. You must be more positive in your thinking and have faith in my detecting abilities. We must honour the confidentially of our client. Who would hire a private detective who rushed off to the police to solve a case for him? No, Doctor, I'm like a priest in the confessional and my lips are sealed."

"I pity the Prime Minister life expectancy."

"Not with me on the case, surely."

The door opened and Mrs Gooseberry came bustling in with two cups of tea on tray and a side plate with shortbread biscuits. "I thought you'd like a nice cup of tea. Mister Hawes," she said as she placed the tray on the coffee table.

"Thank you, Mrs Gooseberry," replied the detective.

"The convent you visited, Mister Hawes, would it by any chance have been the Convert of the Sisters of Mercy in Watford?" asked Mrs Gooseberry.

"Why, yes, the very same. Why do you ask?"

"There was a report on the radio this morning on the BBC News. It seems a young curate, the Reverend Peter Catchpole, died there and the police are treating it as murder."

"Murder," gasped the doctor shocked, "and to think I sat opposite to the fellow at dinner and shared the salt and pepper with him."

"Murder isn't infectious, Doctor," exclaimed Hawes. "You can't catch it like a cold bug otherwise the world would be full of murdered people lying about willy-nilly making the place look untidy."

"I know, Hawes, I'm a medical man and know murder isn't an infection. I was merely pointing out how bizarre it was that I had sat opposite to a murder victim at dinner."

"Life's full of bizarre coincidences, Doctor."

"Did I ever ask you . . .," began Mrs Gooseberry, thinking to ask the detective a question to change the topic of conversation from murder which always gave her goosebumps.

"Yes, I'm sure you have," interrupted Hawes impatiently, "many times."

"But I was only going to . . ."

"Please, Mrs Gooseberry, not now," retorted the detective trying to assert his authority over the housekeeper.

"I only wanted to ask," persisted Mrs Gooseberry, who was determined not to be browbeaten by the great detective, "if you knew what's the maximum penalty for a man who commits bigamy?"

"No, Mrs Gooseberry, I don't know, replied the detective, "what is the maximum penalty for a man committing bigamy?"

"Having two mother-in-laws instead of one," giggled Mrs Gooseberry enjoying herself. The detective sighed, shrugged his shoulders, glanced at the doctor shook his head showing his annoyance with the housekeeper.

"Would you like dinner at the usual time, Mister Hawes?" asked Mrs Gooseberry.

"Ah, yes, dinner," exclaimed the doctor gleefully who loved food and especially Mrs Gooseberry's cooking. "What delights are you preparing for our dinner tonight, Mrs Gooseberry?"

"Fish and chips," declared Mrs Gooseberry, "with mushy peas and pickled onions if you want them."

"We must stop tycoon Sidney Frogmorton from carrying out his evil plan," exclaimed Hawes, "and find the mysterious Miss Marion Pringle. We haven't a moment to lose."

"Well, gentleman?" asked Mrs Gooseberry. "What's it to be?"

"What's what to be, Mrs Gooseberry?" asked Hawes, impatient to be out the door and solving the case of great national importance.

"Onions," replied Mrs Gooseberry.

"Pardon?"

"Onions," repeated Mrs Gooseberry stoically. "Do you want them or not. They're not everybody's taste with fish and chips."

"Two onions would be proficient for me," declared the doctor with a smile. "Pickled onions tend to make me fart."

"And that's why there'll to be no pickled onions for the doctor, Mrs Gooseberry," declared Hawes grimly. "I'm the one who has to sit at the dinner table with him."

"I understand, Mister Hawes," replied Mrs Gooseberry, "there'll be no pickled onions for the doctor." She left the room and closed the door behind her.

"Come, Doctor, put on your coat and hat for the game's a foot and we've work to do to find Miss Marion Pringle. She's lead us to the killer of that, I'm sure."

"How do we find her, Hawes, old chap?"

"She's made contact by phone to Sydney Frogmorton and so we'll bug his home telephone and wait for her to call him."

"That's illegal, Hawes, bugging a phone."

"So is murdering the Prime Mister. I think a wiretap is called for to save him."

"I don't want to end up in prison, Hawes."

"It won't come to that, trust me. The Prime Minister will be grateful we saved his life and won't allow the police to prosecute us for bugging a phone. You might even get a knighthood."

"Ah, yes, a knighthood, I'd like that, Hawes. Sir Albert Windrush, yes, it has a nice ring to it and would make my mother proud and impress my patients."

Next day Perkins drove to Bumstead-on-the-Wold and stopped at a telephone box. He had arranged to call Sidney Frogmorton at 3.30pm precisely, and was disguised in a grey trilby hat, brown sports jacket and grey trousers, and posing as Bertie Smith a
travelling salesman selling vacuum cleaners. He sat in his parked car for twenty minutes until the allotted time for the phone call then went to the phone box and dialed Sidney Frogmorton's home number. The phone rang five times before it was picked up, the arranged signal between the two men. "Sidney Frogmorton speaking," whispered a voice hardly audible.

"Speak up," replied Perkins speaking in the high-pitched female voice he used when playing the role of Miss Marion Pringle. "My hearing isn't too good."

"Who's speaking?" demanded Sidney Frogmorton in a louder and deeper voice.

"You're speaking too loud now, tone it down."

"Who are you?" asked Sidney Frogmorton speaking normally.

"It's me, Miss Marion Pringle."

"Then give the prearranged password?"

"Silly Arse."

"Correct. Good afternoon, Miss Pringle."

"We must meet face to face. It's too dangerous to discuss our business over the telephone. You never know who might be listening."

"I agree, Miss Pringle."

"Meet me Monday night at 9pm in the public bar of the Saucy Gander pub in Lower Bingley, East Sussex, and wear a yellow carnation in your buttonhole so that I'll know it's you, and I'll do the same so you'll know me."

"What about a password?"

"We'll keep to Silly Arse."

"Then Silly Arse it shall be, Miss Pringle."

Chapter Fifteen

Four days later in the early afternoon a battered rickety white van with black smoke bellowing from the exhaust pipe, drove slowly up the gravel driveway towards Frogmorton manor house. Driving the van Doctor Albert Windrush and sat next to him Allan Hawes, both in disguise wearing denim overalls, brown flat caps, and to add to the illusion of being workmen they had not shaved for two days. On the sides of the van, 'TELEPHONE REPAIRS' painted in black. The van pulled up outside the front door of the manor house and they got out with Hawes carrying a grey canvas tool bag, with an unlit cigarette dangling from the corner of his mouth. The detective thinking the cigarette gave his portrayal of being a workman more conviction. He knocked on the front door which opened and there stood the Irish podgy butler Higgins wearing black tails and bow tie. He looked at the two men disdainfully slowly up and down then declared, "Workmen enter by the back door. The front door is only for family and house guests."

"Your mistress is expecting us," replied Hawes curtly, "kindly step aside and let us enter."

"No, you must use the back door," retorted the butler haughtily.

"Tell your mistress the telephone repairmen are here," replied the detective angrily. He had taken a dislike of the butler and thought he was over doing his authority.

"Go to the back door," replied the butler and closed the door on them."

Five minutes later the detective knocked on the back door which was opened by the butler who asked in haughty tones, "And what might I do for you?"

"You know what you can do," retorted Hawes angrily not saying what he really wanted the butler to do without it sounding crude and rude in front of the doctor, who was an educated man with refined sensibilities. "We're telephone repairmen and here to see your mistress."

"Have you an appointment?"

"We do," retorted Hawes. "Why else would we be here?"

"Follow me," replied the butler curtly. "The mistress is in the study. Wipe your feet on the doormat. We don't want to upset cook.

she's proud of her kitchen and keeps the floor immaculately clean." The detective and the doctor dutifully wiped their feet on a coconut mat inside the door then followed the butler on through the kitchen passing the cook, a scowling red-faced dumpy woman in a piney who pointed at their feet and scowled, and on down a long-arched hallway with oil paintings hanging on the walls. Higgins stopped outside an oak door and knocked twice on it. "The telephone repairmen, Madam," he called in a servile tone of voice used when speaking to his employers.

"Enter," called out Mrs Frogmorton from inside the room.

The butler opened the door and he entered followed by the detective and the doctor, and gave his mistress a slight bow of the head who sat in an armchair reading a magazine.

"Thank you, Higgins," replied Mrs Frogmorton putting down the magazine, "you may go."

"Very good, Madam." The butler turned and left the room closing the door behind him.

"Ah, Mister Hawes," cried Mrs Frogmorton getting to her feet, "you've come at last. I was beginning to think that you had changed your mind about doing the wiretap."

"No, dear lady, our van broke down on the motorway and we had to call the AA. The patrolman said we had dirty plugs."

"Oh, but how frightful," said Mrs Frogmorton sympathetically, "I hope it isn't too serious a medical condition and can be easily treated."

"No, it's isn't a medical condition but dirty car plugs which the patrolman removed, cleaned and put back."

"Well, you're here now and that's what counts."

"Your husband's away as you said he would be?" asked Hawes.

She nodded. "Yes, and he won't be home until tea time."

"Good, then let's get the job done before he returns. I'd like you to keep watch outside the door and stop your staff entering until we've finished bugging the phone."

Mrs Frogmorton nodded and left the room and for the next half-an-hour she paced nervously up and down the corridor stopping occasionally to look up at one of the oil paintings hanging on the wall.

Meanwhile, back in the study the detective and the doctor had unscrewed the bottom of the telephone cradle and inserted a tiny transmitter. Two wires, one red and one black soldered into place by the doctor using an electric hot iron size of a pencil, He found to his surprise that he was more skilled soldering wires to the telephone bug than he was soldering wires on the penis correctors he was inserting on patients in the operating theatre. Indeed, on a couple of occasions he has mixed-up the wires during the procedure with disastrous results causing the hospital to have power cuts with electric shocks for the theatre staff and patient on the operating table. "There," he proclaimed proudly beaming with satisfaction when he finished soldering. "All done and tickety-boo."

"What's the range of the transmitter, Doctor?"

"Six hundred yards."

"What? Only six hundred yards? But I told you to get a transmitter with a three-mile range!"

"Sorry, Hawes, but I thought they all had a three-mile range. It was only when we got here and I took it out of its box did I see my mistake."

"Now, we'll have to camp out all night in a tent in the grounds of the manor to be sure we're in range to receive and record the phone calls for evidence."

"No, Hawes, not a tent," replied the doctor gloomily. "It'll play havoc with my lumbago to say nothing of my toilet arrangements."

The sun was setting as Hawes and doctor Windrush wearing false beards and looking like disgruntled boy scout leaders in light brown shorts and shirts, heavy walking boots, socks rolled down to their ankles, finally managed to erected a small two-man tent after an hour of trying. The instruction manual with the tent claimed a six-year-old child could erect the tent within ten minutes. Hawes hoped if they were seen by anybody passing bye would think he and the doctor were hikers on a walking holiday and camping for the night. They were two hundred yards from the back door of the manor house.

Two hours later as night fell they sat crossed-legged next to a crackling wood fire. Hawes cooking sizzling pork sausages in a frying pan. The doctor miserable and cold and experiencing what he considered was the worse experience of his life, sleeping under canvas after eating sausages cooked by Hawes. The great detective was by no means a cook and was known to have difficulty boiling an egg.

"Supper's ready, Doctor," declared Hawes brightly, showing the frying pan to the doctor with the sausages burnt cinder black.

"I'm not hungry, Hawes."

"Of course, you are," replied the detective as he put four sausages with a fork onto a tin plate and handed the plate to the doctor. "Now get that down you, there's a good fellow." Meekly with a forced smile the doctor took the plate and speared a sausage with the fork and bite off a small piece and chewed. It was like chewing a piece of coal. "What's it like, Doctor, tasty?" asked Hawes brightly.

"I've tasted worse," lied the doctor not wanting to offend his friend.

"There are more sausages if you want them? I don't feel hungry myself. I had a big meal at lunch time."

"No, thanks, Hawes. I mustn't make a glutton of myself, too much of a good thing don't you know." When Hawes was not looking the doctor discreetly slipped the sausages into his coat pocket. He would flush them down the toilet when he got home.

It was dark when a drunken Sidney Frogmorton arrived home from the golf course after having drunk too champagne in the club bar and was unsteady on his feet. He had been celebrating his first hole-in-one after thirty-three years of playing golf. He arrived in his gleaming Rolls Royce driven by a peaked cap chauffeur. Hawes watched through a pair of binoculars as the chauffeur helped his drunken master into the house half-carrying and half-dragging him. Moments later the chauffeur reappeared from the house and collected a bag of golf clubs from the boot of the car.

Hawes and doctor Windrush crawled back into the tent and switched on the black box receiver which began buzzing with sparks flying from it. The doctor promptly received an electrical shock and screamed. "No screaming, Doctor," whispered Hawes urgently. "We mustn't be discovered."

"Sorry, Hawes," whispered the doctor. "Do you think they heard up at the house?"

"Quick, man, hoot like an owl so they'll think it was an owl making a kill."

"Twit-to-woo, twit-to-woo," hooted the doctor doing a poor imitation of a hooting owl.

"No, doctor, hoot like this," said the exasperated detective cupping his hands to his mouth and producing an acceptable hooting of an owl."

"Hawes, once again you astound me with your brilliance. That hooting would have fooled a real owl."

Hawes smiled basking in the doctor's praise. "I doubt Sydney Frogmorton will use the telephone tonight," he said. "He looked too drunk for doing anything but going to bed and sleeping it off."

"What if Miss Marion Pringle calls?"

"We'll be ready for her and take turns to listen with earphones. I suggest three hours on and three hours off, Doctor, with you taking the first three hours."

"That's not fair, Hawes. Why is it always me who goes first? I say we flip a coin to see who goes first with the earphones?"

"Alright, Doctor. Have you got a coin?"

"No, of course not, you know I never carry small change. It makes my trouser pockets bulge and rattle when I walk."

"I haven't a coin either, Doctor, so wake me in three hours."

Chief Inspector Edgar 'Lanky' Briggs was in the mortuary with Sergeant Jenny Hopper and police pathologist Arthur Dean. They stood looking at the naked dead body of curate Peter Catchpole stretched out on the mortuary slab. There was a line of stitches from throat to belly button where he had been sliced open for the heart and other major organs to be removed, examined and placed into glass jars. "Poor devil," exclaimed the Chief Inspector, "at least he was in bed when his time came."

"I've never seen anything like it," exclaimed the sergeant shaking her head looking puzzled.

"What are you talking about?" asked Briggs intrigued, he too, was surprised at its size. "His penis?"

"No, I was talking about his death and with him being injected with an air bubble."

"I've seen a death like it before," said the pathologist, it was during my fourth year at medical school when I was studying under Professor Bertie Brown at the London School of Pathology. I assisted him with a secret post-mortem for the Government on the body of a Russian double agent brought in by MI6. The agent murdered by the KGB with a syringe and an air bubble. When the heart was examined it was found to have imploded exactly the same as Peter Catchpole's heart imploded."

"Are you saying the KGB killed Peter Catchpole?" asked Briggs.

"No, Chief Inspector, I'm not saying they did. I'm saying the killer who murdered Peter Catchpole was no amateur but a professional assassin."

Hawes lay in darkness tucked inside a warm sleeping bag. He had given up listening through earphones thinking Sidney Frogmorton too drunk to answer any phone call coming from the mysterious Miss Marion Pringle. He was going over in his mind his case of national importance when the image of Archdeacon Jonathan Needham suddenly popped into his thoughts. The clergyman he met on retreat at the Convent of the Sisters of Mercy. There was something familiar about the eyes and high cheekbones. Hawes knew they had met before but could not place where or when. Finally, it came to him. He had seen that face at the Braddock Towers hotel twenty-five years earlier when he was employed there as a desk clerk. The Archdeacon had the same facial bone structure and those unforgettable eyes as the mysterious American tourist Roger Shepherd the Third. The detective's mind began to race in overdrive and there was a tingling in his toes, the same tingling he experienced when solving a dastardly crime. In the morning, when he was back home in London, he would write an anonymous letter to New Scotland Yard telling them about the Archdeacon and that he was not a clergyman and should be investigated as a suspect for the curate's murder. "Doctor," he cried excitedly giving his sleeping friend a jab in the ribs with his elbow to wake him, wanting him to share in his eureka moment of detection and for it to written down in his notebook for prosperity.

The doctor, wearing candy striped pyjamas, peered out from his sleeping bag. "What's happening?" he asked startled and alarmed, is the tent on fire?"

"No, Doctor, I've found a murderer."

"You have? Not outside the tent waiting to murder us?"

"No, I've figured out who might have murdered the curate, Peter Catchpole. Come, Doctor, we must return to London without delay. I've a letter to write. Put your trousers on there's a good fellow." The doctor, disgruntled and muttering under his breath about being woken from the best dream he had for years. In the dream he was being seduced by two gorgeous naked nymphomaniac, young women determined to have their way with him. With a yawn he struggled out of his sleeping bag and picked up a pair of trousers and pulled them on over his pyjama bottoms. "No, Doctor, put on your own trousers not mine," cried Hawes tugging at the trousers and making the doctor fall over.

Mrs Gooseberry, bustling cheery cockney housekeeper at 202B Bakery Street, greeted Allan Hawes and Doctor Windrush on their return to London on the doorstep. The men still disguised as hikers in shorts with false beards, and to pander to their egos she pretended not to recognize them. "Away with you both," she cried throwing up her hands in mock disgust, "no doorstep salesmen or people posting junk mail through the letterbox here."

"It's me, Mrs Gooseberry," declared Hawes brightly removing his beard with a flourish and turning his head in profile so she would see it was him.

"Goodness gracious me, but it's you, Mister Hawes," declared the housekeeper in fake surprise looking suitably shocked.

Hawes nodded happily.

"And who's this gentleman with you?"

"Why it's me, Mrs Gooseberry, "Doctor Windrush," proclaimed he doctor removing his false beard and waving it at her.

"Why are you gentlemen in disguise?"

"We've been camping," responded the doctor brightly.

"Well, the less said about that the better I think," replied Mrs Gooseberry raising her eyebrow's knowing 'camping' was a term used by homosexuals for visiting gentlemen's toilets for brief sexual encounters.

"You misunderstood, Mrs Gooseberry," replied Hawes embarrassed. "We slept together in a tent!"

"As I said, Mister Hawes, the less said about that the better."

"Oh, for goodness' sake, we weren't sleeping together in the biblical sense, Mrs Gooseberry," retorted Hawes exasperated and deliberately speaking in a deeper baritone voice to show he was definitely heterosexual. "We took turns to listen with earphones while the other one slept. We're not gay."

"Gay?" cried the doctor appalled, "who's gay?"

"Most certainly not us," replied Hawes grimly.

"Absolutely not," agreed the doctor, "I like women, my mother was one and so was my auntie Jean."

"Oh, dear," apologized Mrs Gooseberry, "and there was I thinking you were a couple of . . ."

"Yes, quite so, Mrs Gooseberry," interrupted Hawes, "but we aren't that way inclined and never have been." Mrs Gooseberry smiled sweetly at him and nodded but she still had her doubts. Why would they dress up in shorts and go camping together? She led the way up the hallway followed by the two men. "Has there been any messages for me while I was away?" asked Hawes as he followed her up the staircase.

"Yes, there's one from a Mrs Mabel Frogmorton. She rang an hour ago saying she found an entry in her husband's diary for a meeting with a Miss Marion Pringle at the Saucy Gander pub in Lower Bingley, and for you to be told as soon as possible. I've written it all down, the time and date for the meeting on the notepad next to the telephone. Oh, and she said her husband will be wearing a pink carnation to be recognized by Miss Pringle and so will Miss Pringle to be recognized by him."

Chapter Sixteen

Chief Inspector Edgar 'Lanky' Briggs sat at his desk in New Scotland Yard eating his second raspberry jam doughnut. Sergeant Jenny Hopper sat to his right at her desk whispering discreetly into her telephone so he could not overhear the conversation. She was talking to pathologist Arthur Dean who wined and dined her the previous night, treating her to dressed lobster salad with champagne, then taking her home and treating them both to undressed prolonged sexual activity. "No, I can't say it, not now, Arthur," she whispered with a girlish giggle, "He'll hear me."

"What's he doing? "

"Eating a doughnut and reading an anonymous letter he received this morning that was delivered by hand at the front desk by a man wearing a deerstalker hat who refused to give his name. The letter supposedly identifying a murder suspect."

"Who are you talking to, Sergeant," called out Briggs.

"It' a wrong number, Sir," replied the sergeant as she hurriedly put the phone down.

"Funny wrong number. You've been on the phone for ten minutes. I've been timing you."

"Sorry, Sir, the caller was trying to sell life insurance and you know how persistent an insurance salesman can be."

"I certainly do, Sergeant. I'm insured myself against everything except for having the mother-in-law come to stay." He laughed enjoying his own joke. "This anonymous letter," continued Briggs holding up the letter, "claims Jonathan Needham an Archdeacon in the Church of England, might have murdered curate Peter Catchpole at the Convent of the Sisters of Mercy. I think we should visit the convent and speak to the nuns about the Archdeacon."

Mother Superior sister Rosebud was shocked to be told Archdeacon Jonathan Needham was thought by the police to have murdered curate Peter Catchpole. "But are you sure, Chief Inspector," she asked clasping her hands in dismay. "Couldn't you be mistaken? The Archdeacon was such a kind charming polite gentleman who said both please and thank you." She sat in her office at the Convent of the Sisters of Mercy talking to Chief Inspector Edgar Briggs and

Sergeant Jenny Hopper.

"I received an anonymous letter this morning claiming the Archdeacon could be a murderer," replied Briggs grimly.

"But how dreadful if true," replied the nun, distraught and shaking her head. "Whatever will the Archbishop of Canterbury say?"

"Have you an address for the Archdeacon?" asked the sergeant.

Sister Rosebud nodded and opened a red book on her desk and ran her finger down a page then looked up at Briggs, and said, "No, he hasn't put his address in the retreat guest book only that he's between parishes."

"Then we've lost him the slippery devil," muttered Briggs dismally. "He's away on his toes."

"Not necessarily, Sir," replied the sergeant. "We might have more luck with a visit to Church House for an address for the Archdeacon."

Allan Hawes with pink carnation in his buttonhole sat with doctor Windrush in the Saucy Gander pub in Lower Bingley in the public bar. Both disguised in green-checked ill-fitting suits, black bowler hats and heavy brown working boots, hoping to pass themselves off as being tough Irish navies. They sat at a table in a darkened corner sipping glasses of Guinness talking loudly in poor imitations of Irish accents. On the table in front of Hawes a grey canvas bag in which there was a directional microphone with a receiver plugged into a portable tape recorder. "Well, Paddy," said Hawes addressing the doctor as he sipped a glass of Guinness, "and how are you on this fine evening, my bucko?"

The Guinness was too bitter for the doctor's delicate palate with his sweet tooth and he struggled to even sip the beer. Hawes told him that Irish navies drank nothing but Guinness and so they also must drink Guinness to enhance their portrayal as being tough Irish navies. "I'm as happy as a leprechaun with pot of gold at the end of a rainbow, Sean," replied the doctor over-doing his portrayal and saucily winking an eye. "I'd love to be in Galway Bay watching the sun go down and hearing the seagulls' plaintive cries as they dive-bomb sightseers to poo on them."

"Don't wink at me, Doctor," whispered Hawes hastily in his normal voice, "people will get the wrong idea about us just like Mrs Gooseberry."

"Sorry, Hawes, old chap," replied the doctor in his normal voice.

"I wasn't thinking."

"Speak with an Irish accent," whispered Hawes speaking again with an Irish accent and glowering at the doctor.

"And it's the top of the evening to you, Sean," declared the doctor reverting back to a bad Irish accent and slapping the detective heartily on the back making him spill his Guinness.

"The it's the top of the evening back to you too, Paddy," replied Hawes grimly slapping him twice as hard on the shoulder and spilling the doctor's Guinness. They did not know the thickset man in a grey gabardine raincoat and black trilby hat standing at the bar had taken a great interest in them. It was the Irish accents that caught his attention. He was an MI5 officer undercover and was on the lookout for an IRA three-man bombing-team known to be in the area. He watched Hawes and doctor Windrush to confirm his suspicions that they were Irish and possibly two of the men he was seeking, and satisfied they were Irish and IRA asked the barmaid to use the bar telephone saying it was for important government business. He dialed MI5 headquarters in London. "Put me through to major Golightly," he told the operator. "This is captain Larry Parks. I've found two of the IRA bombing team we're been seeking."

"Putting you through," replied the operator.

"Hello, Major Golightly speaking," said a gruff voice with a posh accent.

"Captain Larry Parks reporting in, Sir. I've got two IRA men under surveillance. They're sitting in the public bar of the Saucy Gander pub in Lower Bingley in East Sussex."

"What makes you think they're IRA?"

"They're the only ones in the pub speaking with Irish accents, and one of them is wearing a yellow carnation in his buttonhole. I think he's the IRA commander of the team."

"Have you a gun with you?"

"Yes, sir, I never go on a mission without it."

"Good man. I hope your aim has improved since that nasty business on the shooting range when you shot the instructor in the foot."

"My aim's improved since then, Sir."

"Good man. I'll dispatch a rapid response team to you immediately. They should be with you within thirty minutes depending on the traffic."

"What shall I do if the IRA men try to leave the pub, Sir?"

"Use your gun and stop them."

"They've got a suspicious looking canvas bag, Sir."

"Do you think it's holding a bomb?"

"I do. What else could it be in it, Sir?"

"Don't panic. I'll also send an army bomb disposal squad. Remember, England expects you to keep a stiff upper lip and to do your duty for flag and Queen."

"I know, Sir, I'll make you and the department proud."

"Good man, now hang on in there until help arrives."

"I will, Sir, I'm British to the core and know all the verses of God Save the Queen."

"Best of luck, Captain. There might be a gong in this for you."

Captain Larry Parks put the phone down and reached furtively inside his jacket for the revolver in his shoulder holster and pulled it out, and slipped it into his right raincoat pocket with a finger curled round the trigger ready for a quick draw and to open fire.

Five minutes later Sidney Frogmorton strolled casually into the public bar. He glanced around looking for someone wearing a yellow carnation to identify Miss Marion Pringle and spotted Allan Hawes, and was surprised to see it was a man wearing the flower, and thought Miss Pringle had sent a male accomplice in her place. He went over to the bar and ordered a whiskey with a packet of ready salted crisps. He would be cautious approaching the man wearing the yellow carnation needing to be certain that he was his contact.

Captain Larry Parks eyed Sidney Frogmorton suspiciously spotting the yellow carnation in his button hole and decided he was the third IRA man come to join his two companions.

Perkins, posing as Miss Marion Pringle entered the pub dressed in green tweeds carrying a black handbag with a pink carnation pinned on his breast. Glancing around the public bar he looked for a man wearing a yellow carnation and saw Allan Hawes and thought he was Sidney Frogmorton the man he was to meet. Meanwhile, the doctor had popped out to the toilet for a bowl movement. Perkins went up to Hawes and whispered the agreed password with Sydney Frogmorton on the phone. "Silly Arse."

"I beg your pardon, Madam, what did say?" gasped Hawes, startled and thinking he must have misheard what the plumb woman in green tweeds had said to him.

"Silly Arse," repeated Perkins in the shrill feminine voice he used when doing his impersonation of Miss Marion Pringle.

"Are you drunk, Madam?" retorted Hawes indignantly.

Perkins realizing his mistake and that the man sitting before him wearing the yellow carnation was not Sydney Frogmorton, apologized. "I'm afraid there's been a misunderstanding. I thought you were somebody else, somebody from my old school days who was nicknamed Silly Arse."

The doctor returned from the toilet feeling much relieved pleased after having what he thought was a good bowl movement and sat down.

Perkins went to the bar and ordered a double whisky to steady his nerves which he drank in one quick swallow. It was then he noticed the man standing next to him was wearing a yellow carnation in his buttonhole. He tapped him on the shoulder and whispered the agreed password word, "Silly Arse."

"Miss Pringle?" asked Sydney Frogmorton turning to face him.

Perkins nodded. "Yes, let's go and sit at a table and conclude our business in private. The quicker we're out of here the better." They went to a corner table and sat down.

"Would you like a drink, Miss Pringle?"

"No, I've a long drive home and don't want to be stopped by the police and fail a breathalyzer. Do you still want me to make the demise?"

"Yes, I do."

"And you accept my fee?"

"It's more than I wanted to pay, Miss Pringle. Would you consider giving me a discount?"

"I never give a discount for a first-time client."

"Alright, then I agree. You'll get the full amount you've asked for. How do I settle the account, Miss Pringle?"

"Pay half within four days into my Swiss bank account. I'll give you the account number. Final payment made when you hear Sir Anthony Dingle is dead."

"Agreed, Miss Pringle."

Meanwhile, Hawes had spotted the yellow carnations in Sydney Frogmorton's buttonhole and in Miss Marion Pringle's buttonhole. He reached into the canvas bag on the table in front of him and switched on the tape recorder and pointed the directional microphone towards the two conspirators to pick up their conversation, and listened through a small earpiece inserted in his ear with the other earpiece in the doctor's ear so he could hear too. "Keep on sipping your Guinness, Paddy," said the detective with a poor Irish accent, "we don't want to arouse their suspicions."

Captain Larry Parks sat at the bar with a double whiskey, nervously fingering the revolver in his raincoat pocket. He took a gulp of whiskey and glanced at his wristwatch. He was waiting for the MI5 rapid response team with the army bomb disposal squad to arrive. He looked at the canvas bag on the table in front of Hawes trying to gage how big the bomb was and decided by the size of the bag it must be big enough to blow up the pub. He knew the IRA men would be armed and worried the pub was steadily filling with customers, and to take down the Irishmen he would need the MI5 team. But they were late and most probably caught up in a traffic jam somewhere on the A22.

He decided to wait five more minutes before going into action and then to take the IRA men by surprise before they had time to pull out their guns and turn the pub into a slaughterhouse. It would need careful handling but he was a highly trained MI5 operative and confident of his abilities. Glancing again at his wristwatch he saw there were three minutes to go before going into action.

Perkins concluding his business with Sydney Frogmorton said, "You leave first and I'll follow five minutes later." He handed a piece of folded paper him. "This is my Swiss bank account number, remember it and then destroy the paper. The first half of the money must be paid into my Swiss account within four days."

Sydney Frogmorton nodded and took the paper and slipped it into his pocket. "When will I hear from you again, Miss Pringle."

"You won't not unless you're late in making your final payment."

"The payment will be made."

"I hope so for your sake, otherwise I'll be making a removal that you won't like."

"There's no need for threats, Miss Pringle. I'm a man of my word and once given I never go back on it."

"There's still time to cancel."

"No, I want it carried out."

"Very well, you won't hear from me again unless you fail to keep your side of the bargain."

"Goodbye, Miss Pringle."

"Goodbye, Mister Frogmorton."

Sydney Frogmorton turned and walked rapidly from pub with an icy shiver running up and down his spine. Miss Pringle was the scariest woman he had ever met and he was in no doubt that she meant the threat should he fail to pay the agreed amount for her services. In the morning he would visit his bank to arrange for the first payment to be paid into Miss Pringle's Swiss bank account with the second payment ready to go. He entered the pub's car park and almost reached his car when three black saloon cars followed by an army lorry swept in at high speed to pull up with a squeal of tyres. Men in army uniforms and men in grey gabardine raincoats with black trilby hats, leapt from the vehicles and raced towards the pub. Sydney Frogmorton got into his car and started the engine. "They're in a hurry for a drink," he thought bemused, "and must be alcoholics on a day out," as he pressed his foot down on the accelerator and the car sped away.

Inside the pub, Allan Hawes and doctor Windrush, sat watching Miss Pringle deciding on how they would make a citizen's arrest. She looked to be a big hefty woman who was well able to look after herself in a rough and tumble. "We'll wait for her to stand up, Doctor," whispered the detective, "then we'll take her down together."

"What if she won't come quietly?"

"Did you bring your trusty revolver?"

"No, Hawes, I forgot it. It's at home in my sock drawer."

"You forgot it? Oh, for goodness' sake, man, we're dealing with a dangerous woman who might be a murderer."

"Sorry, Hawes, but guns make me nervous especially when pointed at me."

"Alright then use karate. I'll take her from the front while you take her from behind in a karate hold."

"Behind what?"

"Her back of course."

"Hawes?"

"Yes, Doctor?"

"I don't know karate sufficiently enough to subdue anybody."

"But you took lessons."

"I took them, yes, Hawes, but only the first two lessons on how to relax while sitting on a mat and how to fall without hurting myself. I meant to finish the course but there was always more important things to do like pursuing my medical career and helping you to catch criminals."

"Alright, Doctor, then pin her arms to her side so she can't move and I'll do the rest."

Meanwhile, Perkins had stood up and was walking briskly towards the door of the pub feeling pleased with the contract he made with Sydney Frogmorton. The money would be used for him to retire from the killing business and marry Melody. They would live happily ever after in the sunshine in the south of France. Hawes and the doctor stood up and moved quickly to intercept Miss Pringle before she reached the door. They left the canvas bag on the table containing their recording equipment to keep their hands free for unarmed combat. After Miss Pringle was arrested they would retrieve the bag and hand the tape and her over to the police.

Captain Larry Parks, seeing the two Irish men walking away from the table and leaving the canvas bag behind concluded they had primed the bomb and were making their getaway. The pub was the target and the public and saloon bar full of people. "IRA swine," he muttered, as he hastily pulled the revolver from his raincoat pocket fumbling in his haste ripping a hole with the barrel sticking through it.

"He's a flasher," screamed a woman hysterically pointing at the exposed gun barrel.

Hawes and the doctor had almost reached Miss Pringle and were about to confront her, with the doctor wishing fervently he was back home in bed instead of about to step up behind Miss Pringle to grab her and pin her arms to her side.

"Don't move," shouted captain Parks pulling out the gun and pointing it at Hawes. The detective turned and saw the gun and thinking the captain was Miss Pringle's accomplice raised his hands above his head. Doctor Windrush fainted. "You're under arrest," cried captain Parks. The pub door swung open and in rushed an array of men dressed in army uniforms, grey gabardine raincoats and black trilby hats, and like an unstoppable tidal wave they surged forward carrying captain Parks and Hawes before them crushing them against the bar. The doctor lay unconscious on the floor. Perkins seeing his opportunity to escape pushed his way through the crowd and entered the ladies toilet and escaped through a window.

The officer in charge of the bomb disposal squad, Captain Derek Parsmore, a tall distinguished looking man with a neat black moustache, carrying a swagger stick, screamed in panic as the surging soldiers carried him forward slamming him against the bar.

Striking out wildly with his swagger stick he beat wildly at the soldiers nearest to him trying to force them to back away from him. "Get back," he shouted, "you're squashing the life out of me."

"Permission to move the men back?" called out a barrel-chested sergeant with a bulbous nose, who was squashed up against the officer in an intimate position much favoured by ancient Greek men of a certain sexual persuasion.

"Granted, Sergeant," wheezed the officer going blue in the face.

"Fall back away from the officer," shouted the sergeant in the thunderous voice he used on the parade ground as he pushed back against the throng of soldiers. The soldiers fell back with the exception of lance-corporal Henry Henshaw who hard of hearing thought the sergeant was offering to buy drinks all round. "Thanks, sergeant, I'll have a pint of ale," he cried pushing forward to reach the bar and be the first one served.

"Sergeant, who's that man?" demanded the captain angrily, pinned against the bar by the lance-corporal in an intimate position much favoured by ancient Greek men of a certain sexual persuasion.

"Henshaw, Sir."

"Take his name, Sergeant."

"Yes, Sir." The sergeant unbuttoned his right breast tunic pocket and took out a notepad and pencil. "Right, Henshaw, what's your name?" he demanded briskly.

"Henshaw, Sergeant." The sergeant wrote down the name and returned the notepad to his pocket.

Meanwhile, the MI5 rapid response officers in grey gabardine raincoats and black trilby hats were trying to mingle unnoticed with the people crowding the public and saloon bars.

Captain Parsmore saw captain Parkes with gun pointing at Hawes, the doctor sprawled unconscious on the floor at their feet, and thought he should identify himself and his rank, and called out, "Bomb disposal, Captain Parsmore."

"MI5, Captain Parkes," called back captain Parks.

"I see you've bagged two of the IRA rotters."

"What's happening?" demanded Hawes, confused and bewildered seeing so many soldiers and men in grey gabardine raincoats and black trilby hats milling about the crowded pub.

"Keep your mouth shut, you ghastly IRA rotter," retorted captain Parks, "you're under arrest."

"I'm not IRA," protested Hawes indignantly. "I'm Church of

England. There's been a terrible mistake."

"Yes, and you're the one whose made it," replied captain Parsmore grimly. He turned to captain Parks and pointed to the canvas bag on the table. "Is that the bomb?"

"Yes, and it's primed."

"It isn't a bomb," cried Hawes, "its evidence that I've taped for the police."

"Be quite and speak when you're spoken to," snapped captain Parks angrily, waving his gun in the detective's face. "You're an utter and absolute rotter."

"Clear the pub, Sergeant," ordered captain Parsmore.

"Yes, Sir," replied the sergeant leaping to attention with a click of his heels and giving a salute. The pub was cleared within thirty seconds when the sergeant shouted, "Get out. There's a bomb." People in panic rushed out into the car park. Hawes was hurried out at gunpoint in handcuffs by captain Parks and put into the back of a car under guard. Doctor Windrush carried out unconscious, also handcuffed, and dumped on a grass verge to await an ambulance to take him to hospital.

The patriotic landlord of the Saucy Gander tavern, Clive Highland, a fat balding man with slobbering lips who survived the London blitz and years of bed-wetting, and his wife's cooking, proudly wearing union-jack underpants, gathered his frightened customers into a corner of the car park. He led them in a rousing singsong to keep their spirits up and ten times they sang, "There'll always be an England," the landlord's favourite song and the only one in which he knew all the words.

Captain Derek Parsmore, the army bomb squad officer, the longest serving captain in the British army having joined as a Second lieutenant with a fast-moving mobile unit of latrines and portable baths serving without distinction in the Middle East. "Report to me at the double, Sergeant Barker," he called briskly pointing his swagger stick at an army lorry with 'Bomb Disposal Squad' on the side. Out from the back of the lorry jumped an overweight bulging untidy looking corporal wearing spectacles who hurried over to the captain and stood to attention and gave a half-hearted salute. The captain returned the salute touching the peak of his hat with his swagger stick. "Now, about this bomb, Corporal," he said.

"What about the bomb, Sir?"

"Damn nasty thing an unexploded bomb, Corporal."

"Very nasty, Sir."

"There's bomb in the pub on a table in a grey canvas bag. Go and fetch and bring it out to the car park."

"Might it not explode when I'm carrying it, Sir."

"Not if you're careful, Corporal."

"May I make a suggestion, Sir?"

"Very well, Corporal, speak your piece but be quick about it. The bomb's ticking as we speak."

"Why not leave the bomb where it is, Sir."

"Can't be done, Corporal. It's our job to deal with the bomb. Now, be a good fellow and fetch the bomb for me."

"Couldn't we wait for the next bomb disposal squad to come on duty in morning, sir?"

"Are you a coward, Corporal?"

"No, sir, I'm a Methodist."

"Go and get the bomb, Corporal."

"But, sir, I . . ."

"It's an order, Corporal," interrupted the captain angrily. "Go before I put you on a charge for refusing an order while on active duty."

"I might be blown-up and my mother wouldn't like it."

"Go, Corporal, go."

"Yes, Sir." The corporal saluted and turning on his heel he marched quickly away swinging his arms as if he was on a parade ground, and headed down the road away from the Saucy Gander pub.

"Corporal," shouted the captain after him. "Come back."

The corporal meekly returned and stood to attention in front of the captain. "I thought you dismissed me, Sir."

"Where were you going?"

"Back to barracks, Sir."

"I didn't say you could return to barracks, Corporal."

"But you ordered me to go, sir, and so I went."

"Do you think that I'm a fool?" The corporal made no reply. "Well," insisted the captain, "do you think I'm a fool?"

"Could I have a few moments to think about it, Sir?"

"Corporal, either you go and get the bomb or you'll be in the glass house for the rest of your army career."

"Well, if you insist, Sir."

"I do insist, Corporal. Now, get the bomb."

The corporal saluted, turned on his heel and marched into the pub. He returned moments later carrying the grey canvas bag, walking very slowly holding the bag out before him at arms-length. "Where shall I put it, sir?" he called out as he approached the captain who promptly leapt behind the army lorry.

"Put the bomb in the middle of the car park, Corporal."

"No, don't do it," implored Clive Highland, landlord of the Saucy Gander pub, hysterically. "You can't blow up my car park. Where will my customers park their cars?"

The corporal carried on walking until he reached the middle of the car park where very gingerly he lowered the canvas bag to the ground, then turned and ran as fast as his chubby legs would carry him to the army lorry. "Mission accomplished, Sir," he called as he joined the captain behind the lorry. The captain warily advanced towards the canvas bag carrying a detonator in his right hand. He set the timer for two minutes then placed it on top of the canvas bag, then ran the fastest one hundred yards of his life and dived into a ditch to lay on his belly with hands covering his ears. There was a loud explosion, The grey canvas bag blew-up with a tongue of flame spurting twenty feet in the air followed by black billowing smoke. The receiver and tape-recorder with the 'evidence' tape of Miss Marion Pringle talking to Sidney Frogmorton was blown to smithereens.

Hawes and doctor Windrush, after the doctor was treated in hospital, were taken to New Scotland Yard where they appeared in handcuffs before a custody sergeant at the reception desk, and personal items such as wallets, wristwatches and money put into a prisoner's property bag. One telephone call allowed for each prisoner. Hawes prudently phoned his solicitor while the doctor, feeling hungry phoned for a takeaway pizza. Belts and shoelaces were removed and the hapless pair locked in a cell by a brutish ape looking policewoman with a low brow and long dangling arms. They told her they were not Irish and had never been to Ireland and were true blue Englishmen born and bred, and always stood to attention whenever the national anthem was played. The brutish policewoman grunted in reply and pushed them into the cell with Hawes wishing he had a banana to pacify her. He nicknamed her Grunt Grunt because she had not spoken a word to them only grunted.

When the cell door clanged shut behind them and key turned in the lock, they found themselves confined within a small white tiled cell resembling a public toilet. There was a bunk with a blue mattress, flushing toilet without a seat in the corner with no toilet paper. Both men, distraught and miserable, sat down on the bunk. "What are we going to do now, Hawes?" asked the doctor despondently.

"How are your bowels holding up?"

"Thank you for asking, Hawes, this is the first time you've shown any interest in my bowel movements. Why is that I wonder?"

"Because I don't want you having a bowel movement while were locked in here together, and nor do you."

"I don't? Why not?"

"There's no toilet paper and we're in a confined space."

"What are we going to do, Hawes, this is a ghastly business? Why didn't you tell the police about the death threat to the Prime Minister's life?"

"Because I gave my word of our complete confidentially to Mrs Frogmorton. Only she can give permission for me to talk to the police about her husband."

"How long do you think we'll be kept here?"

"No idea, all we can do is to sit it out and wait, Doctor, unless you've got the key to the cell door?"

"No, of course I haven't, Hawes. What will my mother say when she hears I've been arrested as an IRA terrorist?"

"A great deal knowing your mother, doctor."

Three hours later the sliding grill on the cell door slid open and Grunt Grunt, the brutish ape looking policewoman, peered in at Hawes and the doctor. The doctor lay asleep on the bunk bed snoring quietly. Hawes pacing up and down the cell contemplating on how to clear himself of terrorist charges without implicating his client. "Your solicitor's here to see you, Mister Hawes," called out Grunt Grunt through the grill. "He's proved you're not with the IRA but a private detective." There was the sound of a key turned in the lock and the door opened. Grunt Grunt stood astride the threshold and beckoned to Hawes with a huge paw and he stepped towards the door. "What about him?" asked Grunt Grunt pointing to the sleeping doctor, and again Hawes wished he had a banana to give her.

"Let him sleep on," replied Hawes. "I phoned for a solicitor and he phoned for a pizza. Let the pizza deliveryman set him free."

Chapter Seventeen

When the first half payment of his murder for hire fee was paid into his Swiss bank account by Sydney Frogmorton, Perkins decided to celebrate by marrying Melody Austin. The couple holding hands stood on the doorstep of the vicarage in the village of Bumstead-on-the-Wold to see the vicar to discuss their wedding plans. Perkins rang the doorbell. The Reverend Sidney Bloom opened the door greeting them with a beaming welcoming smile. "Are you collecting for charity?" he joked. "If so, then please take the wife." The vicar laughed at his own joke. He liked to greet visitors with a cheery smile and a joke thinking it put them at their ease.

Melody forced a weak smile. She was not amused by the vicar's joke about a wife especially as she was about to become one herself. "We've come to discuss our wedding plans, Vicar," she said.

"Oh, and whose wedding might that be?" replied the vicar brightly looking at Perkins and winking an eye. "Some lucky fellow whose heart has been captured by his fair lady love, I shouldn't wonder?"

"You're such a tease, Vicar," retorted Perkins impatiently wanting to get the wedding organized and sorted so he could return home to smoke a Cuban cigar and have a double Brandy.

"I know," chuckled the vicar enjoying what he thought was his ready wit and sense of humour which had been deplored at Theological Collage by his fellow students who did their best to keep clear of him outside of lectures. "I couldn't resist it. My wife thinks I should have been in show business, a comedian would you believe. Please come in and we'll discuss your wedding plans in the comfort of my study."

In the study Perkins and Melody sat holding hands sitting on a brown leather sofa with the vicar sat opposite to them on a matching brown leather armchair. "Now, let's begin," beamed the vicar, looking at Melody, "tell me, my dear, what denomination are you?"

"I'm English."

The vicar laughed, "No, what religion are you?"

"Does that matter?"

"It does. You have to be Church of England to be married at St Freda the Eveready."

"I was christened in a Church of England church. I know because my mother embarrasses me at family gatherings by telling the story of how I weed on the vicar as a baby as he was christening me at the font."

"Sounds like it was a wee experience for you both," chuckled the vicar, who continued chuckling until he saw Perkins and Melody looking stony-faced at him and not amused by his wit. "Are you confirmed?" he asked.

"As what?" asked Melody with a smile, "I was once a dancer and I could . . ."

"The vicar doesn't want to know about that, darling," interrupted Perkins thinking Melody was about to tell the vicar of her experiences as an exotic striptease dancer performing with a snake called Brian.

"How interesting, "beamed the vicar, "I was once a tap dancer before I fell off into the sink." He laughed uproariously at his joke.

"Please, Vicar," said Perkins, "can we continue. I've got things to do at home."

"Sorry, yes of course," replied the vicar, smile fading from his face. "Were you christened in the faith as member of the Church of England, Ronald?"

"Most definitely I was," declared Perkins.

"Confirmed too?"

"Yes, when I was thirteen at public school."

"Is there any reason to prevent you being married in church?"

"Only if you say we can't."

"No, Ronald, I mean are you already married."

"No, I've never been married."

"And what about you, Melody?"

"Of course not, Vicar."

The vicar smiled and nodded. "Good, then we can proceed with making the arrangements for your wedding and book a date for the church. Have you decided on what music you'd like? I take it you want the church choir with our organist Miss Jessica Bowls? She's eighty-one and boasts she can still handle an upright organ with the most amazing skill and agility."

"We'd like everything that's on offer, Vicar," replied Perkins, "including the church to be full of flowers. Money's no object when it comes to Melody's happiness."

"Have you a date in mind? I'll need three weeks for calling the bans in church."

Perkins, disguised as Miss Marion Pringle in green tweeds, jacket and skirt, carrying a black handbag, stepped briskly onto the tube train. He was going to West Minister to visit the House of Commons to see Sir Anthony Dingle at Prime Minister's Question Time. He wanted to see the great man in the flesh and size him up to get some ideas on ways to murder him without being caught. The Prime Minister, rotund with flabby jowls, face like a boxer dog, bald with hardly any neck on slumped shoulders. Perkins wanted the murder to be committed before he married Melody with the church booked for a month on Saturday and time was ticking away.

Forty minutes later Perkins sat in the visitor's balcony in the House of Commons. Prime Mister Sir Anthony Dingle below him was up his feet amidst a furious barrage of howls and catcalls coming from the opposition benches. "Sit down before you fall down, you're drunk again," called out a squat horse-faced woman waving her arms, the ferocious Miss Judy Upstarter-Brown, a dedicated career virgin who despised the entire male gender of the animal kingdom. She was Opposition Shadow Cabinet Minister for Women's Rights, and when a student at Cambridge University had campaigned vigorously against the over use of penises. "Penises only be used for passing urine and making babies," was her rallying cry.

"If I looked like you, Miss Upstarter-Brown," retorted the Prime Mister enjoying himself immensely, "then I'd be sitting in a cage at London Zoo eating a banana." The Government benches cheered and waved their order papers.

"Order, order," shouted the Speaker of the House.

"What about the workers?" called a shrill wailing voice from the Liberal Democrat Party benches.

"There aren't any workers in this House," shouted back the Prime Minister, "except for the members seated on the on the Government benches." There was a cascade of deafening booing from the Opposition benches.

"Order, order," shouted the Speaker of the House.

"What about the workers?" repeated the shrill wailing voice from the Liberal Democrat Party benches, determined to be taken seriously.

"I can hear the honourable member of Ducksbury is back from his holiday in Bognor," shouted the Prime Minister. "I'd know his wailing voice anywhere."

"I'm not back from holiday!"

"Oh, yes you are," chorused the Government and Opposition benches together in unison as if they were an audience encouraging a pantomime Dame on stage.

"Oh, no I'm not," called back the shrill wailing voice indignantly.

"Oh, yes, you are," shouted back the Government and Opposition benches.

"Loony," shouted a Government backbencher.

"I'm not a loony," shouted back the shrill wailing voice. "I've got my army demob papers to prove it." The Government and Opposition benches broke into thunderous applause and cheering stamped their feet. Perkins watched the Prime Minister through a pair of opera glasses then crept silently away and returned to the hotel where he was staying.

Hetty Perkins behaviour had become stranger and more bizarre since she learnt of her son's wedding plans, and was giving Melody spine chilling icy looks whenever they met in the house. The wedding plans of her son unbalanced the old lady's mind replacing reason with festering insanity. She harbored dark thoughts on murdering Melody before she could become a bride.

Melody lay alone on the big double bed sleeping. Perkins was away in London on business. The midnight hour chimed on the grandfather clock downstairs in the hallway and a light breeze fluttered the curtains of the quarter open bedroom window. Moonlight cast a pale orange glow over Melody's face and there was no sound heard but the faint tick toc of the bedside alarm clock.

The bedroom door knob slowly turned and the door opened and a deranged looking figure, wild-eyed and bare foot, unkempt hair falling to bony shoulders, wearing pale a blue nightie, advanced on tip toe into the room. It was Hetty with a bread knife raised in her right hand ready to strike. Melody sighed wistfully in her sleep dreaming of her dead lover, the young robust curate Peter Catchpole, snug between her thighs thrusting steadily away bringing them both to orgasm.

Hetty stood poised in the moonlight standing over the sleeping Melody and thought when the maid discovered her dead body in the morning it would be thought a burglar broke in and stabbed her.

Nobody, least of all the police would suspect her of committing the murder. She would put on an Oscar winning performance of grief to look as if she loved and cherished Melody.

Hetty tried but could not bring the knife down to stab Melody. Indeed, all her years of church going would not allow her to break the commandment 'Thou shalt not kill,' and trembling with frustration and seething with fury she turned and hurried from the bedroom closing the door behind her. The sound of the door being closed woke Melody from her slumbers. She sat up in bed with an overwhelming feeling of dread thinking there was somebody in the room with her. "Who's there?" she called out switching on the bedside lamp and was relieved to see she was alone. Getting out of bed she locked the door leaving the key in the lock. Climbing back in bed she switched off the light and returned to the arms of her dream lover, the rampant young curate, who stiff as a poker was waiting to mount her for a second time.

Chief Inspector Edgar 'Lanky' Briggs sat in the back of an unmarked police car with Sergeant Jenny Hopper. The driver police constable Douglas Higgins, a young man of average height who had been the police force less than three months. He served in the army before joining the police and drove a tank in a desert in North African. When he entered Hendon for police training he told his instructors that he was a licensed driver trained by the army but not that it was for driving tanks only. When he graduated from Hendon as a constable he was assigned to be a police car driver.

Higgins drove the unmarked police car as if it was a tank with a grinding of gears and travelling at less than 15mph. "Can't you go any faster, Constable?" asked Briggs impatiently. "It's taken over an hour to go sixteen miles."

"It's the traffic, Sir," replied Higgins with a grinding of gears, "I'm not used to driving in traffic. It unsettles me. When I was in the army and driving in the desert there was only camels to worry about. I'm new to car driving. But don't worry I'm getting the hang of it now."

"New to car driving?" replied Briggs alarmed. "You've got a driving licence, haven't you?"

"For driving a tank, Sir."

"Driving a tank? You took your driving test to drive a tank?"

"Yes, Sir, there wasn't a car handy and so the sergeant in charge of transport said I could use a tank instead. He passed me on my fifth attempt. I blame my failures on the camels being too slow in getting out of my way and the pyramid shouldn't have been there."

"You hit a pyramid?"

"I didn't see it until it was too late, Sir. There's only a small slit in a tank to see through."

"Oh, my God," muttered Briggs, face turning a deathly pale.

"Would you like me to drive, Sir?" asked Sergeant Jenny Hopper.

"Please, Sergeant, I can't think of anything I'd like more."

"Pull over, Higgins," cried Jenny Hooper, "I'll drive from here on."

"Yes, Sergeant," replied Higgins, relieved to be handing over driving the car. London traffic was too much for him and was nothing like driving in a desert with its wide its open spaces and occasional hazards such as camels and pyramids. He turned the steering wheel taking the car closer to the pavement and to bring it to a halt for the hand over. In his haste instead of pressing his foot down on the brake pedal he pressed it down on the accelerator. The car shot forward onto the pavement hitting a middle-aged woman dressed in green tweeds, jacket and skirt, waiting to cross the road. The front bumper caught and tossed Miss Marion Pringle into the air like a rag doll to somersault and land with a dull thud denting the bonnet of the car. Slowly he slid down to sit slumped on the road.

Briggs, fearing the woman was seriously injured, opened the door and leapt out of the car, visibly trembling having seen Miss Marion Pringle's with legs akimbo flying through the air exposing her bloomers, the sight badly shaking his faith both in mankind's mortality and ladies underwear. Miss Marion Pringle lay in front of the car stunned. It was Perkins army training in the parachute regiment that had saved him from serious injury. He rolled sideways as he landed on the car's bonnet. With a groan he opened his eyes and saw Briggs bending over him with an anxious look on his face. "Don't move, Madam," said Briggs anxiously thinking the woman before him was seriously injured and possibly dying.

"I'm not hurt," muttered Perkins weakly in the high pitched squeaky feminine voice he used when posing as Miss Marion Pringle. Then he remembered he had been wearing a hat and a wig reached up to feel if they were still in place. The hat was missing but the wig was still in place. He breathed a sigh of relief. He still resembled a woman.

"I'm a police officer, Madam."

"I must go home and cook my father's tea," lied Perkins alarmed to hear the man bending over her was a policeman. "He's having smoked haddock with brown bread and butter."

"Don't worry about your father. He can get his own tea."

"No, he can't. He's bedridden."

"What's your name?"

"Marion . . . Marion Pringle. I'm a Miss, you know. Are you married?"

"Miss Pringle, I'm taking you to hospital."

"No, please, I don't need a doctor." Perkins got to his feet feeling dazed and bruised and as he did so his wig slipped slightly to the left. He quickly adjusted it with a sweep of his right hand.

Meanwhile, Briggs called for Higgins to come and help him with Miss Pringle. The two men took hold of Perkins arms thinking to stop him falling over. "Oh, look, over there," cried Perkins nodding his head in the direction of a red double-decker bus that had pulled up at a bus stop on the opposite side of the road. "There's my bus. I must go or I'll miss it."

"There's no bus for you, Miss Pringle," declared Briggs, "you're coming with us to hospital. I want you seen by a doctor."

Perkins knew if he went to hospital then a doctor would quickly discover that everything was not where it should be on a woman but would be on a man. "But I must go home to my father. He'll be wondering what's happened to me. The haddock will go off if I go to hospital."

"She's delirious, Constable," muttered Briggs looking at Higgins. "Help me to get her into the back of the car." Perkins struggled as Briggs and Higgins manhandled him to the car and onto the back seat. "You've laddered my stockings," he cried.

"Never mind your stockings, Miss Pringle," said Briggs as he sat next to Perkins and held his hand. "Let's get you to hospital and examined by a doctor."

"But they're nylon," protested Perkins, and he was about to leap out of the other rear door when Higgins got in and sat next to him and he was squeezed between the two policemen on the back seat.

"Put your foot down, Sergeant," called out Briggs. "Miss Pringle's in need of urgent medical treatment. She's delirious and keeps talking about her stockings."

Jenny Hopper slipped the car into first gear and pressed her foot down on the accelerator pedal and the car sped away into the rush hour traffic. "It's a pity this is an unmarked police car, Sir," she called out. "We could have used a marked police car with siren going full blast to get us quickly through the traffic."

"I can lean out the window and blow my whistle," offered constable Higgins.

"Good thinking," replied Briggs, "get whistling, Constable, this is a life-or-death emergency."

Chapter Eighteen

Casualty Doctor Percy Mackey was tired, very tired, it had been a long grueling shift and he was almost asleep on his feet. There had been a series of emergencies including a boy with a marble up his nose and a drunk man with a beer bottle up his bottom. The doctor was thirty-one, brown haired, hazel eyed, and of average height with delicate hands and slim fingers, the fingers which his mother maintained were those of a world class concert pianist. She was disappointed when he chose medicine instead of playing the piano. "And to think you could be tinkling the ivories with those delicate fingers before an enraptured concert hall audience, Percy," she would chide him whenever he visited her, "instead of using them to examine and poke about prostrates and hemorrhoids."

He yawned and glanced at his wristwatch. There were twenty minutes to go before he was off duty and wearily he slumped onto a chair and closed his eyes for a few minutes rest. "Coffee, Doctor?" asked a familiar female voice.

Opening his eyes, he looked up and saw the smiling face of staff nurse Caroline Westbrooke holding two plastic cups of steaming coffee. The staff nurse a beautiful Yorkshire girl, brunette with a bright bubbling personality. "Thank you, Staff," he muttered gratefully, taking a mug. "It'll help to keep me awake until I get to my bed. I'm about all done in." He sipped the coffee.

"Not long is it now, Doctor?" asked the nurse referring to how long it was before they would be off duty.

He almost choked on his coffee thinking she was referring to the size of his penis. Two days earlier he had made love to her best friend staff nurse Trudy Rollings who had made derogatory remarks about the miniature size of his penis. He knew women, especially best friends, shared with each other the intimate details of their lovers and how good or bad the love making had been.

"Not long is it now, Doctor?" repeated the staff nurse speaking louder thinking he had not heard her the first time.

"Please don't tell anyone, Caroline," he pleaded red-faced with embarrassment. "It's bad enough that you and Trudy know."

"Know what?"

"I've got a small penis."

"I didn't know, Doctor, but I do now."

Sergeant Jenny Hopper drove at speed to the hospital with constable Higgins leaning out a rear window blowing his police whistle for all he was worth. The car came to a halt with squealing tyres outside the main doors of the casualty department. Perkins, disguised as Miss Marion Pringle, desperate to escape before a doctor examined him and find that all was not what it should be under his bloomers. He sat forlornly in the back of the car wedged between Chief Inspector Briggs and Constable Higgins. "I feel sick," he muttered as a delaying tactic trying to gather his thoughts on how to make an escape bide.

"Quick, she's going to be sick," cried Briggs grabbing Higgin's hat and thrusting it under Perkins chin. "Use this, Miss Pringle," he said sympathetically. Perkins felt he should oblige and leant forward and buried his face in the hat and made being sick noises.

"That's my best hat," protested Higgins indignantly.

"Stop fussing, Constable," replied Briggs, "help the lady from the car." Higgins opened the door and stepped out. Perkins seeing his chance to escape pushed past the constable and holding up his skirt above his knees fled down the driveway heading towards the hospital gates. "After her, Constable," shouted Briggs, giving chase. "She's concussed and doesn't know what's she's doing."

Higgins ran after Perkins and being fitter and faster gradually closed the gap between them, and with a flying rugby tackle brought him down. "It's alright, Miss Pringle," he said sympathetically helping the disguised murderer to his feet. "You don't know what you're doing. Trust me. I'll look after you." Perkins promptly kneed him between the legs and down he went groaning onto his knees clutching his groin. Perkins ran for the hospital gate but had run only a few yards when Briggs and Jenny Hopper caught him and held him in restraining arm locks. Complaining bitterly about police brutality Perkins was frog-marched back up the driveway and into the hospital. The casualty department crowded with people sitting on chairs waiting to be seen by a doctor. "Let me go," protested Perkins shrilly. "What about my haddock?"

"What? You've injured your haddock?" asked Briggs anxiously thinking Miss Pringle's 'haddock' was her pet name for her vagina, knowing some women like some men often had pet names for their genitals. He called his penis 'Bunny' because it always leapt about in the presence of a beautiful woman. "Don't worry, Miss Pringle, I'll get a gynecologist to see you." Perkins stopped struggling hoping the two police officers would relax their hold and he could make a run for it. But they continued to apply the half nelsons and marched him over to the reception desk.

At the reception desk sat a bored looking young woman receptionist with orange hair set in a beehive style with purple painted fingernails, wearing too much make-up giving her a clownish appearance. She was talking on the telephone. "Oh, yes, and I've heard that about her too, she's insatiable and has an open marriage with legs to match," she said brightly into the telephone, "and she's . . ."

"Excuse me," interrupted Briggs. "But this is an emergency."

"Can't you see I'm on the phone? Wait your turn and I'll see you when I'm ready."

"No, you'll see me now"

"Pardon?"

"I said you'll see me now," repeated Briggs angrily.

"You'll wait your turn like everybody else."

"I'm a police officer," replied Briggs showing his warrant card, "and I'll arrest you for obstructing a police officer in the performance of his duty if you don't get me a doctor immediately."

The receptionist scowled showing her contempt. "I'll have to call you back, Jackie," she said into the phone, "something's come up that needs my attention." She replaced the phone on its cradle and looked the Chief Inspector directly in the eyes. "What's wrong with you?" she asked. "Are you drunk?"

"No, I'm teetotal."

"Well, you could have fooled me."

"This lady," replied Briggs pointing at Perkins, "needs to see a doctor urgently."

"What's wrong with her?"

"She was hit by a car."

"Whose car?"

"A police car."

"Were you the driver?"

"No."

"Who was the driver?"

"This is an emergency. Get a doctor. I fear this lady's has serious injuries."

"What's her name?"

"Marion Pringle."

"Miss," added Perkins meekly. "I'm not married."

"I don't blame you, dear," replied the receptionist sardonically. "Men are such pigs and a girl is better off staying single. I could tell you stories about my Errol and his appetites that would curl your hair."

"Will you get a doctor?" cried Briggs, his patience gone.

"No."

"No?"

"Miss Pringle must first be seen by a staff nurse to determine how serious her injuries are and only then can a doctor see her. If you'll follow me I'll show you to a cubicle." The receptionist led the way through swing doors and into the treatment area with curtained cubicles on either side of a brightly-lit room smelling of disinfectant. Staff nurse Caroline Westbrooke stepped forward with a smile to welcome them. "What have we here?" she asked, running an expert eye over the blue-rinse haired roly-poly woman in green tweeds who was still firmly held by both arms by police officers.

"Road accident," said the receptionist.

"Serious?" asked the staff nurse.

The receptionist pointed to Briggs. "He says it's an emergency and he'll arrest me if I don't get a doctor to see her."

"Bring the lady into the cubicle," said the staff nurse as she pulled aside the white plastic curtain. "She's looks pretty rough to me," she added. Indeed, the nurse had never seen a more rougher looking woman and if she had not been told she was female then she would have sworn it was a man in drag.

"Please, Nurse, I'm not injured," implored Perkins as he was hauled into the cubicle. "I' worried about my haddock."

"Haddock?" asked the nurse, wondering what fish had to do with a road accident.

"She needs to see a gynecologist," explained Briggs. "She calls her intimate lady part her haddock."

"Oh, I see," replied the nurse.

"I want to go home," implored Briggs. "This is madness."

"Help me to lift her onto the trolley," said the nurse. Perkins was lifted by the three police officers and the nurse onto the trolley. The nurse then hurried away to fetch the doctor while the officers restrained Perkins.

"Let go," pleaded Perkins. "I won't try to get off the trolley." But it was a lie and he was going to leap from the trolley and make a run for it the moment the officers relaxed their hold.

The cubical curtain was pulled aside and Doctor Percy Mackey strode in followed by nurse Westbrooke, and stepping up to the trolley he put a stethoscope in his ears and looking at the three police officers said, "Wait outside. I need privacy to conduct my examination. You'll find a coffee vending machine down the corridor."

"Thank you, Doctor, we could do with a hot drink," said Briggs releasing his hold on Perkins.

"I'll come with you," exclaimed Perkin. "I'm feeling better now and don't want to waste your time, Doctor. I'll just pop off home and get my father's tea."

"Don't worry about your father's tea, Miss Pringle," replied Briggs. "You're in the best possible hands here. Just relax and do what the doctor tells you."

"Leave her to me," said the doctor.

"But of course," replied Briggs, "we'll get ourselves a coffee." He left the cubical followed by the other two police officers. The nurse closed the curtain after them.

"Right, now let's have a look at you," said the doctor and blew on the end of his stethoscope to warm it. "Can you tell me what happened?"

"There's no need to waste your valuable time. I'll take a couple of aspirin when I get home." Perkins sat up and swung his legs over the side of the trolley.

"Let me be the judge of your injuries," replied the doctor as he pushed Perkins back on the trolley. "Relax Mrs eh . . ."

"Miss Marion Pringle," said the nurse. "She was hit by a police car."

"Sounds serious," replied the doctor. "Was the car badly damaged?"

"Please I'm not hurt," pleaded Perkins. "I want to go home and have a hot cup of cocoa and pop into bed. I'll be right as rain in the morning."

"You're not going anywhere until I've examined you, Miss Pringle." The doctor turned to the nurse, and said, "Loosen Miss Pringle's clothing, Nurse, I want to listen to her heart." Perkins was gripped with overwhelming panic. The nurse was about to discover his true gender.

The nurse bent over Perkins and unbuttoned the top button of the green tweed jacket and then glancing at the doctor, asked: "Do you want all clothing removed, Doctor?"

"Yes, I need to see her injuries." The staff nurse returned to her task of unbuttoning the green tweed jacket, buttons two and three unbuttoned and the jacket fell open revealing a huge bosom covered by a pink blouse. She began unbuttoning the blouse and as each button was unbuttoned Perkins gave a nervous little squeak. "Go gently, Nurse," said the doctor. "Miss Pringle might have a broken a rib or two."

The nurse opened the blouse exposing a white brassiere and sticking out from the top of the right cup was a single strand of cotton wool. Taking hold of the strand of cotton wool she began to tug it from the cup and watched in amazement as the cup steadily deflated as she pulled out more and more of the cotton wool. "Doctor," she gasped, "I think you should see this --- all is not what it should be."

The doctor looked at the deflated bra cup and made a quick medical diagnosis thinking Miss Pringle must have had breast cancer with a breast removed, and asked, "Was a breast surgically removed?" Perkins moved his head and as he did so his blue-rinsed wig slipped forward and the nurse seeing it fall over Miss Pringle's eyes reached up to brush it back into place. The wig came away in hand. Holding the wig, she stared at it in horror and screamed.

Perkins seeing his chance leapt off the trolley and fled from the cubicle and saw the police officers down the corridor standing at a coffee vending machine drinking coffee from white plastic cups ran in the opposite direction, climbed out of a window and dropped into a back ally. Minutes later he was seated in the back of a taxi speeding towards his hotel. The cabbie, Alfie Boil, was not shocked to see such a bizarre looking male figure in female clothing clamber into his taxi knowing there were lots of transvestites in London who were mostly good tippers. He drove Perkins to his hotel where Perkins paid the fare but without giving a tip. "What? No tip?" asked Boil disgruntled and holding out his hand.

"Yes, bet on Perky Lad running tomorrow in the three-thirty at Epsom."

Perkins hurried away and crept unseen up a fire escape and into his room on the sixth floor where he stripped out of his female clothing and bungled it into a suitcase. He dressed in male clothing and within the hour was seated in a train chugging home to Bumstead-on-the-Wold.

The blue-rinsed wig Perkins left behind in the hospital was handed to Chief Inspector Briggs with the nurse telling him, "I was suspicious before the wig came off in my hand that Miss Pringle was really a man in drag especially when I saw the hairy legs come swinging off the trolley." Briggs wanted to hand the wig into lost property at New Scotland Yard thinking Miss Pringle was a harmless cross-dresser who fled from an embarrassing situation in the hospital and would claim the wig back from lost property. But Sergeant Jenny Hopper thought otherwise and sent the wig off to forensics to be tested for DNA thinking the DNA might match with other DNA held on the police national DNA data bank.

Chapter Nineteen

Chief Inspector Briggs sat in his office with Sergeant Jenny Hopper reading the forensic report on Miss Marion Pringle's wig. The DNA taken from the blue-rinsed wig matched with the DNA samples taken from four murder investigations spread over a twenty-five-year period. The four murders, two historic murders of the river police constable Robert McDougal and railway employee David Penrose, and the recent murders of Group Captain Huey Luey Lampton and Church of England curate Peter Catchpole. Briggs was worried expecting to be reprimanded and demoted in the ranks for letting a killer slip through his fingers. Standing up he paced up and down the squad room and finally he turned to Jenny Hopper, and exclaimed, "I never thought for a moment that Miss Pringle was really a man."

"I did, Sir, that he was a cross-dresser in drag."

"Who the doctor? Damn it, Sergeant, he really was a man. He wore trousers and needed a shave."

"I mean Miss Marion Pringle was in drag, Sir."

"This is a nightmare. What will the Chief Constable think?"

"Probably the same as me, Sir."

"What do you think?"

"Your copper's nose wasn't working too well when you met Miss Marion Pringle, Sir."

Melody Austin lay relaxing in a bubble bath enjoying the soothing warm caress of water on her naked body, and she wriggled her toes and gently nudged with her right hand a little yellow plastic duck bobbing about between her knees. She called the duck Petey after her dead lover the late Peter Catchpole, the duck was a love gift from him. Since his murder she had been doing her best to hide her grief from Perkins keeping tears for moments of solitude when walking alone in the garden. There came a gentle knock on the bathroom door. "May I come in, Mel?" called out Perkins. "I need to talk to you."

"Only if you behave yourself, Ronnie, I'm not in the mood for patty fingers." The door opened and Perkins entered smoking a Cuban cigar. He wore a black evening jacket and bow tie and he liked to dress for dinner. With a smile he walked over to the bath and stood gazing down at Melody enjoying her nakedness, "You look like a gorgeous pink mermaid," he said brightly as he reached down and touched her right breast and gently caressed the nipple.

"No, Ronnie, I said no patty fingers," she said brushing his hand away.

"Sorry, Mel, but you look so sexy and inviting."

"We'll make love tonight in bed, Ronnie, but not in the bath. The last time we had sex in the bath I almost drowned."

He nodded and forced a smile, disappointed. "I'm going away tomorrow for a few days on a special removal business."

"How long will you be gone?"

"Two to three days at most."

"Must you go? I don't like being alone with your mother."

"Sorry, Mel, but it's the biggest removal of my career. When I return we'll get married and go and live in the sunshine in the South of France."

"What are you moving, Ronnie, furniture, jewelry, a priceless painting?"

He bent down and kissed the tip of her nose. "That's for me to know, Mel. I can't tell you and break a client's confidentially, sorry darling."

"Couldn't you arrange for your mother to go and stay in a five-star hotel while you're away, Ronnie? It could be another birthday treat for her."

"It's not her birthday."

"I don't like being alone with your mother."

"Why not?"

"She frightens me the way that she stares at me. I'm afraid she's going to hurt me."

"That's silly talk, Mel, mother wouldn't hurt a fly."

"Well, I get icy shivers whenever she's in a room alone with me. Yesterday she dropped a flowerpot from her bedroom window narrowly missing me, and said it was an accident but I don't think it was."

"Oh, come now, Mel, you're letting your imagination run away with you."

"When I'm in the sitting room watching TV she's comes in and sits down . . ."

"But that's good, Mel," interrupted Perkins, "the two of you sitting watching TV together."

"But she doesn't watch TV she watches me."

"Oh, well, that's bad. I'll talk to her."

"Please don't be away too long, Ronnie, our wedding's only a month away."

"I know, Mel, but I've must go, it's an important removal that can't be delayed. I'll hurry home when it's done, I promise."

Allan Hawes and doctor Windrush were taking an evening stroll over London Bridge after a late supper of cod fish cakes, bake beans, and a mug of cocoa. The only sound heard the river lapping against the bridge. "Pity the tape of Miss Pringle and Frogmorton was blown up by the bomb disposal squad at the Saucy Gander pub," said Hawes grimly. "Now we've no evidence to prove Miss Pringle is the go-between with Sydney Frogmorton arranging for the murder the Prime Minister, and Frogmorton's wife will deny hiring us because she wants no publicity or police involvement."

"Yes," agreed the doctor, "the soldiers thought your canvas bag held an IRA bomb and blew it up."

"The War Office are refusing to replace the bag."

"I think we've no choice, Hawes, but to go to the police and tell them all we know about the attempt to be made on the Prime Minister's life. If we don't and he's murdered then we could be charged with conspiracy for withholding evidence. I don't want to go to prison. Come on, old chap, after all you did vote for Sir Anthony Dingle at the last election and so you should try your best to keep him alive."

"But there's client confidentiality to consider."

"That won't help the Prime Minister, Hawes. We must go to the police. You know it's the right thing to do."

"What about Mrs Frogmorton? Shouldn't we respect her wishes?"

"Not if you're going to save the Prime Minister's life."

"Give me three days, Doctor, to track down the elusive Miss Marion Pringle and if I fail then we'll go to the police."

"The Prime Minister could be dead by then. Surely you don't want his death on your conscience?"

"Alright, Doctor, you've persuaded me. We'll go to the police."

It was a hot sunny day and Perkins, disguised as a rambler in baggy grey shorts, open neck white shirt, walking shoes with grey socks rolled down to the ankles, false grey goatee beard and black horn-rimmed spectacles, with a green knitted woolly hat. On his back a haversack containing a change of clothing, cheese sandwiches, pickle some without pickle, flask of hot coffee with a bottle of spring water. He was within seven miles of the Prime Minister's country residence of Checkers and strolling down a twisting country lane. The purpose of the walk to carry out surveillance on Checkers to ascertain the security there.

Perkins was in a relaxed mood and whistled as he strode along. Birds chirped among the hedgerows and cows and sheep munched grass in fields and meadows. It was a hot cloudless day and Perkins was sweating slightly as he stopped at farm-gate. He took out a compass and map and took directional readings for finding Checkers. After making the readings he put away the compass and map and climbed over the farm gate into a field, crossed the field and entered a wood. He walked for half-an-hour through the wood and came to a style at the edge of the wood and clambered over the style into a meadow. At the top of the meadow a pigpen next to a corrugated hut, and as he approached the pigpen he heard the squealing and grunting of pigs. When he reached the pigpen he glanced in and was startled to see there were no pigs. The sound of squealing grunting pigs came from two loud speakers standing in the empty pigpen.

The door of the corrugated hut opened and a man stepped out. He was in his early twenties and dressed in grubby overalls with a straw dangling from the corner of his mouth. "Hello, there," he called out in a Cornish accent as he walked towards Perkins.

"Lovely day isn't it," replied Perkins putting on a Welsh accent.

"Aye," agreed the man, "it is to be sure. This is private land and I'm a pig farmer with my prize sow Freda about to give litter and I don't want strangers upsetting her. Where are you going? Are you lost?"

"No, I'm heading for the next town to catch a train home. How far is it?"

"Eight miles as the crow flies."

"Thank you."

"Might I ask your name?"

Perkins forced a smile. "David Morris."

"I can tell by your accent you're Welsh."

"Yes, I'm a school teacher from Cardiff on a walking holiday."

"Are you alone?"

"Yes, I prefer it that way. I like to walk our beautiful countryside alone with my thoughts. I write poetry, nothing like Dylan Thomas you'll understand, and once I had a poem published in in the Cardiff Trumpet my local paper."

"Enjoy your walk, Mister Morris, and have a good day."

Perkins nodded and strode off across the field having an uneasy feeling about the man and the lack of pigs in the pigpen. The man watched him go until he was out of sight and then took out a mobile radio from his pocket and switched it on. "Nothing to worry about, Sir," he said in a crisp public-school accent into the phone. "The chap's a Welsh rambler, a school teacher on a walking holiday. He said he's walking to the next town to catch a train."

"Alright, Captain, keep your eyes peeled for intruders," replied a voice on the mobile phone. "We can't take any chances with strangers so close to Checkers not with the Prime Minister making a surprise visit for the weekend."

"Yes, Sir." The captain switched off the radio and walked back into the hut. On a table a tape-recorder with wires leading to the loudspeakers set up in the pigpen. Seated at the table was a burly man dressed in army camouflage with sergeant stripes on his arms drinking tea from a mug. He glanced up as the captain entered "Tea, Sir?" he asked in a cockney accent. The two men were SAS men working undercover on surveillance protecting Checkers from the South East approach. The pigpen their cover as pig farmers.

Meanwhile, Perkins had clambered over a stone wall and entered a meadow with primroses growing among the swaying grass. There was a snaking river at the bottom of the meadow. He walked halfway towards down the slope towards the river then sat down to eat a cheese and pickle sandwich and drink a cup of coffee. He heard the sound of thundering hooves behind him and glancing over his shoulder was panicked to see a bull at the top of the meadow charging down towards him. He ran towards the river throwing aside the haversack thinking the weight would slow him down. The bull was fast and rapidly closed the gap between them. Perkins felt hot breath on his neck and dived into the river. The murky water engulfed him. He surfaced and saw the bull standing on the riverbank pawing angry and frustrated at the ground. The bull remained at the riverbank for a long time before losing interest and trotting away trotted back up the meadow to the haversack. The haversack was tossed into the air several times and trampled upon.

The bull sauntered away to munch grass beside the stone wall at the top of the meadow.

Perkins decided not to leave the river until the bull had gone away. An hour passed with him still waiting and feeling miserable and cold in the water, when the bull returned and stood watching him before returning back up the slope to chew grass at the stone wall. When night began to fall the bull was nowhere to be seen and Perkins decided to risk leaving the river.

He retrieved his haversack with most of the contents having been scattered. There was the change of dry clothes including socks, five badly squashed cheese sandwiches, some with pickle some without pickle, but no flask of coffee or bottle of spring water. In the haversack a box of matches. He made a fire to warm himself and dry his clothes, then waited miserably for daylight and the warmth of the sun before venturing on to Checkers.

Chapter Twenty

Melody Austin sat opposite to Hetty Perkins eating dinner, shepherd's pie with green peas followed with dessert of scoops of strawberry and vanilla ice cream covered with hot chocolate sauce, Melody's favourite desert next to bread-and-butter pudding. The atmosphere charged with animosity with the two women having not spoken all evening. There was something menacing and chilling in the way Hetty was staring at Melody across the table who was upset and frightened tempted to leave the table before Cobblers the butler served the ice cream.

Up in Hetty's bedroom the voodoo doll of Melody was covered with so many pins it resembled a hedgehog. Was it Melody's imagination or was Hetty looking at her through the eyes of madness? The women finished the shepherd's pie and peas and Melody rung the service bell to summon Cobblers to serve the ice cream. Hetty unable to control herself any longer leapt to her feet shouting, "Sow the wind and reap the storm."

"What's wrong, Hetty?" cried Melody, ashen faced, trying to remain calm, "Don't you want your ice cream?"

"It's you that's wrong."

"Me? Surely not."

"Leave my son and his money alone, you gold digger."

Cobblers the butler entered the room carrying a silver tray on which were two tall glasses of strawberry ice cream covered with hot chocolate sauce. Hetty, breathing heavily and looking demented sat down and glared at Melody. Cobblers placed a glass of ice cream in front of each woman. "Will there be anything else, Madam?" he asked looking at Melody.

"No, thank you, Cobblers, you may go."

"Yes, Madam." Cobblers went out the door and closed it behind him. Melody felt a sudden desperate urge to call him back but stifled the impulse. How could she explain why she wanted him to remain in the dining room while she ate her ice cream, to protect her from Hetty? The two women faced each other across the dining room table. Hetty stood up and took a step around the table towards Melody holding a table spoon in her right hand raised like a knife to stab her. "I won't let you marry my Ronnie," she cried hysterically.

You're after his money and won't get it. I'll see you dead first."

"More ice cream?" asked Melody, her knees trembling under the table and fearing for her life.

"You know what you can do with your ice cream," screamed Hetty, as she advanced round the table towards Melody.

Melody stood up and began to back away keeping the table between them. "Please Hetty," she pleaded, "think of what you're doing? You don't really want to hurt me, now do you?"

"Yes, I do, I've thought of nothing else for weeks."

"Can't we sit down and talk it over calmly like rational people?"

Hetty howled like a wounded animal and quickened her step as did Melody backing away from her. "You're not marrying my Ronnie," she screamed.

"Please don't do this."

"Yes, and I'm going to dance on your grave." Hetty broke into a run and Melody screaming turned and ran for her life. She ran round and round the table pursued by Hetty. They circled the table seven times before the door opened and Cobblers the butler entered carrying a silver tray with two coffee cups. He closed the door and seemed oblivious to what was happening between the two women and put the tray down on the table. "Will that be all, Madam," he asked looking at Melody running round the table pursued by Hetty with spoon raised to stab.

"Open the door, Cobblers, and stand clear," shouted Melody knowing she could not outpace Hetty for much longer.

"Yes, Madam," replied Cobblers, and opening the door he stepped aside allowing Melody to run out into the corridor. She did not stop running until she reached her bedroom where she slammed the door behind her and turned the key in the lock. Gasping for breath she sat on the bed and with her head in hands and sobbed.

Moments later there was a furious knocking on the door. "Melody," called out Hetty shrilly, "let me in I've something here for you." Melody picked-up the telephone on the bedside table and dialed 999 and asked for the police, and as she spoke to the operator she heard Hetty babbling incoherently as she pounded upon the door beating it with the spoon.

Twenty minutes later the police arrived and Hetty was subdued by police officers outside the bedroom door and hauled downstairs screaming threats at Melody into the living room where she was put in a straightjacket and sat in an armchair. The family doctor, George

Pegg, a bulky little Fatman, was summoned who administered a sedative and arranged for her to be taken as an emergency by ambulance to St Biddy's Hospital for the mentally ill in Romford. On arrival Hetty was sectioned by two doctors who diagnosed her insane.

Perkins slept the night under an elm tree using his haversack as a pillow and covered himself with grass to keep warm. He woke at first light to a chorus of chirping birds and sitting up stretched and yawned, then watched the first rays of sunrise creep above the treetops. Standing up he found every muscle in his body ached and his feet felt like blocks of ice. He knew it was not good for a man of his age to have spent the night sleeping rough without tent or sleeping bag, and so he did press-ups and running on the spot for twenty minutes, then feeling warmer he ate the last cheese sandwich with pickle then set off towards Checkers.

Allan Hawes and doctor Windrush were shown into Chief Inspector Edgar Briggs office at New Scotland Yard. The Chief Inspector sat at his desk and stood up to greet them. Sergeant Jenny Hopper sat at her desk typing a report and glanced up and nodded her greeting. "Thank you for coming, gentlemen," said Briggs holding out his hand for them to shake. "It's about the statements you made last night at Tower Bridge police station regarding an attempt to be made on the life of the Prime Minister, and alleging the assassin's identity is known by a middle-aged woman called Miss Marion Pringle. Do you know when and where the murder attempt will take place?"

"No, only it'll be sooner rather than later," replied Allan Hawes.

"Who's behind it? The IRA?"

"No, Chief Inspector, Freddy Frogmorton the supermarket chain multi-millionaire. He's hired a professional assassin using Miss Pringle as his intermediary."

"What evidence have to support that?"

"We had evidence but sadly no more."

"No more? What happened to it?"

"The army blew it up in a pub's car park."

"Blew it up? What do you mean blew it up?"

"An army bomb disposal squad thought my bag was holding an IRA bomb."

"So, your bag was the evidence?"

"No, Chief Inspector, the evidence was inside the bag, a taped conversation on a tape-recorder between two people of interest to the police."

"You and doctor Windrush?"

"No, Chief Inspector, the man who hired the assassin and the mediator Miss Marion Pringle the killer's contact."

"You taped their conversation?"

"We did on my tape recorder using a directional microphone, which I might add I want replaced by the army with a new bag and tape-recorder. So far, the War Office have refused to do so and so I've written to my MP to complain."

"Your statement said you were disguised and working undercover."

"Yes, posing as Irish navies with my trusty companion Doctor Windrush. We were on surveillance to observe the meeting between Sidney Frogmorton and the elusive Miss Marion Pringle."

"Can you describe Miss Pringle?" asked the sergeant taking an interest in the conversation and wondering if Hawes's Miss Pringle might be the same Miss Pringle, a man in drag, who fled wigless from the hospital casualty unit."

"She's rotund, middle aged, closer to fifty than forty, with blue-rinsed hair, dressed in green tweeds, jacket and skirt, and carried a black handbag."

Jenny Hopper leapt to her feet. The description matched. "I've news for you, Mister Hawes," she cried excitedly, "Your Miss Marion Pringle is none other than our Miss Marion Pringle who fled the hospital."

"My God, then she's a . . ."

"Twin," interrupted Briggs brightly.

Jenny Hopper sighed and shook her head. "No, Sir, it's the same person we took to hospital. We carried out a DNA test on the blue rinsed wig left behind by Miss Marion Pringle at the hospital. The result matched with DNA murder evidence kept on police files for four murders committed over a twenty-five-year period."

"What are you going to do, Chief Inspector?" asked Hawes.

"Call Superintendent Lionel Harper of Special Branch and tell him there's to be a murder attempt made on the Prime Minister. He's responsible for the Prime Minister's protection, and then I'm going to arrest Freddy Frogmorton."

Prime Minister Sir Anthony Dingle sat in the back of a silver fox Rolls Royce drinking a double whiskey he poured himself from a well-stocked drinks cabinet. He was on his way to Checkers to join his wife for the weekend. The Rolls Royce in convoy with two black saloon cars, one in front of the Rolls the other behind. Seated in the saloon cars armed security men, and leading the convoy two motorcycle police outriders. The convoy had left far behind the crowded streets of London and were entering the lush green countryside of the Surrey hills.

Sat in the front of the Rolls Royce next to the driver a grim-faced MI5 officer in civilian clothes, bowler hat, pinstripe trousers, and on his lap covered by a folded grey gabardine raincoat a light machine gun. The car reinforced with armor plating with windows bullet proof. In the back of the car sitting next to the Prime Minister and looking queasy because she never travelled well was his personal secretary Miss Constance Goodbody.

Miss Goodbody, middle-aged and single, a brunette with body shaped like a pear drop, big bottom but no breasts, had put her career before that of having a husband and children, and dedicated to serving the Prime Minister been with Sir Anthony for twelve years from his first cabinet post as Minister of Fish and Veg. She has her hair pulled back into a bun at the back of the head, wears glasses and kill-joy bloomers, with a two-piece navy-blue suit, jacket buttoned to the throat, skirt reaching to the ankles. The great man is dictating a speech which she scribbles down in shorthand on a notebook balanced on her knee. He speaks so quickly she has difficulty in keeping pace with him. Sir Anthony Dingle is to make an important speech on Tuesday afternoon in the House of Commons on 'Taxes and even more taxes.' He paused and took a sip of whiskey. "Tell me, Miss Goodbody," he asked, hoping to use her as a sounding board for public opinion, "what do you think of Income Tax? Do you think you pay too much or pay too little tax?"

"I'd rather not say, Prime Minister," replied Miss Goodbody knowing how frail his ego was when it came to being criticized. He expected his staff to agree with all his decisions and never speak against them.

"Come now, Miss Goodbody, I'd value your opinion as a voter."

"The British people are the most heavily taxed people in the world, Sir, and you're planning to tax them even more. That's wrong in my opinion, and as for myself, well, I find my own tax bill is far too high and crippling."

The Prime Minister took a puff of his cigar and frowned regretting having asked her opinion knowing people without much money hated being made to pay more. "I want you to type up the notes I made yesterday on my memoirs when we reach Checkers," he said to change the subject not liking the angry glint in her eyes. "I've completed chapter five of volume three. I think the British people deserve to have a record of my life and thoughts as seen from my own perspective, don't you think so, Miss Goodbody?"

"Who else but you would undertake such a work, Prime Minister?" replied Miss Goodbody curtly, wanting to tell him what she really thought, that he had an inflated idea of his own importance but had not the courage to do so.

The Prime Minister sipped his whiskey and smiled. "You're right of course, Miss Goodbody. Indeed, history deserves to have my own account as a statesman of world renown and a much-loved leader of Great Britain."

"Have you a title for your memoirs, Sir?"

"Yes, Miss Goodbody, I'm going to call it 'Greatness Was His Calling."

"Don't you think that's rather brazen, Sir?"

"Brazen? What do you mean?"

Miss Goodbody realized her mistake by using the word brazen and thought quickly, and said, "Well, aren't you giving away the plot in the title for your readers? It would be like reading a murder mystery and being told in the title who did the murder!"

Chapter twenty-one

The IRA in Ireland sent a three-man bombing team to England with orders to blow up the Prime Minister, the team from the Falls Road, Belfast. The commander, Sean O'Leary twenty-five, bachelor, a small thick-set bearded man whose job in Ireland was to stack supermarket shelves at night. He is considered by IRA high command to be a safe pair of hands and reliable in a crisis, a man dedicated to the cause of a united Ireland who never fails to carry out orders. The other two men in the team, Patrick Dodds and Roy McCluster. The three men had grown-up together in the back streets of Belfast and went to the same school, played football using dustbins as goal posts and were angelic altar boys serving Father Barry Mackey at mass in St James church.

Roy McCluster, twenty-three, hospital theatre porter and bachelor, sandy haired, bearded, a jovial man with hands like shovels and a singing voice like an angel. Patrick Dodds, twenty-five, fishmonger's assistant, married with two children under the age of four, team's bomb-maker who had learnt the art of bomb-making from a book he borrowed from the Belfast library, titled, "Easy Bomb Making for Beginners.'

The IRA team had been in England less than a week and they were staying in a safe house in Dorking, Surrey, when Commander O'Leary received a phone call at 10am on a Friday morning from Jean McNeely, working undercover for the IRA near the House of Commons as a traffic warden. She had been writing out a ticket for an illegally parked car when the Prime Minister's convoy swept passed heading for Checkers. She did not finish writing out the ticket and hurried to the nearest telephone box and called the IRA commander. "The big man's on his way," she told him, "and he's travelling in a Rolls Royce with police outriders."

"Good work, Jean, you've done well," replied O'Leary. "We're ready for him. Ireland forever."

"Ireland forever," responded the traffic warden brightly. She replaced the phone and hurried back to finish writing out the ticket to find the car gone. The IRA team had already placed a bomb, primed to detonate, packed in a biscuit tin with a radio receiver with two pounds of syntax. The bomb buried near a bend on a lonely stretch of country road eight miles south of Checkers on the route the Prime Minster would have to take to reach the house. The bomb buried at midnight a week earlier with one of the team keeping watch while the other two Irishmen dug a hole ten inches deep and fourteen inches square. The bomb placed into the hole and covered over with a layer of tarmac.

Forty minutes after Jean McNeely's phone-call, the three IRA men, grim and determined, were concealed behind bushes two hundred yards from where the bomb was buried ready to detonate with a remote control. The site of the bomb marked with a white chalk cross scrawled on the road. Commander O'Leary watched the chalk cross through binoculars. "Right, lads," he said grimly, "the big man will soon be here and then we'll blast him to Hell, so we will."

"Where is he?" muttered Dodds looking at his wristwatch, "he should be here by now."

"He'd be late for his own funeral," muttered McCluster with a chuckle.

"Remember, lads," said O'Leary hoping to stir the patriotic hearts of his companions, "this is an historical moment for Ireland. We'll be remembered as heroes and have pubs named after us."

"Shouldn't we say a prayer for his soul?" asked Dobbs. "It's the right and decent thing to do. Father Barry would expect it of us."

"Hell bells, no," retorted McCluster indignantly. "The British Prime Minister wouldn't pray for me if he was going to kill me. He wouldn't care less."

"That's an embittered attitude you've got there," replied Dodds.

"Be quiet lads," cried O'Leary, "I hear motorbikes. It'll be the police outriders, so it will."

"Aye, and the big man himself," muttered McCluster nervously.

"Ready with your thumb on the button, Pat?" asked O'Leary.

"Ready, Sean," replied Dodds.

"Don't explode the bomb until the car is over the chalk mark," said O'Leary, and added patriotically, "Ireland forever."

The sound of motorbikes became louder and two police outriders appeared coming at speed around the bend followed by the Rolls Royce. "Steady, Pat, steady," cried O'Leary, heart beating like a drum.

"The Brits certainly know how to build good cars," muttered McCluster, impressed by the silent running of the Rolls Royce engine.

"Steady . . . steady . . . steady," whispered Dodds, thumb poised ready to press the button on the remote control. He pressed the button and the three Irishmen threw themselves down onto their stomachs. There was no explosion. The convoy continued on its way up the road and was quickly lost to sight. The three Irish men stood up and dusted themselves down. "What happened?" asked O'Leary, "Why didn't the bomb go off?"

"I don't know," muttered Dobbs shaking his head. "I pushed the button and nothing happened."

"Well, that's blown it and shame to us," stormed O'Leary clenching his fists and thinking miserably what the IRA high command in Dublin would say when they heard of his team's failure to carry out the 'big one' for a united Ireland. The team would be ridiculed with no patriotic songs sung about them and women weeping at the mention of their names.

"But it didn't blow," retorted McCluster.

O'Leary turned to Dobbs and shoved him hard in the chest with both hands. "It was you, wasn't it?" he demanded.

"Me? What are you talking about, Sean?" Dobbs took a hasty step backwards and put his fists up in a boxing stance to defend himself. "I'll not be bullied by you, Sean, not like I was as a wee boy back in the school playground and you demanded my dinner money to buy sweets."

"I know it was you," retorted O'Leary putting up his fists to fight.

"Steady there, boys, steady," cried McCluster stepping between them. "We mustn't fight among ourselves not while we're on active duty. Alright, so the bomb's a dud but nobody's to blame for that. These things happen in war. It's unfortunate but there's nothing we can do about it. We had our chance and now it's over."

"It didn't just happen," fumed O'Leary glaring at Dobbs. "He knows it didn't."

"What do you mean?" demanded Dobbs waving a fist under O'Leary's nose. "You're asking for it so you are, and I'm the very man to be giving it to you."

"You forgot to put batteries in the remote control, didn't you," fumed O'Leary, "just like you did in the training session back in Ireland."

"Don't talk nonsense. I wouldn't make the same mistake on a combat mission."

"Turn out your pockets."

Dobbs reached into his pocket and pulled out two AA batteries. "Oops," he gasped, face going the colour of beetroot, "I was certain that I'd put them into the remote control."

"Idiot," screamed O'Leary throwing a punch and missing Dodd's nose who pulled away in time. Dobbs turned and fled up the road pursued by O'Leary determined to land a punch.

Prime Minister Sir Anthony Dingle sat in the back of the Rolls Royce unaware his life had been saved because the IRA bomber forgot to put batteries into the bomb's remote control. "It's been a long tiring day, Miss Goodbody," he said, taking a puff of his cigar.

"Yes, it most certainly has, Prime Minister," agreed the overworked Miss Goodbody,. Who was tired, hungry and overworked.

"How much longer before we reach Checkers?"

Constance Goodbody glanced at her wristwatch. "About twenty minutes. Prime Minister."

"Good. I want you to type up what I've dictated and to have the draft ready for me to correct before dinner."

"Yes, Prime Minister," replied Miss Goodbody as she closed her notepad. "Will you be doing any oil paintings over the weekend?" she knew he liked relax by painting on canvas, which he claimed were beautiful landscapes although it was difficult to tell as they mostly looked like badly scrambled eggs.

"Yes, I'm going to paint the back garden of Checkers. Have you a hobby, Miss Goodbody?" He smiled to encourage her. "I've known you for twelve years and you've never mentioned having a hobby."

"Yes, I like to knit, do jigsaws, visit museums and zoos, and watch the news on TV."

The smile faded from his face. "How interesting," he muttered, stifling a yawn with his hand, and thinking quite the opposite. It confirmed for him how boring and drab Miss Goodbody's private life was. "See that I have the draft before dinner. It's important I make the necessary corrections for you to type up a finished speech ready for me to deliver on Tuesday in Parliament."

"Yes, Prime Minister."

The convoy of cars with police outriders turned off the road passing between the open iron grill gates guarded by armed police in bullet proof vests carrying light machine guns. The Rolls continued up a long winding gravel driveway. They had arrived at Checkers.

Freddy Frogmorton with his wife spent an enjoyable evening at the theatre seeing 'The Importance of being Ernest," by Oscar Wilde in London's West End. After the theatre they went to a restaurant for a late supper where Freddy told his wife he had booked a sea cruise to celebrate their twelfth marriage anniversary. "In two days, darling," he said, "we'll be at sea on board the ocean liner SS Lulu of the Pritchard line cruising the Caribbean for a month." But the real reason for the cruise was for him to be out of the country when the Prime Minster was assassinated. He took his wife to Alfonso's the best Italian restaurant in London with five stars and a portrait of the Queen on the wall. The owner Marcus Alfonso, overweight, a jolly bearded man with bald spot on the back of his head giving him a monk like appearance, stood smiling as he served the couple at table insisting they accept with his compliments a bottle of champagne on the house. "It's always good to see you, Mister and Mrs Frogmorton," he told them with a heavy Italian accent as he poured bubbly champagne into two long-stem glasses. "Would you like to order now?"

"Later, thank you, Marcus," replied Freddy with a smile.

Marcus Alfonso bowed slightly from the waist. "But of course, sir, and when you're ready to order might I suggest chef's specialty? Spaghetti with beef meatballs swimming in a rich spicy tomato sauce and sprinkled with mature cheddar cheese, and for dessert, a sponge suet pudding covered with golden syrup. He turned and walked away to the kitchen leaving the couple alone at their corner table.

"Well, it seems that we'll be having spaghetti and meatballs," muttered Freddy with a smile, as he leant across the table and kissed the back of his wife's hand.

"I'm sorry, Freddy," she replied, "but I don't think a sea cruise is a good idea at this time of year. It's too cold to be sitting out on deck."

"Please come on the cruise, darling," he implored, "you've always loved cruises and sitting at the captain's table. I've already brought the tickets and we'd be having the best cabin with champagne and caviar for breakfast. You'll love it."

She placed her hand on his hand and gave it a gentle squeeze. "I love you, Freddy," she said, her eyes moist. "You know that, don't you?"

"Oh, God," he thought, ashen faced, and thinking she had found out about his monthly visits to a prostitute called Madam Whiplash in London's Soho, a domineering woman who tickled his fancy by giving him six of the best on the bottom with a bamboo cane while telling him he had been a very naughty boy.

"What's the matter, Freddy? You look awful."

"I'm alright, darling. I was thinking how terrible it would be if you left me."

"I'd never leave you, Freddy. I'll always stand by you no matter what you did."

"What I did?" His worse fear was confirmed. She did know about Madam Whiplash.

"Isn't there something you'd like . . ." her voice faltered momentarily, "to share with me but find it difficult to do so?" She was thinking about Miss Marion Pringle and the murder attempt to be made on the Prime Minister.

"Like what, dear? I don't understand," he muttered feeling sick to his stomach and desperately trying to think a plausible lie she would believe denying he knew Madam Whiplash.

"I was hoping you'd tell me, Freddy."

"Sorry, darling, but I haven't the faintest idea what you're talking about." He was playing for time hoping a good lie would suddenly pop into his head.

"Please, Freddy, I'm your wife. Things are never so bad that they can't be resolved." She wanted to tell him she knew he had hired a professional killer to murder the Prime Minister and she had hired a private detective to stop the killing. But now, face to face with him in a restaurant, she could not say what she wanted to say with waiters hovering about the table and people sitting at nearby tables. She would wait until they returned home where she could be sure of complete privacy.

Marcus Alfonso returned to the table. "Are you ready to order?" he asked with a broad smile showing his gleaming teeth.

"We're ready, Marcus, thank you," replied Freddy. "We'll have spaghetti and meat balls followed by sponge pudding covered with syrup. Have you a suggestion what we might have for starters?"

"Might I suggest king pawns and mussels on a bed of seaweed covered with a delicious parsley sauce made with fresh cream."

Perkins was in a wood close to Checkers and he could see smoke wafting above the treetops and knew the smoke was coming from the chimneys of the house. He moved towards the smoke and in the distance heard voices and dived into the nearest thicket and lay on his stomach. Moments later two armed policemen strolled bye discussing a football match to be played between Liverpool and Manchester United on Saturday. "I won't see the game although I've got tickets for myself and my brother-in-law," complained the shorter of the two policemen, "not with the Prime Minister coming to Checkers for the weekend. It's going to be overtime for us until he returns to London on Monday." The two policemen walked on and were soon lost to sight among the trees. Perkins felt the hairs rise on the nap of his neck bristle up at the mention of the Prime Minister. He had been planning only to reconnoiter Checkers but now knowing the Prime Minister would be in residence for the weekend he had an opportunity to kill him.

The three IRA bombers sat at a table in McAllister's pub 'The Jolly Irish Man,' in Oxted, Surrey. Roy McCluster trying to make peace between Commander Sean O'Leary and Patrick Dodds, with Dodds having forgotten to put batteries into the remote control to explode the bomb. Dobbs sported a black eye showing he had not outrun O'Leary when he was chased up the road after the bomb failed to explode. There was a brief fistfight with O'Leary, the bigger and stronger of the two, knocking Dobbs down twice before being stopped by McCluster reminding him they were on an important mission for the IRA and suggested they should retire to the pub to discuss peace terms between him and Dodds.

After drinking four pints of Guinness each and becoming unsteady on their feet with slurred voices, they agreed never to fall out again and to remain loyal friends. "Now, lads," said O'Leary cheerily, "we're still in with a chance to put things right with the bombing. We know Sir Anthony Dingle is at Checkers, don't we?" The other two Irishmen nodded and grinned sheepishly. "Alright, lads, then I say that we go to Checkers and finish the job. What do you say?"

"Ireland forever," cried McCluster patriotically getting to his feet and raising his glass of Guinness and almost falling over.

"Ireland forever," chorused his companions standing up and raising their glasses and then falling over.

The IRA team knew the Prime minister was at Checkers but not that Robert R Rooker the fourth, who wanted Britain's help to invade an Island nineteen miles north of Cuba to build an air base with a hotdog takeaway concession. It was the American President's desire to expand the American Empire and hotdog concessions world-wide before his term of office ended in two years.

"If we're going after Sir Anthony Dingle at Checkers then we'll need a bomb," said O'Leary looking at Dobbs, "a bomb that has batteries inserted into the remote control so it'll go off as planned."

"There he goes again," protested Dodds angrily, "going on about the batteries again. Haven't I said I'm sorry? What more can I do?"

"Have the new bomb explode," retorted O'Leary angrily.

"You're asking for it you really are," retorted Dobbs waving a fist under O'Leary's nose, "and I'm the very man to be giving it to you."

"Is that so? And I'll be putting you on your back again," replied O'Leary red-faced leaping to his feet and putting up his fists to fight.

"You and whose army?"

"I don't need an army. I'll be doing it myself."

"Oh, yeah."

"Yeah."

"Stop arguing both of you," cried McCluster. "We're republican soldiers on a dangerous mission and must forget the first bomb didn't go off and move on. We've on a vital mission for Ireland."

"Forget it?" exclaimed O'Leary indignantly. "I'm Commander and man responsible to High Command in Dublin for success or failure of our mission, and I won't forget or forgive what Pat did with the batteries. Oh, the shame of it. What a laugh the lads will have back in Belfast when they hear about it. I won't be able to hold my head high again walking down the Falls Road without having fingers pointed at me."

"They won't hear about it, Sean," declared McCluster grimly, "because we won't tell anyone. There's no need once we've blown up the British Prime Minister. We'll return home as heroes."

"I like it," said O'Leary, "but I can see flaw in your plan, Roy."

"Which is?"

"We still have Pat to mess up the bomb and stop it from going off."

"Haven't I said that I'm sorry," replied Dobbs glumly. "What more can I say?"

"How about I'm away home to Ireland?" suggested O'Leary thinking there was a better chance for blowing up the Prime Minister without him.

"I won't stay where I'm not wanted," retorted Dobbs getting to his feet. "Sit down, Pat," said McCluster grabbing his arm and retraining him, "finish your Guinness like the good man you are. Sean didn't mean it. He's just a little upset."

"Let him go," insisted O'Leary. "We don't need him. He's more trouble than he's worth."

"We can't make a bomb without him, Sean," replied McCluster. "He's the only one of us who has read the book on bomb making. We need him. We're a team aren't we? The best team the IRA have, and each of us handpicked. We grew up together and we've been friends since childhood. Come on, lads, we can't let a few batteries take all that away. Shake hands like the good men you are and together we'll blow-up the British Prime Minister at Checkers."

"Do really think we can do it?" asked O'Leary.

"I'm certain that we can, Sean. If we work as a team we can't fail." O'Leary solemnly shook hands with Dobbs.

"Good, then that's to be the way of it, lads," beamed McCluster wiping a tear from his eye, "you've made me a very proud Irishman."

"Can you build another bomb, Pat?" asked O'Leary.

"Sure, I can, Sean, but why bother when we can dig up the old bomb."

"Good man," cried McCluster, "then let's do it."

The three men raised their glasses and chorused, "One for all and all for Ireland," and tears flowed down their patriotic cheeks. The conversation between the IRA team had been loud and it was lucky for them the only other occupant in McAllister's bar was McAllister himself, already too drunk to hear or see what was happening and lay slumped behind the bar in a stupor with a silly grin on his face.

It was midnight when Freddy Frogmorton and his wife returned home from London after their meal at Alfonso's restaurant, and as they drove up the driveway they saw cars with headlights on parked outside the house. Illuminated within the beams of light were uniformed police officers. "What the Hell's going on," exclaimed Freddy Frogmorton, alarmed. His wife burst into tears and buried her face in her hands knowing why the police were there, they had come to arrest her husband. But how did they know Freddy had hired a killer to murder the Prime Minister? The car came to halt behind a police car and a man wearing a deerstalker hat stood talking to another man with a stethoscope dangling from his coat pocket. Mrs Frogmorton recognised the two men as super sleuth Allan Hawes and his trusted companion Doctor Windrush, and felt betrayed having hired Hawes to protect her family from public disgrace, and now he had gone to the police and told them everything.

Freddy Frogmorton switched off the car engine and applied the handbrake, then taking a deep breath to steady himself stepped from the car to be confronted by two plain clothed CID officers, Chief Inspector Edgar Briggs and Sergeant Jenny Hooper. "Freddy Frogmorton?" asked Briggs holding up his warrant card.

"Yes. What's wrong?"

"I need you to accompany me to New Scotland Yard to answer some questions."

"Questions? Am I under arrest?"

"No, Sir."

"I see, and what if I refuse to come with you?"

"Then you'll be arrested."

Chapter Twenty-Two

Prime Minister Sir Anthony Dingle sat in a bath at Checkers smoking a cigar having just finished dictating two letters to his personal secretary Constance Goodbody, who sat on a stool on the other side of the drawn blue plastic shower curtain so she would not be traumatized by seeing him naked. It was his custom sometimes to dictate while having a bath which was a traumatic experience for her. "Get the letters typed and ready for my signature, Miss Goodbody," he called out brightly from behind the curtain. "I want them sent by motorbike courier within the hour to Downing Street."

"Yes, Prime Minister," she replied, and standing up to leave the bathroom shaded her eyes so she would not inadvertently glimpse the naked plumpness of the Prime Minister in the bath and so be put off her dinner, which had happened on more than one occasion before.

"When is the American President arriving, Miss Goodbody?"

"President Rooker arrives at Stanstead airport at eleven o'clock tomorrow morning and he'll be at Checkers in time for lunch."

"Good, the President's visit must be kept a secret from the Press."

"Yes, Prime Minister," replied Miss Goodbody with a grimace smelling cigar smoke. She hated the smell of cigars and wished she had the courage to tell him not to smoke while in her company.

"Will the First Lady be accompanying the President?"

"Yes, she'll be with him."

"Good, then I can sell her another oil-painting."

"I'm sure she'll know where to hang it in the White House," replied Miss Goodbody with a grimace. The Prime Minister had insisted on giving her a painting for her birthday and she had known exactly where to hang it --- on a toilet room door to inspire anyone wanting to sit for too long on the loo when faced with an appalling eye-sore of a painting.

Caroline Ann Rooker, America's first lady, beautiful, slim with spouting rose bud lips, brunette with long hair falling to her shoulders, graceful and charming, a woman who most men except for those who preferred other men, and some women to catch their breath in admiration on seeing her gorgeous hour-glass-figure. She was kind, thoughtful and generous, a woman easily sweet-talked, which was how she found herself made pregnant aged twenty after being impregnated three times in less than half-an-hour on the back seat of her boyfriend's car. The boyfriend the future United States President Robert R Rooker, then a budding young lawyer with an over active libido. They were married seven months later so the baby would be born safely within wedlock.

The First lady the only owner of a Sir Anthony Dingle's oil-painting who paid for it and not having it dumped on them as an unwanted gift. The painting purchased not as an investment but to appease the British Prime Minister's huge ego and make him more pliable to be America's friend in a crisis.

Freddy Frogmorton was questioned for three hours in the presence of his legal representative Sir Hilary Harker QC. The interview held at New Scotland Yard where he was charged with conspiracy to murder the British Prime Minister and was remanded in custody at Brixton prison. In the hope of leniency told the police everything he knew about the elusive Miss Marion Pringle, which was not very much. He said the attempt on the Prime Minister life was to be made 'very soon,' but could not give a date, location, nor the time.

Chief Inspector Edgar Briggs sat in his office at New Scotland Yard drinking coffee with Sergeant Jenny Hopper, Allan Hawes and doctor Windrush. They were discussing the taped interview with Freddy Frogmorton after listening to the copy sent by Superintendent Lionel Harper of Special Branch, who was now leading the investigation. "Sadly," began Briggs grimly, "we're still no closer to finding the killer's identity than we were before arresting Freddy Frogmorton. All we know is that the assassin might or might not be a man in drag who is posing as Miss Marion Pringle."

"Ah, yes, the mysterious Miss Marion Pringle," exclaimed super sleuth Allan Hawes thinking the killer was of equal genius to own brilliance, and how it was an intriguing intellectual mind game being played out between them, a game he was determined to win.

"Could Miss Pringle be a transvestite with a thrill for wearing frocks and silk undies?" asked doctor Windrush, excited by the thought. He had said nothing for five minutes and thought it was time his voice was heard. "I've read about such people in medical books. They're not gay you'll understand, no, but simply love putting on lipstick, high heels and a dress. Oh, but the joy and delightful thrill of feeling smooth cool silk of ladies undies next to the skin, it feels so. . ." The doctor's voice trailed off when he noticed the others were looking at him with shocked expressions on their faces, and realizing he had said too much, far too much. "So, I've heard," he added in a hardly audible voice.

"We don't think Miss Pringle is a transvestite, Doctor," said Jenny Hopper. "The dress is merely a disguise to fool us, simple and effective for covering a man's tracks and make us think he's a dowdy middle-aged woman."

"What a tricky blighter," exclaimed the doctor aghast. "Good thing my brilliant friend Hawes is on the case, don't you think?"

"I beg your pardon," retorted Briggs indignantly, jealous of Allan Hawes reputation as being a super sleuth, spread by Hawes himself and the doctor, and as far as he was concerned there was only one brilliant detective in the room and that was himself. He would be the one who arrested the elusive killer and not a third-rate private detective wearing a deerstalker hat.

Perkins sat with legs astride a bough high up an oak tree overlooking the rear garden of Checkers. The tree in a wood and less ten yards from the twelve-foot-high brick wall surrounding the house and grounds. Perkins had a clear view across the lawn up to the French windows. It was Saturday afternoon and he was surprised there were no security people to be seen.

The outer perimeter of surveillance was sealed tighter than a drum with armed police patrolling outside the wall, and gardens and house guarded by the SAS watching on monitors through hidden cameras dotted around the garden. This was to give the Prime Minister and his wife, lady Jane Dingle, a feeling they were alone. The wife wanting to relax in house and gardens without being watched by dozens of SAS lurking hidden among the shrubbery.

The three IRA men in green tracksuits, black baseball caps, and running shoes, had passed without hindrance through the SAS outer ring of surveillance surrounding Checkers hidden in the back of a dustcart on its way to empty the dustbins. The dustcart having been stopped at a police checkpoint at the main gate. But the police did not want to rake through the stinking rubbish and so a police dog handler had approached the dustcart with his dog. The dog sniffed at the dustcart and smelt the three IRA men hiding inside and barked to draw attention to them. But the police dog handler thinking the dog was barking because of the awful stench of the rubbish waved the dustcart on towards Checkers.

The dustcart had travelled less than a hundred yards from the checkpoint up the long driveway when a head popped up from the rubbish with rotting cabbage leaves draped over it. "All clear, lads," cried Commander Sean O'Leary gleefully. "We're through the check-point." Two other heads emerged from the rubbish beside him heads also covered with rotting cabbage leaves. "Ireland forever," exclaimed O'Leary proudly.

"Ireland forever," chorused his two companions.

"Have you remembered the batteries, Pat?" asked O'Leary.

"Of course, Sean. I won't be bitten twice by the same dog."

"Good, then we'll succeed this time," chuckled O'Leary. "There's going to be a big bang and then its goodbye to Sir Anthony Dingle."

"I've been thinking, Sean," said Dodds. "After the bomb's exploded how are we getting home to Ireland? I haven't heard you mention any escape plan. You do have an escape plan, haven't you?"

O'Leary did not answer. There was no escape plan and for him it was now a do and die mission for the glory of a united Ireland.

"We're going home after blowing up the Prime Minister, aren't we?" demanded Dodds looking worried.

"We're in God's hands," replied O'Leary making the sign of the cross on his chest. McCluster and Dodds looked uneasily at each other and said nothing. They too made the sign of the cross.

Prime Minister Sir Anthony Dingle dressed in blue boiler suit, white straw hat, smoking a cigar, strolled relaxing in the back garden of Checkers following the manicured lawn heading towards the red rose bushes. He picked a red rose and sniffed it, then smiling put it in a buttonhole of his boiler suit, and sighing wistfully, thought happily, "Ah, England's fair red rose and national flower. How fortunate for the British people having me as their beloved leader." He turned and sauntered back towards the house pondering on his forthcoming talk with the American President Robert R. Rooker and the possibility of selling his wife another oil painting.

Perkins was surprised to see the Prime Mister walking in the garden from his advantage up an oak tree, his prey so close and lone, vulnerable, unaware he was being watched by the assassin hired to kill him. The Prime Minister walked slowly and leisurely across the lawn and entered the house through the open French windows. Perkins settled down for the night with legs astride a branch with head and shoulders resting against the tree trunk, and closed his eyes. In the morning he would enter Checkers and find Sir Anthony Dingle and complete his assignment of murder.

Superintendent Lionel Harper of Special Branch stood in his office before a large wall map of Surrey, a balding squat middle-aged man of average height, narrow face with beady eyes, who walks with a slight limp, a car driven by a little old lady with poor eyesight had run over his left foot when he a young constable on zebra crossing duty. Sitting on chairs facing the wall map Chief Inspector Edgar Briggs, Sergeant Jenny Hopper, Allan Hawes and his trusted companion Doctor Albert Windrush. Harper pointed at Checkers at the map with a finger. "Checkers," he declared with a smile.

"Well done, old chap," exclaimed the doctor, impressed being a poor map reader the Superintendent found the location of Checkers so quickly on a huge map. Indeed, he once went on a cycling holiday as a young medical student to Italy to see Rome using by mistake a map of France, and got himself hopelessly lost and was repatriated with his bicycle back to England by the British Embassy in Paris.

"The Prime Minister's at Checkers," continued Harper, pausing and expecting a reaction of surprise to his disclosure. There was no reaction. "This is classified information and mustn't go outside this room." He strode over to the door and opened it and peered outside to make sure there was no one listening outside. Satisfied there was no one he closed the door and returned to stand in front of the wall map. "We mustn't take chances with security," he explained ruefully, "not with the Prime Minister's life at stake."

"Do you think the killer will try to kill the Prime Minister at Checkers?" asked Briggs.

"No, I don't. How could the killer possibly know the Prime Minister will be at Checkers this weekend? It's a code red secret. Not only will the Prime Minister be at Checkers but also the President of the United States with his lady wife.

"I don't agree, Superintendent," said Hawes, standing up. "We're dealing with a fiendishly clever killer, a killer who's unpredictable and we should expect the impossible to be possible."

"Meaning?"
"I think the killer will be at Checkers!"

Chapter Twenty-Three

The dustcart drove slowly up the long driveway towards the big country house of Checkers. Hidden in the back under piles of stinking rubbish, disheveled and filthy, were the three-man IRA bombing team preparing to abandon the dustcart. "Right, lads," called Commander Sean O'Leary brightly, "get ready to leap over the tailboard when the dustcart comes to a halt. Keep your heads down and run to the nearest cover."

"Won't we be seen jumping off the back of the dustcart?" asked McCluster. "There'll be security men everywhere."

"They won't bother with a dustcart that's already been stopped by the police at the main gate."

"I hope you're right, Sean."

The dustcart reached the house and drove around to the back and stopped beside a dozen dustbins outside the kitchen door. The IRA men quickly clambered over the dustcart tailboard and dropped to the ground and sprinted across to the dustbins, and crouched down out of sight behind them. "Won't the dustmen come to empty the bins?" asked Dobbs nervously.

"You're right, Pat," replied O'Leary, "that's good thinking. Now be quick lads, and let's get out of here before they come." But it was too late and four dustmen had climbed out of the dustcart's cab and were walking towards the dustbins to empty them.

"That's torn it," muttered Dobbs, "here they come."

"Follow my lead," cried O'Leary, and leaping to his feet he confronted the dustmen with a pistol in hand. The dustmen, terrified and ashen-faced, raised their hands above their heads.

"Don't shoot," pleaded a squat short dustman. "We're only emptying the bins." The other two Irishmen sprang up to confront the dustmen holding pistols.

"We're SAS," declared O'Leary putting on a posh English accent, "and we're checking the dustbins for explosives. I'm Captain Cyril Masters. Put down your hands you've nothing to fear." The dustmen lowered their hands. "These bins have now been checked," added O'Leary with a cheery smile, "and are guaranteed to be free of any explosive
device. You can safely empty them without fear of being blown-up."

"Thank you, Captain," said the squat short dustman, looking much relieved and thinking how wonderful the SAS were in action.

"Good show," replied O'Leary putting away his pistol, "we'll let you gentlemen get on with emptying the dustbins. Don't say a word about seeing us. We don't want to alarm the staff here who would panic if they knew there might be explosive devises hidden at Checkers."

"Not a word," replied the squat short dustman.

"Keep up the good work," replied O'Leary and he ran to the nearest door, a green door, opened it and stepped quickly over the threshold and promptly fell twelve feet into the inky darkness of a coal cellar. The two other IRA men following closely on his heels suffering the same fate landing on top of their hapless commander. The wooden stairs leading into the cellar had been removed because of woodworm to be replaced at the end of the month. The last IRA man to pass through the door pulled it shut behind him shutting off the only source of light. The dustmen heard muffled groans as the Irishmen landed followed by silence.

"Amazing those SAS blokes aren't they," said the squat dustman in an awed tone of voice, "appearing and disappearing as if by magic."

"That's because they're highly trained," replied a tall dustman.

"Yes," agreed the squat short dustman, "and heroes to a man and the best in the world." The four dustmen feeling privileged and patriotic having witnessed the elite SAS in action, and smiling happily emptied the bins into the back of the dustcart then climbed into the driver's cab and drove away down the driveway.

Meanwhile, down in the inky darkness of the coal cellar O'Leary was speaking in a whisper to his companions trying to make contact with them in the inky darkness, "Are you alright, lads?" There was no response. "Lads," he whispered slightly louder than before, "are you there? Speak to me?"

"Of course, we're here, Sean," retorted McCluster angrily. "Where else would we be?"

"When I took the oath to follow you back in Belfast, Sean," added Dodds gloomily, "I never thought it meant down a coal cellar!"

"How do you know it's a coal cellar?" asked McCluster indignantly. "It's too dark to see."

"Because I'm sitting on lumps of coal."

"What do we do now, Sean?" asked McCluster.

"We'll carry on regardless for Ireland," replied O'Leary. "What do you say, lads?" There was an ominous silence. "Come now, this isn't the time to sulk. I'm sorry for leading you down a coal cellar. Will you forgive me?"

"Yes," replied his companions in unison half-heartedly knowing Father Barry would expect forgiveness from them.

"Try and look on the bright side," continued O'Leary trying to boost his companions' morale, "at least we're alive and . . ."

"Stuck down a coal cellar," interrupted Dodds gloomily.

"Yes, and we're staying here until we're ready to enter the house and place our bomb," replied O'Leary. "There's no rush now. Just think what we've achieved so far? We're under the same roof as the British Prime Minister."

"Aren't you forgetting the SAS, Sean?" asked Dodds despondently. "They'll be buzzing about the house like flies around a turd. We're stuck down a cellar with nowhere to go."

"You've got the bomb haven't you, Pat?" asked O'Leary.

"Sure, I have."

"And it's operational?"

"No, Sean, it isn't operational."

"No? Why not?"

"Because it needs two wires attached to the live and neutral connections on the detonator. There's more than enough syntax to blow up a fair-sized room. I wasn't going to carry a primed and armed bomb around in my trouser pocket."

"Then make it operational."

"Can't do it."

"Why not?"

"It's too dark to see."

"Haven't you got a torch?"

"No. I didn't think that we'd end-up down a coal cellar."

"Matches?"

"No."

"Lighter? "

"I don't smoke, Sean, as well you know."

"Alright, then let's consider our situation shall we? We're down a coal cellar with a bomb that we can't make operational because we can't see to arm it. Tell me, Pat, did you remember the batteries for the bomb detonator?"

"They're in the detonator."

"Where's the detonator?"

"I lost it, Sean, it fell from my pocket as I leapt from the dustcart." There was the sound of fists being slammed into flesh in the darkness as O'Leary struck out wildly at Dodds. McCluster sitting between them took all the punches and shouted desperately, "Stop, Sean, it's me Roy you're hitting not Pat."

"Where is he?" cried O'Leary. "I'll malaise him this time for sure."

Perkins, hidden up an oak tree, watched the two-man armed police patrol passing below him. The officers were regular as clockwork appearing every thirty-eight minutes patrolling the wall surrounding Checkers.

Meanwhile, in a room in Checkers a meeting of senior security staff was being held. "Not even a bird can enter the perimeter without us knowing about it," proclaimed Colonel Derek Slattery proudly, the officer commanding the SAS guarding the British Prime Minister. "We've got a ring of steel a mile in radius surrounding Checkers." But he did not know as he was speaking Perkins was entering the garden to hunt down his prey.

Perkins moved along a branch reaching over the wall crawling on his belly, and dropped down onto a flowerbed rolling sideways as he landed using the skill he learnt in the parachute regiment. Getting to his feet he ran for cover to an apple tree and climbed out of sight among the foliage, and feeling hungry helped himself to some apples.

The coal lorry backed slowly making warning tooting sounds towards an open manhole at the rear of Checkers leading down to the coal cellar below. Two SAS men in battle fatigues armed with sub-machine guns stood outside the kitchen door watching the lorry. The driver's mate, Henry Broadbent, a tall leathery faced muscular man, shouted to the driver, "Keep coming, Ken, keep coming. That's it, bit move to the left . . . stop." The lorry crunched to a stop and stepping forward he pulled a metal chute on the back of the lorry over the open manhole. "Right, Ken," he cried, "let it go." The driver pulled a red lever in his cab and three tons of best Welsh coal tumbled down the chute into the cellar with thunderous roar that muffled the screams of the three IRA men below as they were engulfed by the black avalanche.

The driver, Ken Duffy, a fat man with blubbery lips and a weak chin, got out of the cab to help Henry Broadbent lift the heavy manhole cover back into place with lifting tongs. They were about to lower the manhole cover into position when they heard a squeaky cry coming from the coal cellar depths below. "What's that?" asked Henry Broadbent nervously peering down into the inky darkness of the cellar. The cry was a muffled "Ireland forever," gasped by Sean O'Leary as he struggled to stop himself from being buried alive.

"Only a rat," said Ken Duffy, "filthy little beggars."

"Yes, they make my flesh creep," agreed Henry Broadbent with a shudder. The two men lowered the manhole cover into position and drove away.

Perkins climbed down the apple tree to explore the garden and crossed a large lawn leading to an orchard of fruit trees, apple, plum and cherry, and a goldfish pond with waterlilies and reeds. Goldfish swam in the crystal-clear water. Perkins knelt and using both hands as a cup drank some water which tasted slightly bitter but was refreshing. He continued to walk around the edge of the pond until he came to a large greenhouse and entering the greenhouse was hoping to find something to eat, but it was full of flowers in flowerpots, and disappointed he retraced his steps towards the orchard. "Who are you?" called out a voice from behind him and turning he saw the British Prime Minister Sir Anthony Dingle dressed in an artist's white smock smudged with various colours of oil paint, in baggy shorts reaching below the knees, and open toed sandals without socks, on his head a white fedora hat.

Perkins thought quickly knowing Checkers with its vast garden would employ several gardeners. "I'm the new gardener," he said touching his forelock humbly.

The Prime Minister smiled warmly thinking everyone he met over the age of eighteen was a potential voter, and it never did any harm to do a little canvassing. "What's your name?"

"Rupert Quemby."

"Well, Rupert, I hope that I can rely on your vote for the next election?"

"But of course, I've always voted for you."

"Good man, that's what I like to hear a man who's loyal to his convictions and remains steadfast in his politics. Tell me, how do you find your work here?"

"Hard but satisfying,"
"What work are you doing now?"
"Rhubarb."
"Ah, yes, rhubarb, there's nothing like rhubarb crumble with custard. Couldn't get enough when I was a boy. Nanny said it was a most wonderful purgative for a boy and would keep him regular." The Prime Minister held out his hand for Perkins to shake. "It was nice talking to you, Rupert," he said. Perkins took the hand and shook it. "I suppose," continued the great man with a smile, "that with you chatting to me like this it's got to be an experience that you'll be telling your grandchildren with pride?"

"I haven't got any grandchildren."

"I meant when you do have grandchildren that you spoke to me in the garden of Checkers about rhubarb."

Perkins forced a smile and nodded amazed at the conceit of the man. "Yes, I'll be doing that of course," he lied.

"Well, I must get back to my oil painting," said the Prime Minister as he began walking away, "I want to get the roses onto canvas before the light fades. Goodbye, Rupert."

"Goodbye." Perkins watched the portly figure walking away and thought he that he might never have a better opportunity to be alone with the Prime Minister to kill him. One bash on the head with a rock with body found floating in the goldfish pond and it would look like an accident the same as it had when he murdered sister Tulip at the convent of the Sister of Mercy. It would be thought Sir Antony Dingle had been watching the goldfish, slipped and hit his head and drowned. Perkins picked up a rock the size of a house brick and followed him.

The Prime Minister sat down before his easel on a stool under a sun umbrella, picked up his pallet of paints and dabbed away with a brush at the canvas. Perkins crept up behind him with the rock held above his head in both hands ready to strike. The Prime Minister was relaxed and happy. Perkins paused startled to see the painting, a blurred mess of assorted colours unrecognizable as the garden landscape it was supposed to be. The Prime Minister was painting the south view of the house from the lawn down to the goldfish pond with none of the distinctive features visible and looking more like the handiwork of a constipated chimpanzee.

Perkins took a step forward to bring the rock smashing down on the Prime Minister's head. "Hi, there, Sir Anthony," called a voice with an American accent. Perkins promptly dropped the rock and glanced in the direction of the voice. American President Robert R. Rooker with two Secret Service agents were striding towards the Prime Minister across the lawn. The secret service agents in black suits and wearing dark glasses. The President in a three-piece grey suit, white shirt with blue bow tie, smiling broadly showing his gleaming white teeth. The British Prime waved a paintbrush in greeting. "Ah, Mister President," he called out brightly, "what a delight and pleasure to see you."

"Still painting I see, Sir Anthony," chuckled the President, standing beside the Prime Minister and looking at the painting and wondering what it was supposed to be and then deciding it was either a self-portrait of Sir Anthony Dingle or a bowl of decaying fruit. The Secret Service agents moved to stand on either side of the President protecting him with right hands inside jackets gripping revolver butts, each man ready to draw and fire. The proud motto of the American Secret Service agents guarding the President, "I'll take one for the Man." This was a bullet and not reference to an activity that was much favoured by men in ancient Greece of a certain sexual persuasion.

"Perhaps you'd like to have the painting when it's finished for the Oval office, Mister President?" beamed the Prime Minister with a twinkle in his eye hoping for a quick sale.

The smile faded from the President's face and for a moment he looked uneasy and lost for words. "We'll talk about it later, Sir Anthony."

"As you wish, Mister President." It was then the Prime Minister saw Perkins standing behind him looking sheepish and hoping to go unnoticed. "Ah, Rupert the gardener. Now, this has got to be another great moment for you to tell your grandchildren you witnessed both President Rooker and myself talking in the garden of Checkers? History in the making wouldn't you say?"

"Yes, history in the making," agreed Perkins, thinking it was time he made himself scarce before the secret service agents took an interest in him.

"Well, what is it, Rupert?" asked the Prime Minister with a smile.

"What is what, Sir?"

"Why have you followed me?"

Perkins thought quickly. "Rhubarb, Sir," he said, "I was wondering if you'd like me to pick some rhubarb for you to have a rhubarb crumble dessert at dinner tonight?"

"Oh, but how thoughtful of you. Yes, I'd love having a rhubarb crumble. See to it there's a good fellow. Give the rhubarb to the chef and say it's for my dessert tonight."

"I'll see to it right away." Perkins touched his forelock humbly and turned and walked quickly away across the lawn towards the greenhouse.

"Salt of the earth that fellow," said the Prime Minister proudly, "and he's not just my gardener but also a voter who supports me. I wonder if any of your gardeners at the White House, Mister President, would think of going out their way to specially pick rhubarb for you to have a rhubarb crumble?"

"None of them would," replied the President. "I don't like rhubarb."

Chapter Twenty-Four

Superintendent Lionel Harper of Special Branch with four companions departed in haste from London in a police car with siren blaring and lights flashing heading for Checkers. The four companions Chief Inspector Edgar Briggs, Sergeant Jenny Hopper, and super sleuth Allan Hawes with his trusted companion doctor Windrush. Superintendent Harper arranged the trip but he did not expect to find the assassin at Checkers but felt the possibility of doing so should not be overlooked with the Prime Minister's life at stake. "Always cover your back," was his policy for any crisis so he would not be blamed if things went wrong.

"Do you think we'll find the killer at Checkers, Hawes?" asked the doctor, who had his revolver with him and hoped he would not have to use it. He was a bad shot at the best of times and only carried the gun to impress the super sleuth.

"No doubt about it," replied Hawes grimly. "The game's a foot, my dear Doctor, and I think we'll find the mysterious Miss Marion Pringle and the killer are the very same person."

"My God," gasped the doctor shocked, "the same person!"

"Yes, we know the killer's a master of disguise," continued Hawes glibly, "who could be disguised as anybody at Checkers, male or female, and we're dealing with a highly intelligent, devious and cunning master criminal."

"Aha, a genius in your own league, Hawes," responded the doctor brightly.

Hawes smiled and nodded enjoying the praise.

"The killer doesn't know the net's closing in," added Briggs not wanting to be left out of the conversation. "Master of disguise the killer might be but it'll be my experienced copper's nose that'll catch the villain in the end. My nose has never let me down. I can sniff out a master criminal from fifty yards away."

"How long before we reach Checkers?" asked Jenny Hopper convinced there was no chance of them finding the would-be killer at Checkers, not with the Prime Minister so well guarded and only a fool would try to kill him there and Miss Pringle certainly was no fool."

"About two hours," replied Harper glancing at his wristwatch, "as long as we don't run into traffic jams and roadworks or are held up at red lights."

The three IRA men, miserable and despondent, sat in the inky darkness of the coal cellar, battered, bruised, with clothes, faces and hands blackened with coal dust. "Are you all safe? No one injured?" called out Commander Sean O'Leary, worried he might be the sole survivor from the avalanche of falling coal.
"I'm here," replied Dobbs, voice faint.
"Me, too," added McCluster, "I'm here too."
"Good," replied the O'Leary, relieved to hear their voices. "Do you know what this means, lads? It means we're operational again and back in business." The other two Irishmen sighed audibly having hoped the Commander would now admit defeat and take them back home to Ireland. "We can still get the British Prime Minister," continued O'Leary. "All we need is a good plan."
"How about a plan for getting us out of here?" asked Dodds glumly, feeling an increasing need to go to the toilet.
"You've still got the bomb, Pat?" asked O'Leary fearing it was lost under the heap of coal.
"Yes, Sean."
"Good man, then we're in business."
"Yes, but first we have to get out of here," replied Dodds, the urge to pee so overpowering he crossed his legs. "Some of us are more desperate than others to do so."
"Right, then," said O'Leary, "let's find a way out of here and explode our bomb. Are you with me?"
"Yes," chorused his two companions but without much enthusiasm. The mission so far had been one disaster after another and they were homesick for Ireland.
"Let me hear it, lads?" cried O'Leary with gusto, hoping to brighten his companions sagging spirits and inspire their patriotic feelings for Ireland. "Ireland forever," he cried with tears of pride running down his cheeks thinking the lads would follow him into Hell and back if he asked them.
"Ireland forever," chorused his companions half-heartily reluctant to follow him anywhere after he had led them down a coal cellar.

Perkins searched the lower garden looking for the rhubarb patch. He would use the rhubarb as his reason for entering the house by way of the kitchen, thinking if stopped and questioned his story of getting rhubarb for the Prime Minister dessert would be confirmed by the Prime Minister himself. He found the rhubarb patch and picked a dozen sticks and holding them cradled in his arm proceeded to the house. There was a small cobbled courtyard on the left of the house leading into the kitchen area from where there wafted the smell of freshly baked bread. He saw a green door near some dustbins and wondered what lay behind it? Perhaps an outside cold larder containing fresh bread or cooked meat? He was hungry and going to the door, opened it and peered inside. It was inky black and he could not see a thing. "Hello, up there," called a voice from the darkness below him speaking in a posh English accent. It was the IRA Commander Sean O'Leary disguising his Irish accent.

"Hello, down there," replied Perkins nervously, ready to turn and run.

"Who are you?" asked the voice from the darkness.

"Rupert Quemby," replied Perkins.

"SAS?" asked O'Leary, prepared to die for Ireland thinking the SAS had arrived at the cellar door and were about to demand his surrender. He would never be taken alive and eased back the safety catch on his revolver and took aim at the shaft of sunlight coming through the doorway illuminating the shadowy figure of Perkins.

"I'm a gardener," replied Perkins.

"Gardener?"

"Yes, and I've got sticks of rhubarb for the chef. Who are you?"

There was a momentarily hesitation before O'Leary replied. "I'm SAS. There are three of us down here."

"What are you doing down there?"

"Checking for explosive devices. I'm captain Cyril Masters."

The word SAS sent chills through Perkins. "I must be going," he said hastily, "the chef's waiting for the rhubarb."

"Before you go, Rupert," called out O'Leary. "It's Rupert, isn't it?"

"Yes."

"Good man. I don't suppose you've got a ladder handy? We're trapped down here. My sergeant took away the ladder when he went back to barracks to fetch our survival rations. That was three hours ago. Something must have happened to delay him."

"Sorry, no."

"Could you be a good chap and find a ladder for me?"

"Alright," agreed Perkins reluctantly thinking he needed to keep the SAS men trapped down the cellar.

"Be quick, there's a good chap."

"I won't be long." Perkins hurried away closing the door behind him, and moments later he was entering the nearby kitchen door carrying the rhubarb. He walked past a range of ovens on which pots and pans steamed and bubbling away. Men and women looking harassed and anxious wearing white overalls were busily preparing food and cooking. Perkins put the rhubarb on a table next to some cauliflowers and cabbages.

"What are you doing?" demanded a shrill squeaky voice with a French accent from behind him. Perkins turned and saw a diminutive little man with neat trimmed black moustache, in white jacket, candy and stripped trousers, with a tall chef's hat on his head giving him a bizarre look. He was red faced and looked angry.

"I've bought the rhubarb."

"Rhubarb? What rhubarb? I didn't ask for rhubarb? Why do you bring me rhubarb?"

"The Prime Minister wants to rhubarb crumble for dessert tonight."

"Oh, does he? Well, I'm a gourmet chef, best in all of France if not the world, and I came to this cold miserable land of fish and chips and rain, lots of rain, to cook for the British Prime Minster, and what does he want? Not gourmet dishes of world excellence but rhubarb crumble any simpleton can make from a cheap nasty cook book."

"Then you're not making the Prime Minister his rhubarb crumble?"

"I'm Claude Monte renowned chef of brilliance who can create any gourmet dish you care to mention." The chef's voice was steadily becoming more hysterical as he spoke, "and now, I'm expected to waste my culinary brilliance making a rhubarb crumble. The Prime Minister will be asking next for that dreadful sausage and mash or even worse the appalling fish and chips. I despair of such food that's fit only for people without refined taste buds."

"I'm sorry. Please don't upset yourself."

"I'll make the rhubarb crumple but I'm most unhappy about doing it. Are you the vegetable chef I'm expecting from the London Best Cooks Agency?"

"No, I'm Rupert Quemby, the new gardener."

"What? You're a gardener? How dare you. I won't allow a gardener in my kitchen," screamed the chef waving his arms wildly above his head as if beating off a persistent fly, "with dirty hands and muddy boots. Get out of my kitchen." Perkins hurried away heading for the nearest door and opening the door he glanced back over his shoulder. The little French chef was no longer standing at the table with the rhubarb but had moved on to check on the food being prepared and cooked by his harassed looking assistants.

Perkins opened the door and stepped out into a corridor with doors on either side, and followed the corridor until he came to a domed hallway with a glass chandelier and a red carpeted staircase with marble banisters. Unkempt in disheveled grubby clothes and needing a shave he wanted to find a bathroom to clean himself up and change his appearance. Hearing voices he pressed himself into an alcove behind a statue of the Duke of Wellington as two maids hurried passed chatting without seeing him. He dashed up the stairway to the first landing and entered the first bedroom door he came to and inside found a double bed. There was another door leading to a pale blue tiled bathroom with a toilet, bidet, shower and bath.

In the bathroom cabinet he found a razor with a shaving brush and stick of shaving soap, and locking the bathroom door he stripped off his clothes and put them in a linen basket, filled the bath with hot water and climbed in. He washed himself with a soapy sponge, rinsed off the soap, then stepping from the bath dried himself with a white bath towel. Using the mirror on the bathroom cabinet to shave, then combed his hair. "What I need are clothes that won't rouse suspicion as I move about the house," he thought, as he wrapped the towel around his waist and going into the bedroom he searched a chest of drawers and a wardrobe, and in the chest of drawers found underwear with a white shirt, and in the wardrobe a choice of three expensively tailored suits with ties to match, and three pairs of shoes. He chose a charcoal three-piece suit with a pale blue tie and black shoes. The man to whom the clothing belonged was shorter and thinner than Perkins but they fitted him well enough to pass off at glance as being a fairly good fit. When he was dressed he studied his appearance in a full-length mirror in the bedroom and was satisfied with what he saw, a gentleman of wealth and good taste. Opening the door, he stepped briskly out onto the landing and proceeded at a leisurely pace up the stairway to the next floor to hunt down his prey Sir Antony Dingle.

President Robert R. Rooker was in his bedroom with his wife, America's first lady, the gorgeous willowy Caroline. The Rookers were changing for dinner. "I hope the Prime Minister won't try to sell you another of his horrendous paintings," said the President glibly as he stood behind his wife looking over her shoulder at the dressing table mirror while adjusting his black bow-tie. She was applying her lipstick.

She smiled sweetly looking at his reflection in the mirror. "You know me, Robbie, I'm a real softie when it comes to Sir Anthony. I like the guy and he makes me laugh and I find him charming and witty."

"Sure, I like the guy too, honey, but we don't want another of his paintings hanging in the White House. That painting you brought from him frightened the cat and it ran away and hasn't been seen since. If only your mother would react in the same way I'd fill the White House with his paintings."

"Don't be naughty, Robbie. Mother loves you."

"Only because I'm the President."

"No, she really loves you but doesn't like your politics."

"I know, honey, I was only teasing."

"Well, don't, I don't like it."

"Promise me, Caroline, you won't weaken and buy another painting from Sir Antony?"

"But he's such a good persuader, Robbie, the same as you, and like you he can charm the birds off the trees."

"If you say so, honey."

"The paintings aren't so bad really. I've seen worse but can't remember where or when."

"Whenever Sir Anthony visits the White House we have to hang his painting on a prominent wall to appease his ego and then take it down when he leaves."

"Never mind, Robbie, surely that's not too high a price to pay for his friendship and support. America needs friends especially the Brits."

"I'm having my talk with Sir Anthony after dinner about America invading the island of Gela north of Cuba and setting up a hotdog concession there. I hope he'll support me with his vote with NATO."

"I'm sure Sir Anthony will support you."

"Yeah, but he'll want something in return."
"That's politics, Robbie."
"And he's damn good at it. Better than me I sometimes think."
"What necklace should I wear? Pearls or diamonds?"
"Diamonds, darling, they sparkle like your eyes."
She laughed. "Diamonds are a girl's best friend."
The President went over to a wardrobe and opened the door. Inside stood a grim-faced secret service agent in a black suit wearing dark glasses, ready to take one for the man, a bullet not an activity much favoured by men in ancient Greece of a certain sexual persuasion. The President reached into the wardrobe and lifted out a dinner jacket on a coat hanger. The secret service man saluted. "Gee, Caroline," muttered the President proudly, saluting the man, "we've got the best security men in the world, haven't we?" He closed the wardrobe door.

Prime Minister Sir Anthony Dingle sat at a desk having just finished working on the eighth draft of his speech for Tuesday in the House of Commons making final corrections. He smoked a cigar and held a glass of brandy. The door opened and his secretary Constance Goodbody entered. "I'd like you to take dictation, Miss Goodbody," said the Prime Minister, "I want to do more work on my memoirs before my talk with President Rooker."
"Yes, Prime Minister," replied Miss Goodbody wearily. She was tired and hungry having typed up draft after draft of the Prime Minister's speech since arriving at Checkers without a break or refreshment.
It must be hard keeping up with an old workhorse like me, Miss Goodbody, but as you know how I thrive on work and the more work the better for me. I seem to have hardly a moment these days to relax because I'm a man of historical destiny with great things to achieve on the world stage."
"Yes, a man of historical destiny," greed Miss Goodbody tongue in cheek knowing it was all in his delusional head. "You work too hard," she lied to appease his ego, "and you're an icon for the world." Flattery always delighted and pleased him.
"Tell Jackson to run my bath, Miss Goodbody, "it'll help me relax." Jackson, his personal valet, an elderly Scotsman who had been with him fourteen years, and wore a kilt even in the chilliest of weather.

"It must be nice to relax, Prime Minister."

"Yes, Miss Goodbody, I know, but Britain expects me to work tirelessly, and I do my duty without complaint. After you've told Jackson to run my bath I want you to type up my speech with the corrections that I've just made. I want the speech polished so it'll stir and inspire the hearts of voters and win their support for me. There's an election in the New Year and I want another five years in office."

"I need to take a short break so can I . . ."

"My bath, Miss Goodbody, tell Jackson to run it," interrupted the Prime Minister impatiently.

"Yes, Prime Minister."

The three IRA men trapped down a coal cellar were still waiting half-an-hour later for gardener Rupert Quemby to return with a ladder. Finally, Commander Sean O'Leary with patience gone, decided they must escape without a ladder. They would form a human ladder with O'Leary standing at the bottom supporting his two companions, Dodds standing on his shoulders, McCluster, the most agile of the three, to clamber up his two companions like a monkey up a tree. McCluster then to haul himself clear of the cellar and then help his friends out. It took five attempts before Dodds managed to balance himself perilously on O'Leary's shoulders, and seven more attempts before the agile McCluster hauled himself clear of the coal cellar. He reached down to pull Dodds up after him but O'Leary could not reach the helping hand stretched down to him and ordered Dodds and McCluster to remove their trousers and belts and tie them together and make a rope. O'Leary was then hauled out of the coal cellar. "Well, done, lads," he exclaimed enthusiastically. "I'm proud of you. Now put your trousers back on. We don't want the lads back in Belfast to hear that we were together in a dark cellar without our trousers on. They might reach the wrong conclusion about what we were doing in the dark."

"Are we going home now, Sean?" asked Dodds hopefully who had enough of the mission and was homesick for family and friends. "Home?" gasped the shocked O'Leary thinking of the shame and disgrace of returning home and reporting the mission a failure. No, that would never do. It was for him now a 'do and die' mission. There would be a successful bombing with the British Prime Minister blown-up whatever the cost was to himself and to his two companions. It was for him now a death and glory mission for the

IRA team.

"We're done our best, Sean," said McCluster glumly, "we can't do more. I say that we call it a day and go back home to Belfast."

"Done our best?" echoed O'Leary indignantly. "Not yet, and we're not going home until we've completed our mission."

"Then we're done for," muttered McCluster gloomily, and decided that never again would he volunteer for an IRA mission. He might end up with Sean O'Leary as his team commander again.

"What did you say, Roy?" demanded O'Leary angrily.

"I said Ireland forever."

"Good man, that's what I want to hear from a patriotic Irishman."

"What are we going to do now?" asked Dodds.

"We've got a bomb," replied O'Leary, "and now we're going to use it."

"Yes, we've got a bomb but no detonator, Sean," said McCluster, "It fell out of my pocket when I leapt from the back of the dustcart and hide behind the dustbins."

"Then we'll search around the dustbins until we find the detonator."

Jonathan Jackson, personal valet of Sir Anthony Dingle, a tall slender beanpole of a man in valet's black jacket and black bow-tie, and a kilt with sporran, had run the Prime Minister's bath. He poured in half-a-bottle of rose scented bubble bath. The Prime Minister liked to smell nice. Jackson, grey haired and balding, with a long-pointed nose and thin spiderly legs. He removed his jacket and rolled up his right shirtsleeve to test the water temperature with his right elbow. It was slightly too hot for Sir Anthony Dingle and he turned on the cold tap allowing water to flow for thirty seconds. Sir Anthony Dingle was fussy about his bath water temperature having as a young student at University got into a bath after a drinking binge with water too hot and had scalded his pride and joy. Satisfied with the water temperature Jackson rolled down his sleeve and put on his jacket. "Bath's ready for you, Sir," he called out in a servile tone of voice.

Prime Minister Sir Anthony Dingle naked as the day he was born strutted into the bathroom smoking a cigar. "Thank you, Jackson," he said briskly as he stepped into the bath and sat down with a splash. "Put a decanter of whiskey on the stool beside the bath so I can help myself?"

"Yes, Sir," replied the valet, and put a silver tray with a decanter three quarters full of whiskey with an empty glass on the stool. There was no jug of water because Sir Anthony liked his whiskey neat. "Will there be anything else, Sir?"

"Yes, there's a Party-Political talk given by the Opposition Leader Clive Hurst on the radio following the concert on the Home Service. Bring a radio so I can hear what the old fool has to say. It'll amuse me to hear what he has to say to the British people to try and win their votes."

"Yes, Sir," replied Jackson, bowing his head slightly. He turned and left the bathroom and returned carrying a small white plastic radio which he positioned above the hot and cold taps of the bath. There was a black power cable with a three-point plug. "Where shall I plug it in?"

"Above the bathroom cabinet you'll see a socket where I plug-in my electric razor." Jackson plugged in the radio and tuned the radio to the home service. Classical music was playing "Ah, how delightful," sighed the Prime Minister wistfully closing his eyes and humming along with the music.

"Shall I pour you a whiskey, Sir?"

"What a splendid idea. Make it a double."

Jackson poured whiskey from the decanter into the glass. "Is there anything else, Sir? "

"Come back in an hour and switch off the radio."

"Yes, Sir. "

"Thank you. You may go."

Jackson left the bathroom and closed the door behind him.

The little French chef, Claude Monte, stressed and overexcited, rushed about the kitchen urging on his cooks as they prepared his gourmet meal for the Prime Minister. Food cooked by him had to be a work of art with every dish a masterpiece. The little chef hurried from cook-to-cook tasting pots and pans scolding some cooks while encouraging others as he went. "Good, good," he would cry, "just a little more seasoning," or angrily wagging a finger scolding and scream, "This s foul. Throw it away and start again."

The minutes ticked away and the main dish had to be ready to serve at table in less than two hours. Claude Monte worked hard creating his culinary masterpiece of roast pheasant stuffed inside a duck, with an assortment of nuts, red onions, blue berries and sultanas, a dish that was a great favourite with America's First lady who particularly liked nuts and especially her husband's nuts. The little French chef was peering at a roasting duck through a glass panel on the door of an oven when the three IRA men burst into the kitchen waving pistols. The Irishmen's clothes, faces and hands covered in coal dust. "Hands up," cried Commander Sean O'Leary.

The kitchen staff with exception of the little French chef raised their hands. "What's the meaning of this?" demanded the chef furiously, eyes bulging from sockets like organ stops.

"We're IRA," declared O'Leary as he advanced towards the chef pointing his gun at him.

"I don't care if you're RAC," stormed the chef worried the cooking would spoil if it was not constantly being attended to. "This is my kitchen and nobody can enter without my permission. I've a dinner to prepare for the Prime Minster and the President of the United States of America."

Dodds stepped forward and waved his gun under his nose. "This gives us permission," he exclaimed grimly.

The chef was unabashed. There was nothing more important for him than saving the gourmet dinner and he was not going to be cowered. "I order you to leave my kitchen. I won't allow strangers in my cooking area."

"Be quiet," retorted O'Leary.

"We must be quick, Sean," said McCluster, worried the SAS might appear at any moment and come bursting through the kitchen doors firing a hail of bullets.

"We've time enough," replied O'Leary. "Gather the cooks and herd them to the far end of the kitchen." The cooks with the little French chef complaining bitterly were marched at gunpoint and made to stand facing a wall with hands raised. "Have you made the bomb operational, Pat?" asked O'Leary.

"I have, Sean, so I have."

"Good man, and the detonator's set to go off?"

"In fourteen minutes."

"Hide the bomb where it'll be difficult to find. We don't want it rendered harmless." Dodds walked down the line of ovens looking for somewhere to hide the bomb and was about to drop the bomb into a saucepan of tomato soup simmering on a hotplate, when he remembered liquid would ruin the electrical connections of the timer and detonator. What he needed was somewhere dry to hide the bomb. He saw an oven-ready turkey laid on a table waiting to be stuffed with sage and onion stuffing, and placed the bomb inside the turkey and used handfuls of stuffing to plug it in, then put the turkey into an oven at electric setting mark 180.

Dodds returned to O'Leary, standing guard over the cooks, and whispered in his ear where he had placed the bomb. O'Leary nodded, smiled, and said, "That's good thinking, Pat, it's the last place that the SAS will think of looking for a bomb that's been stuffed up a turkey's bum."

"What about my gourmet dinner. It's being ruined?" wailed the little French chef close to tears as he turned to confront McCluster. Please, let me save it."

"The dinner's the least of your worries."

"But I've spent hours preparing it."

"Your dinner's blown or soon will be," replied McCluster. The chef made no reply and turned his face the wall and sobbed.

"Right, lads," called out O'Leary, "time to go."

"What about us?" called out a woman cook hysterically, eyes wide with terror.

"Leave or you'll be blown-up with the bomb," replied O'Leary curtly. The cooks in wild panic rushed towards the door followed by the sobbing French chef with the IRA men running after them.

Chapter Twenty-five

Perkins went from bedroom to bedroom looking for Sir Anthony Dingle, knocking on doors, speaking with an American accent to anyone who answered the door saying he was a secret service agent looking for the Prime Minister with an urgent message from President Rooker. But nobody knew the whereabouts of Sir Antony Dingle and he had reached the third floor after visiting all the bedrooms on the first and second floors when he met the Prime Minister's personal valet Jonathan Jackson. The valet coming out of a bedroom. "Excuse me, Sir," called out Perkins, "I'm looking for the Prime Minister. Have you seen him?"

"Indeed, I have," replied Jackson brightly. "Might I enquire why you want him?"

"President Rooker has sent me with an urgent message for him."

"Can I pass the message on for you. I'm the Prime Minister's personal valet."

"No, the message for the Prime Minister's ears only."

"Who are you?"

"Secret service agent, Eric Gatwood."

"Well, agent Gatwood, you'll find the Prime Minister having a bath. The bathroom adjoins the bedroom behind me. You can go in and speak to him."

"Thank you."

Jackson stepped aside and opened the bedroom door for Perkins to enter. "Try not to be too long, agent Gatwood, the Prime Minister's trying to relax and rest before dinner. He needs all the peace and quiet he can get."

"I won't disturb him for longer than is necessary."

"Thank you, agent Gatwood."

Perkins entered the bedroom and Jackson closed the door behind him and hurried away down the stairway. There was the sound of a radio coming from the bathroom as Perkins moved silently forward on tiptoe towards the bathroom.

Meanwhile, terrified cooks followed by the sobbing French chef rushed out through the kitchen door into the courtyard. "There's a bomb," was their frenzied cry as they milled about in a wild panic. The three IRA men had run around the side of the house and on down the long gravel driveway in an effort to get as far away as possible before the bomb went off.

"What about my gourmet dinner?" wailed the French chef hysterically and overwhelmed at the prospect of losing his masterpiece to an IRA bomb.

"What bomb?" demanded an SAS man in army fatigues with corporal strips on the sleeves holding a sub-machine gun who had popped up from behind a dustbin.

"In the kitchen," exclaimed a fat male cook, face white as his hat, pointing a trembling finger at the kitchen door.

"Are you sure?" asked the SAS man.

The cook nodded. "They said they're IRA."

"Blimey," gasped the SAS man his trigger finger twitching. "The real thing at last." He pulled a whistle from his left breast pocket and blew it three times. Dozens of SAS soldiers appeared in the courtyard milling about among the cooks adding to the panic and confusion. The little French chef had to be restrained from trying to return to the kitchen to rescue his culinary masterpiece.

"Clear the area," shouted an SAS officer with a crown and three pips on his shoulders. Whistles blew as the cooks were ushered away from the back of the house to the front of the house where they stood on the front lawn fearfully awaiting the explosion and wanting to witness it.

Sir Anthony Dingle sitting in his bath heard the three whistle blasts of the SAS sergeant knowing it meant a dangerous situation had arisen. but paid no heed thinking if something was wrong concerning him then he would be notified soon enough. He settled back into his bath with a smile, water lapping round his bulging belly listening to the talk on the radio by his political rival, leader of the opposition Clive Hurst. The man making his usual political patter trying to outscore Sir Anthony and blaming him and his party for all the bad things that had happened in British politics in recent years, while praising his own Party for all the good things. He promised to reduce taxes and to put more money into the National Health Service and Education, and increase the old age pension with free incontinence pads.

The Prime Minister took a puff on his cigar and scowled as he listened and closing his eyes he sank lower in the bath, his huge belly looking like an island surrounded by water. There was a faint rustling sound from the other side of the drawn plastic bath curtain. "Is that you, Jackson?" he called out opening his eyes and sitting up. There was no reply. The rustling of the curtain continued. "Jackson?" he called again.

Perkins pulled the curtain aside and looked down at the Prime Minister. "Good afternoon," he said curtly.

Sir Anthony Dingle took another puff of his cigar. "Where's Jackson?" he asked.

"He's been called away. His mother has been taken ill and I'm here to look after you in his place."

"There's something familiar about your face. Haven't we met before?"

"We have."

"I knew it. I've a good memory for faces. When was it?"

"In the back garden an hour ago when you were painting. We discussed you having rhubarb crumble for desert tonight?"

"Rhubarb crumble? Then you're Rupert the gardener."

"That's right."

"Didn't I say that I had a good memory for faces?"

"You did. Now, what are your last words?"

"My last words?"

"Your final words before you depart from this vale of tears."

"What are you talking about?"

"I'm going to kill you."

Sir Anthony Dingle sat bolt upright in the bath. "What the hell are you talking about?" he cried, "is this some kind of sick joke?"

"No, I'm deadly seriously. Have you some last words you'd like to say? You know like King George Vll's famous last words spoken on his deathbed in reply to his doctor telling him he would soon be better and could go on holiday to Bognor, the king's favourite seaside holiday retreat. "Bugger Bognor," exclaimed the king and promptly died.

"Help," cried the Prime Minister.

Perkins reached forward and knocked the radio into the bath. "Oops," he exclaimed with a smile, "butterfingers." There was a splash as the radio entered the bath between the Prime Minister's spread knees followed by a loud sizzling sound as water bubbled. The Prime Minister, cigar clenched in his teeth, went into convulsions, the hair on his head stood up on end and electric sparks shot out from the end of his penis like a Roman candle. He was dead

213

in thirty seconds with steam coming out of both ears. Perkins timed it with his wristwatch. This was he thought a perfect murder looking like a tragic accident happening with the Prime Minister listening to a radio in the bath and having accidentally knocked the radio into the water to pass 250,000 volts through his body.

"Well," thought Perkins looking at the body of the late Sir Anthony Dingle, "you were a bright spark right up to the end." Suddenly there came an almighty explosion shaking the house to its foundations. Perkins ran from the bedroom and on down the stairway into the hallway and joined a crowd of people, staff and house guests all milling about shouting and screaming in panic.

"Let's get out of here," shouted a voice, and they all rushed towards the front door.

"Don't panic, don't panic," shouted a police officer as he was pushed aside in the stampede to get out of the house.

When Perkins got outside he hurried round to the back of the house to be confronted with the kitchen ablaze, black smoke poured from shattered windows. There was a crowd of onlookers, mostly cooks, who had run from the front lawn and stood staring transfixed at the fire. One little man wearing a chef's tall hat sobbing hysterically and exclaiming in a French accent "Bastards, the bastards. Oh, my beautiful gourmet dinner, my beautiful gourmet dinner, all ruined and blown away."

The three IRA men, faces and hands covered with coal dust, had run less than a hundred yards down the driveway when the bomb exploded, and they threw themselves down on their stomachs. An armed policeman, a sergeant, at the main gates, seeing them laid on the ground ran up the driveway towards them thinking they had been seriously injured in the explosion and in urgent need of medical attention. When he reached the Irishmen he knelt beside Patrick Dodds who was pretending to be unconscious, felt for a pulse on the Irishman's neck. The pulse was good and strong. He checked on the pulses of the other two Irishmen who were also pretending to be unconscious, and their pulses too were good and strong.

The three IRA men opened their eyes and sat up all emitting a series of low moans to give credence to be being injured. "We need to go to hospital," muttered O'Leary weakly with an English accent not wanting the policeman to know he was Irish and arouse his suspicions that they were IRA.

"Don't worry," replied the policeman grimly, "you're in safe hands."

Meanwhile, Superintendent Lionel Harper of Special Branch was wedged in the back of a speeding police car squashed between super sleuth Allan Hawes and his trusted companion doctor Windrush. Sitting in the front driving Sergeant Jenny Hopper, and next to her Chief Inspector Edgar Briggs. They were less than a quarter of a mile from Checkers when they heard the explosion. "We're too late," exclaimed Briggs, "the killer's done the deadly work."

"There goes my pension," muttered Superintendent Harper, thinking he would be blamed for not providing the Prime Minister with better security.

"I've been outwitted by the dastardly killer," exclaimed Hawes shocked and disappointed he had not outwitted the assassin.

"Who? The archbishop of Canterbury?" asked the doctor brightly.

"No, Miss Marion Pringle."

Perkins stood with the cooks watching the burning kitchen. There was an ambulance that was kept at Checkers whenever the Prime Minister was in residence for emergencies. The ambulance drew up beside the cooks and two ambulance men leapt out. "Anyone hurt?" asked a fat ambulance man with horn-rim glasses.

Perkins stepped forward. "I'm a doctor," he declared, thinking he had found a possible means for escaping from Checkers by getting a ride in the ambulance.

"Anyone hurt, Doctor?" asked the fat ambulance man looking at the cooks who stood shocked and sullen faced watching the burning kitchen.

Perkins pointed to the little French chef who was on his knees wringing his hands and sobbing uncontrollably. "Oh, my beautiful dinner, my beautiful dinner," he wailing hysterically. "The bastards, the bastards."

"What's wrong with him, Doctor?"

"He's having a mental breakdown and in urgent need of hospital treatment."

"Poor devil," replied the fat ambulance man. He turned to his colleague a tall willowy. "The doctor says this man needs urgent hospital treatment, Eric."

"Right, let's get him there pronto." The two ambulance men grabbed the sobbing chef who struggled as they manhandled into the back of the ambulance where they strapped him down on a trolley.

Perkins climbed into the ambulance. "I'd better come with you," he said grimly. "He might have a relapse with serious complications on the way to hospital."

"Glad to have you on board, Doctor," replied the fat ambulance man. "Are you going to give him an injection to sedate him?"

"Not at this stage. It would do more harm than good. What he needs is to get to hospital as fast as possible for emergency treatment."

"Alright, Doctor, let's go."

"Put on the siren and flashing lights," said Perkins hoping an ambulance with siren going and lights flashing would not be stopped at the main gates by the police. The ambulance sped away down the driveway towards the main gates.

The ambulance came to a halt a hundred yards down the driveway with a squeal of brakes waved down by a policeman, a sergeant. The policeman walked round to the rear of the ambulance and knocked on the door. The door opened and the policeman stared up at the face of Perkins who held up his hands expecting to be arrested. The little French chef lay on a trolley behind him sobbing and wailing, "The bastards, Oh, the bastards."

"Room for three more?" asked the policeman. "I've got three men here who are badly burnt."

"We'll squeeze them in won't we, Doctor?" asked the fat ambulance man looking at Perkins who lowered his hands and meekly nodded.

"Get on board," said the policeman as he ushered the three IRA men into the ambulance. They sat on a trolley opposite the little French chef, groaning occasionally to give the pretense of being badly burnt. "God speed," called the policeman as he closed the ambulance door. The ambulance sped away down the driveway with siren going and lights flashing.

There was a police car driving at speed entering through the main gates forcing the ambulance to stop to allow it to continue on up the driveway. In the police car, Superintendent Lionel Harper of Special Branch, Chief Inspector Edgar Briggs, Sergeant Jenny Hopper, super sleuth Allan Hawes and his trusted colleague doctor Windrush. An armed woman police officer in bullet-proof vest at the gate holding a light machine gun waved the ambulance on through and it sped away down the road at top speed.

When the ambulance arrived at the hospital casualty department the two ambulance men wheeled away the little French chef on the trolley, still babbling hysterically over and over, "The bastards, the bastards."

Perkins remained in the ambulance with the IRA men and when the ambulance men returned five minutes later with nurses and three wheelchairs, they found the back of the ambulance empty with the three IRA men and doctor missing.

The end

Printed in Great Britain
by Amazon